LAURA ZIEPE lives in Brentwood in Essex with her husband Terry, three-year-old twins Harry and Darcey, and two dogs. Laura has always loved writing from a young age and was often writing stories from as young as eight. After leaving sixth form and working in office jobs for a year in London, Laura decided to go to university. Unsure what to study, Laura's oldest friend asked her what her ideal job would be. Immediately answering 'author', Laura followed her dreams and chose a degree in Creative Writing and English at St Mary's University in Twickenham. As well as writing books, she is a freelance make-up artist and loves travelling as much as she can. She has previously written three novels, *'Tis the Season to be Single*, *Essex Girls* and *Made in Essex* and hopes to be writing for many years to come. You can follow Laura on Twitter @lauraziepe or on Instagram @lauraziepewriter.

The Morning After the Wedding Before

LAURA ZIEPE

ONE PLACE. MANY STORIES

HQ
An imprint of HarperCollins*Publishers* Ltd
1 London Bridge Street
London SE1 9GF

This edition 2019

First published in Great Britain by
HQ, an imprint of HarperCollins*Publishers* Ltd 2019

ISBN: PB: 978-0-00-833095-8
EB: 978-0-00-831849-9

MIX
Paper from
responsible sources
FSC
www.fsc.org   FSC˚ C007454

This book is produced from independently certified FSC™ paper
to ensure responsible forest management.

For more information visit: www.harpercollins.co.uk/green

Printed and bound by CPI Group (UK) Ltd, Croydon, CR0 4YY

To Stacey.
Always in my thoughts.
Forever in my heart.

Chapter 1

Holly

As Holly looked around, hypnotized by the scene in front of her, she had a good feeling about this trip. It wasn't as though she hadn't been to a pool party on holiday before; she'd been to dozens when she'd been in her early twenties. It was just she'd never been to Las Vegas before; the swimming pool was absolutely enormous, the sun blazing, music blasting, the place was heaving with young people and it was a twenty-four-hour party paradise. She felt so pleased that her college friend, Emma Langford, had chosen Vegas as her wedding destination. Holly being a single mother to two young children, it was exactly the kind of place the doctor ordered. The wedding was the perfect excuse to escape toddler tantrums for this oasis of indulgence.

'Emma?' Holly called out hesitantly, as she made her way over to the slender girl in the white bikini taking a selfie. The girl she was calling had her back to Holly and hadn't heard her voice over the loud music. Holly knew Emma had lost tons of weight, but they hadn't seen each other in six months. Was that *really* her?

Emma turned round, her pretty face exploding into a huge

smile. 'Holly, you came!' She laughed, gripping her in a tight hug, pushing her sunglasses back into her long, dark hair. 'It's so good to see you. I'm glad you found us okay, especially seeing as this place is so packed. Where's Kim?' she questioned, suddenly noticing that Holly was alone.

'She's taking a nap in the hotel room,' Holly explained. They'd only landed about two hours ago and her best friend, Kim, had felt too tired to venture out. Kim was also a mother to two children: Mylo who was three, and Willow, nine months. They were a similar age to Holly's children, Lottie and Jacob. Kim had been more excited about catching up on some sleep than anything else and had sprawled out the moment they got into the hotel room and discovered their giant beds. 'I'm hoping Kim will come out later. You look amazing, Emma, honestly, absolutely stunning. I hardly recognize you,' Holly told her earnestly, her eyes sweeping up and down in admiration. 'I can't believe you have nearly half a million followers on Instagram now too; it's absolutely amazing. You must be *so* proud of yourself.'

Emma was a lifestyle blogger; Holly often checked out her page, lusting over the exotic trips abroad Emma posted about. It had all started with Emma sharing an image of her weight loss and after gaining thousands of followers during her journey, her page had since changed to her general lifestyle. Emma posted about everything: from her new outfit, to the food she was eating or her latest make-up routine. Her Instagram page followers continued to increase, and at a rapid rate too. Emma's images were flawless and aspirational. Sometimes Holly couldn't believe Emma was the same person as the plus-size, curvy teen from college she'd met all those years ago. She appeared to have the dream life and was now making a career just from posting on social media; it was quite incredible and Holly was so happy for her friend who used to have such low self-esteem. Emma was now tiny, Holly realized, astonished by her transformation; she guessed she was now a size eight or maybe even a six. Holly was aware she'd lost even more weight since she'd last seen her, judging by her Instagram feed, but she had always imagined Emma had tweaked her images a little. Taken them from a flattering angle and perhaps added a filter or adjusted the lighting. But here Emma was, looking every bit as polished as she did in her posts. Her hair was glossy, her skin was glowing and Holly couldn't take her eyes off Emma's toned abs. It was almost impossible to remember what Emma had looked like when she'd been a size eighteen. Like when your children grew up and you forgot the memories of them being a newborn baby; Holly simply couldn't imagine it.

'Thank you,' Emma replied, her cheeks reddening with the compliment. 'I wouldn't have been able to do any of it without Charlie though. He's always helped manage my Instagram page and somehow my followers have climbed to half a million. It's been such a mad year. Having a fiancé who is a personal trainer has obviously helped me get into shape, and the wedding has been the motivation I needed too,' she explained before changing the subject. 'That's a shame about Kim, but perhaps she just needs a bit of rest after the long flight. Come, let me introduce you to some of the others.'

Emma introduced Holly to some of her friends lying on the large round sun-bed next to her and she was pleased to see some familiar faces when she noticed Fran and Danni, two girls from college, were also there. She'd never met Charlie, but Holly felt as though she already knew him just from Emma's Instagram. It was strange feeling as though you knew someone just from seeing them on social media. He too, looked every bit as perfect as Emma often displayed, and flashed Holly a warm, welcoming grin.

'This is Frankie, Charlie's cousin,' Emma introduced the man next to Charlie. 'He practically lives with us back home,' Emma laughed good-naturedly, 'we can't seem to get rid of him. He's like part of the furniture.'

Frankie shot Emma a mock-offended look. 'You don't complain when I'm cooking the dinner,' he chuckled.

'To be fair, he's an amazing cook,' Emma flashed him a natural smile. 'You've been a massive help with the wedding too,' she added sweetly, 'even more than Charlie I'd say.' She raised her eyebrows at her fiancé, but it was clear to see that Emma wasn't really bothered.

'Hey, I've done loads of organizing,' Charlie retorted without conviction. 'Frankie's just better than me at planning things, that's all,' he shrugged, 'he seems to like all the girly stuff.'

Frankie elbowed him playfully.

'Come, let's go to the bar and get a drink,' Emma suggested to Holly merrily, 'we have so much to catch up on.'

Holly felt a buzz of excitement as she followed Emma. She hadn't drunk alcohol in the daytime for ages. It felt rebellious and completely alien to her. It was hardly a regular occurrence since she'd become a parent and she felt so free having no children to think about while she was here. No noses to wipe, faces to clean or nappies to change; Holly was determined to enjoy every second and appreciate just thinking about herself for once. This was so far from her usual Wednesday afternoons at Lottie's swimming lesson, chasing after Jacob as he toddled closer and closer towards the swimming pool and trying to feed him as many snacks as possible to keep him occupied.

'Thanks so much for coming all the way out here for my wedding,' Emma said, looking grateful as they ordered some cocktails. 'I know it's not exactly close to home and it must be difficult for you with the children. How are they? I haven't seen them for ages. We must start making sure we meet up more often when we get back,' she said guiltily.

'Definitely,' Holly agreed. Before she and Kim had become parents, they used to see Emma all the time. It wasn't anyone's fault that they didn't spend as much time together any more; it was just one of those things. Their lives had gone in different directions. Kim and Holly often met at the local park or farm with their children, while Emma was extremely busy enjoying

4

her successful career. They'd invited Emma out a few times, but Holly wasn't surprised that Emma had turned their invite down for whatever reason; Holly couldn't imagine she would want to spend time at a soft play if she didn't have kids. Their nights out seemed to have stopped as soon as Holly and Kim had become pregnant, and Holly couldn't even remember the last time they all went out together and had fun like they used to. It was so difficult getting Kim to agree to do something in the evenings without the children, and Holly guessed she'd since just given up asking. Kim was such a worrier. She hated leaving her children alone, even if her husband, Andy, or her mum was watching them. They did need to make much more of an effort though and Holly vowed she would in future. She didn't even know the man that Emma was *marrying*; it had been far too long.

She couldn't resist smiling as she thought of her children. It certainly wasn't easy caring for two little people all the time, especially now that she and their father, Rob, had split up, but she loved her children more than anything. They were the one thing she was really proud of.

'They're good,' Holly replied. 'They're staying with my mum for a few days and then Rob is picking them up. He has a new girlfriend now,' she explained, still unsure how she felt about another woman being around her children. It was still so fresh and raw. 'He told me the day you sent your wedding invites out.'

'Oh wow, really? I was just about to ask how you two are getting on now you're not together any more. Have you met her? I guess it must be so strange.' Emma gazed at Holly, her voice laced with sympathy.

Holly nodded. She and Rob had split up eight months before, and Holly had only seen Emma once, just after it happened. Jacob had only been five months old and had been teething when Emma had come over to see how Holly was doing, and it had been difficult to talk while bouncing a grisly baby on her knee. Emma didn't really know much detail about the split at all.

5

She thought back to that day Rob had told her all about his new girlfriend. Kim had been over that afternoon and they had been discussing Emma's wedding after both receiving invites that day. Holly had been bursting with excitement at the aspect of going to Vegas, but Kim had been reluctant, unhappy about leaving her children to fly halfway across the world. Holly wasn't sure she wanted to go without Kim, so she told herself it probably wasn't going to happen and she hadn't even been thinking about it when Rob knocked that evening to collect the children. They had come to the agreement that he would take them every Thursday night as well as every other weekend. It had always felt so weird letting Rob into the house they once shared together as though he was just a visitor. He no longer let himself in using the front door key, calling out her name so she knew he had arrived back. Instead, he waited until Holly answered the door; something they'd never actually discussed but just something Rob started doing when he moved out. It was the polite thing to do. It was *so* Rob. Holly was pleased they still respected each other and hadn't fallen out. She prided herself on the fact that she was friends with the ex; she wasn't one of those women who sent bitter text messages and used their children as a weapon. They were mature and grown up about it. They put their children first.

Holly thought back to how she handed Rob a bag with the kids' things in, wondering why he was acting so distracted. Questioning why he looked so nervous.

'Erm, I need to speak to you,' he said, suddenly sounding serious.

'Right, okay,' Holly had replied, her brow furrowed. She'd told Lottie and Jacob to go fetch their teddies from the other room so they could be alone and she'd stared at Rob in wonderment, assuming it was going to be about whether he could switch weekends or something trivial. 'Speak away.'

Rob bit his lip looking a bit unsure of himself. His nostrils flared and she could feel the tension emanating from him. 'Errr … I just wanted to tell you that I've met someone,' he stated, looking ill at ease. 'She's called Nikki.'

He was never great in uncomfortable situations. She remembered once when she'd made him question the gardener about charging too much or the time they'd gone into a sex shop together to buy her some new underwear at the start of their relationship and the sales assistant asked him if he needed any help – he simply couldn't make eye contact, shifted on the spot and kept clearing his throat as though it would clear his awkwardness. Looking at him with his flushed cheeks, Holly had almost felt sorry for him. That was, if his words hadn't felt like he'd slapped her hard across the face. She always thought if Rob met someone else, then she would guess long before he told her. She knew him so well, she thought herself wise enough to see the telltale signs. When they'd first became a couple, he couldn't stop smiling. He couldn't even ask her if she wanted a drink without a huge grin on his face. Like the cat that got the cream. When he woke up, he would turn to face her with this *look* on his face. As though he couldn't quite believe that she was there. He couldn't believe his luck. He had made her feel like the most precious, loved person in the whole entire world.

So for him to stand in front of her telling her he had met someone else had been a complete shock. Holly realized then that she hadn't been expecting Rob to meet someone so soon.

'That's nice,' Holly managed to say, forcing her voice to sound bright. Her face felt hot and she knew it wasn't because it was a humid summer's evening. She was irritated that she hadn't been prepared for this and also at herself for not feeling as relaxed about it as she always told herself she would be. She felt a shot of betrayal, even though she knew it was silly, and was slightly embarrassed. Holly hadn't met anyone since they'd split up. She hadn't so much as had a flirty conversation with someone of the opposite sex. Not even a harmless text message. It just wasn't a priority of hers. She had her friends, family and children and that was the most important thing.

Rob had then proceeded to say that Nikki wanted to meet her. Holly couldn't deny it was the mature and sensible thing to do, seeing as Rob wanted to introduce her to their children.

As soon as Holly had agreed, his awkwardness had melted away as quickly as an ice cube on a hot summer's day. Instead, it was Holly left there feeling anxious.

'Where did you meet her? How old is she?' Holly enquired, unable to suppress her curiousness.

He gave a light laugh, looking happy. *There* was the expression she hadn't seen in years and Holly knew at that point it was serious. This wasn't just a casual fling – Rob had fallen in love. It was a strange situation, but Holly was pleased for him. She would always have a special place in her heart for Rob. 'Online. I know you'll find that quite sad, but trust me she's a nice girl. She's twenty-five. She's not a weirdo or anything; she's actually training to be a doctor. You'll like her, I'm certain of it.'

'I have something to tell you too, actually.' The words had just come tumbling out of her mouth impulsively. What was she saying? She hadn't thought any of it through, but it was at that moment that Holly decided she was going to Emma's wedding. Rob could have his doctor and she would have Vegas. For some reason she didn't want him to be the only one with some important news to share that day.

'Okay?' He looked at her questioningly.

'I'm going to Vegas for Emma's wedding,' Holly told him boldly. She was going with or without Kim. She wasn't sure if there were any other people she knew attending the wedding, but Holly would be just fine going alone. She liked to think herself as a friendly, innocuous person who didn't have any problems socializing all by herself. Life was too short and she deserved some fun. Rob was clearly enjoying himself with Nikki and now it was her turn to have a break away and think about herself for once. She'd been pleasantly surprised when Kim had announced the following day that she would join her.

Memories of that day faded as Holly focused on Emma's concerned expression in front of her as she explained what had happened, taking a sip of her frozen strawberry daquiri the barman had just handed her. 'So I met Nikki before I came out here, and she's actually really nice,' she said truthfully. It had been impossible not to like Nikki. She wasn't drop-dead gorgeous, but she was attractive in her own way. She had beautiful hazel eyes, flecked with amber and green (the kind Rob would have called interesting) and a perfect smile (Holly could imagine she took great photos). She was just so *nice*. Holly had been terrified she would hate Nikki. What if she didn't get on with her children? It was a worrying thought that there would be another person playing "Mummy" to Lottie and Jacob when she wasn't around. She'd been worried she'd be envious of her young, toned, stretch mark-free body. She didn't want to resent the fact that she and Rob could go out for dinner whenever it suited them. Or to the cinema. They had time to be alone without having to watch children's programmes like Bing and Mr Tumble. But Holly had felt relieved when it hadn't been like that at all. Nikki's happy, breezy nature was contagious. Holly could just imagine her giving money to charity every month and volunteering in a soup kitchen on Christmas Day. Nikki was understanding and inoffensive. Deep down Holly knew she was very lucky if this was her ex-partner's new girlfriend. Holly instantly trusted her and felt comfortable that her children would be in her presence. Nikki had told her she loved kids and had been excited about getting to know Lottie and Jacob; she'd even gone out to buy them small gifts. 'I actually really liked her. She's mature for a twenty-five-year-old and she couldn't wait to meet the children. She was so easy to get on with and I can see that she and Rob make a great couple. They seem so much better suited than Rob and I ever were.'

'You're handling things great,' Emma said sincerely. 'I can't imagine many people like their ex's new girlfriend. I think it's fantastic if you can be friends.'

'Yes, I really hope we can,' Holly replied truthfully. 'Anyway, tell me about the wedding,' she said eagerly, not wanting to talk all about herself. 'What's the dress like? Or are you keeping it a secret?'

'Charlie sorted a hire company for me and they've leant me one for free providing I tag them in my wedding posts,' she explained. 'I'll show you a photo; it's so pretty,' she said, clicking on her mobile and flicking through her images.

'Wow, Em, that's so good. I can't believe you haven't had to pay for your wedding dress,' Holly said, incredulous.

'Charlie has managed to get free suit hires for all the men too; I'm really lucky to have him,' she explained, flashing Holly the image of a stunning ivory, backless gown. 'He's been great at getting all the free stuff. I still have a few things to do though before the wedding, so I wondered if you and Kim wanted to come along to help me pick things? I'm so indecisive about this kind of thing.'

'Of course. Anything to help, you know that. Your dress is stunning,' she said, her mouth popping open as she took Emma's phone to get a closer look. The material looked so delicate and expensive; it would mould to Emma's slender figure beautifully. It was the kind of dress that Holly would steer well clear of due to an unforgiving tummy area. Since having children, the idea of a flat stomach seemed like a thing of the past; Holly was fine with this though. Personally she'd rather go out with her kids for pizza and ice-cream as a treat without worrying about her bikini body. It just wasn't as important now.

'Thanks Holly. Let's go in the pool for a bit,' she replied, walking ahead. 'I just want everything to be absolutely impeccable, you know?'

Holly nodded. She worked with brides all the time being a hair stylist. Her diary was pretty much fully booked for the rest of the year and she'd offered to do Emma's wedding hair for her on the big day. It had been Edna, Holly's mother, who had suggested taking some time out of her diary in the summer for a break from work, so Holly had made sure she'd left some time where she hadn't booked any weddings in. Holly was grateful she'd listened or she wouldn't have managed to get to Vegas. Being booked up for weddings seemed to dictate her life. 'It's normal to want a faultless day; I think all brides feel like that,' she told her reassuringly.

As they reached the pool, Emma smiled thinly as she placed her drink on the side of the pool. 'It has to be perfect. It's what everyone expects of me. I can't let them all down.'

Holly looked at Emma oddly and just before she could respond, Emma dunked her body into the water and swam off.

Chapter 2

Holly

Holly didn't know which way to look as the taxi drove down the strip to the Planet Hollywood Hotel where they were staying. Her eyes darted from one grand hotel to another, the strip shimmering mesmerizingly, promising excitement and entertainment. Holly was fascinated by the bright lights flashing everywhere she looked. There seemed to be so much going on. It was a place for non-stop adventures, exactly like in films and it felt surreal that she was actually there. The taxi pulled into the hotel and Holly was delighted to reach the icy breeze of the air-conditioning again. The heat outside was stifling and Holly could feel sweat at the nape of her neck; there wasn't even the slightest breeze. She was meeting Emma and the others in a few hours for drinks and she was hoping that Kim would be joining them. Surely she didn't want to stay in the room for the rest of the day? She knew Kim felt tired and jet-lagged, but they weren't in Vegas for long and Holly really felt as though they should be making the most of it.

Kim was sitting up in bed in her silky pyjamas watching the large television when Holly walked back into the room.

'Hey, how you feeling?' Holly asked her. 'The pool parties here are incredible. You really should have come along,' she told her, 'we're going to have the best time.'

Kim stretched out lazily on the bed. 'I haven't actually been to sleep,' she said, 'I've just been chilling out and watching a film. *Bliss*. I can't remember the last time I actually watched a film without being interrupted by something.'

Holly couldn't remember the last time she'd watched a film that wasn't a Disney one. Even when her children were finally asleep she found she was always doing something round the house. Usually tidying up the toy room or catching up on washing. It seemed there was always something that needed doing when you became a parent.

Holly perused the room-service menu. 'Ooh, let's order champagne,' she said, her eyes gleaming as she ran her finger down the menu, 'to get us in the mood for this evening.'

Kim looked unsure. 'I'm not sure I'm feeling up to it.' Her eyes flicked over to the digital clock. 'It's two in the morning. in London right now.'

'So?' Holly replied ebulliently, 'when has that ever stopped us before? It's not like we have the children with us, is it? Emma said we're all meeting at a bar in Caesars Palace tonight, but that's not for another hour or so.'

Kim yawned. 'Oh really? I might give tonight a miss, you know. I'd just like a quiet one to catch up on sleep. That sounds much more appealing than drinking in a bar; I still feel so tired.'

Holly felt a surge of disappointment. She loved her friend with all her heart, but since she'd had children, Kim had really changed. They hadn't been out in ages and she'd so been looking forward to Vegas and spending quality time with her best friend like they used to. She had hoped that without the children, she'd be the old, fun Kim again, instead of this sensible, unenthusiastic new version. Some days Holly wondered what had happened to Kim. Kim had never been the maternal one out of the two of them. She'd always turned her nose up at the thought of having children, saying that she enjoyed her own life too much to give it up for someone else.

'I think I'm more of an animal person,' she'd once said, after they'd been to visit a friend's baby. 'I'd much prefer to hold a kitten or puppy than a baby.'

It had been Holly who had been more interested in babies, excited when someone had a newborn she could cuddle and really looking forward to having her own one day. She'd always had lots of younger cousins and had four younger nephews who she doted on. But Kim? Kim hadn't even planned on having Mylo; it had just happened (a slip-up, she'd said) and then everything had changed. Just like that. It was as though Kim had had a personality transplant, suddenly obsessed with babies and children, wondering how many she could fit in before she hit forty. She suddenly stopped wanting to go out any more. Kim had always been the fun one too. Even since Holly had met Kim at school when they were five, she'd been the mischievous, wild one. The one to get Holly told off for talking in class, encouraging Holly to try her first cigarette and can of cider, and the one to get Holly to stay out until six. Even though she had work the next day. Holly would always wake up with a hangover from hell when she went out with Kim, that was a given. There had never been a dull moment with Kim around and that's why Holly had always loved her. Holly had always been the organized, tidy and sensible one , whereas Kim was much more laid-back, rarely thinking about the consequences of her actions.

Holly adored Kim, they would always be the best of friends, but she couldn't help but miss the spontaneity she'd had before having children, and she hoped that it was just because it was the first night that she was taking it easy.

'You sure you won't come out?' Holly asked hopefully, already knowing the answer.

Kim flapped her hand in Holly's direction. 'No, you go though. Don't miss out just because of me.'

'Are you certain you don't want me to stay in with you?' Holly offered kindly. She didn't want to stay in and had already told Emma she would go out, but she knew she should offer like a good friend would. Holly would do anything for her best friend; so if Kim had wanted her to stay in, watch a film and order room service, she would have done. She honestly couldn't believe that Kim didn't want to go out and meet the others though.

'No, I promise it's fine,' Kim said, turning to her and smiling. 'I'll probably be snoring as soon as my head hits the pillow.'

Holly nodded, shooting Kim a rueful smile.

'I wonder how Andy will cope with the kids all alone,' Kim said, her mind clearly still back home. 'I'll call him as soon as I wake up tomorrow and check he's okay. I'm sure he won't go wrong, seeing as I pretty much left him instructions on every little thing, will he?'

Kim just couldn't seem to relax and switch off like Holly could.

'He'll be fine. Andy's such a good dad,' Holly reassured her. 'I can't imagine him ever doing anything wrong.'

Kim smiled, but Holly noticed it didn't quite reach her eyes. Assuming she was tired, she ignored it, and went to have a shower before getting ready to go out.

Chapter 3

Emma

Emma couldn't believe this was the week she was getting married. She was actually going to be Charlie's *wife*. She still felt far too young to be doing something so grown up, despite being thirty-three. It was strange how her body just kept getting older, even though her brain still didn't feel any different from when she was twenty-one. It was scary and she really wished that time would just *slow down*.

It had been Emma's decision to marry in Vegas and as she glanced out of her balcony at the lively strip and the vibrant colours from the hotels, she felt it was the right choice. There was so much to do and see and she knew that all her guests were going to have fun. Everyone had made such a big effort to get all the way there; it was important to Emma that they enjoyed it. It was bright and sunny too, with temperatures in the high thirties; there definitely wasn't going to be any worry about it raining on her wedding day. Despite being so hot outside, it was never far to escape the heat and cool down in the air-conditioned hotels; it went from one extreme to another.

Emma had never wanted a huge white wedding. She hardly

spoke to her parents who had retired and moved to Gran Canaria. She wasn't particularly surprised when her mother told her on the phone there was no way they could travel all that way due to her father's arthritis, even for their only daughter. As soon as Emma had got herself a job and been able to afford to rent an apartment, it had seemed like they couldn't wait to get away and move abroad.

'The sun will do your father's joints the world of good,' Emma recalled her mother saying. 'You can come visit whenever you want.'

Emma would only see them if *she* made the effort though; her parents hadn't once been back to the UK since they moved and Emma couldn't deny that it hurt. How could they care so little about their only child?

Emma didn't have a large family that wanted to see her get married. Not that she would have wanted anything fancy anyway. Despite what people thought of her due to her career posting pictures of herself, she actually hated all the attention. When she went to university, she had purposely picked courses where she wouldn't have to do presentations; the thought of everyone staring at her was enough to make her palms go clammy and her stomach knot with nerves. A quick, low-key wedding was much more her style. Less pressure. She'd only been with Charlie for two years and hadn't wanted the hassle of planning her big day for months and months on end. Truth be told, the plan was to just get the wedding over with and start trying for a baby. All Emma really longed for was a family of her own. It was strange – she always thought she'd be married with a few children by now. She wasn't so bothered about the marriage part, but not having children was unthinkable for Emma. Emma adored children and imagined there was no way in the world she would ever leave them and move country, even when they had grown up. Her own mother had left it late in life, having a baby at forty-three, having had a successful career as a solicitor. Her parents were always

17

so serious and strict. Holidays were no fun, she had nobody to swap clothes with and she could never join in when her friends complained about being bossed around by their elder siblings. She would have loved to have been bossed around. She wouldn't have cared if her sister took her shoes and never gave them back. It would have beat being alone all the time.

Emma wanted to have at least two children and as much as she hated to say it, she did worry slightly that she might have issues getting pregnant if she left it any later. A woman's fertility was supposed to halve by thirty-five, and that was only a couple of years away. Her friend, Kirsty, had recently had to go through IVF, the reason she wasn't able to make the wedding, and Emma's cousin's wife, Lisa, had also just announced she'd had a second failed round of fertility treatment; it seemed to be coming more and more common for women to get struggle to pregnant. She really hoped it would happen easily for her, although she'd already decided that if it didn't, she'd love to adopt. There was nothing wrong with it, but she really didn't want to be a first-time mother in her forties like her mother. She'd always wanted to be a fun, energetic mother. She imagined going cycling in the park with her children. She didn't want to be one of those mothers who didn't understand the latest app her children were using. She didn't want her kids to snigger when she asked them how to do something online. Emma wanted to be young enough to still be a fairly cool parent.

Emma applied some lip gloss and slipped on a sparkly, strappy silver dress. She ran her fingers across the textured fabric of the dress, which moulded perfectly to her slender figure. She was down to a size eight now. If someone had told her three years ago when she was struggling to get into a size eighteen she would be buying a size eight wedding dress, she would have laughed at them. She wasn't one of those women who pretended she was were happier being larger; she would always have preferred to be slimmer, but the truth was, Emma had just been happy enjoying life and her weight crept up over the years. She loved food. She adored all things bad for her, laden with calories and sugar, and often found herself polishing off a bottle of wine or two after work several times a week. If she wanted to drink a litre bottle of coke, if that was what she'd fancied, she didn't think twice about it. A couple of chocolate doughnuts after lunch? No problem. She hadn't been hurting anyone, had she? She couldn't deny that she'd had low self-esteem and the problem was, when she felt down about herself, she ate to make herself feel better. It had been a vicious cycle. She certainly hadn't loved her wobbly thighs and flabby tummy, but she always managed to cover herself in loose black trousers for work (she had worked for an accountancy firm in London) and she'd always felt that if she just ignored her size, then it didn't really matter. It wasn't as though she had trouble dating; men often said what a lovely face she had, but looking back she realized they rarely mentioned her body. One day, Emma's trouser button had popped off at work and she had to ask for a safety pin. As she saw her colleague's Sue's pitying glance as she handed one over, something came over her. Emma had had enough. She was fed up of constantly being out of breath just walking up the stairs at work. She suddenly felt embarrassed by the fact she seemed to sweat when she'd so much as lifted a finger. She wanted to feel confident in her skin. She went home that night and did a bit of research after Sue insisted she try a weight-loss group that she'd heard about.

'Barbara Seeley lost three stone on it,' she'd told her enthusiastically. Emma was also keen to lose a bit of weight for health reasons. You couldn't listen to the radio or sit in a waiting room without the risks constantly being shoved in your face. Emma didn't want diabetes, high blood pressure or a stroke. 'I think it's a great idea to try it. They do meetings,' Sue had encouraged. 'I could lose a bit too, why don't we try it together?'

Emma had gasped when their scales revealed she was thirteen stone three pounds.

It had taken two years to lose five stone with the help of her weight-loss group and Emma was proud of herself. Everyone was. She was no longer bigger than the women she walked past in the street. She was no longer embarrassed to be seen treating herself to a cake. Losing weight had been the start of a new career, not that she'd known that at the time. After her first month at the weight-loss group, Emma had lost ten pounds and was spurred on further when her name was called out as being achiever of the month. She'd felt a sense of satisfaction. Then after several months she stopped losing as much weight and couldn't hide her frustration when she'd been eating so well. That was when a red-haired lady, Paula, who also attended the group, had pulled her to one side. Emma had noticed her earlier on, as she was probably the slimmest woman in the group and she'd found herself wondering whether Paula really needed to be there.

'You're still going in the right direction, don't be disheartened,' she'd beamed encouragingly. 'Not to put a downer on things, but it does get harder to lose as much weight as when you first started, the longer you diet,' Paula told her sagely. 'If you want to really change shape and drop even more dress sizes, join a gym. The gym I go to has a special offer on at the moment. Here, let me give you the number if you're interested. I have a personal trainer, his name's Charlie. He's fantastic.'

Emma hadn't been too sure about the gym at first. She had assumed it would be full of vain, muscular men looking in the mirrors as they lifted weights and petite women in tiny crop tops. She was more keen on continuing to focus on what she ate. It was all about eating a healthy balance; with her diet plan, she could still eat pretty much whatever she wanted to. Just in moderation. A slice of cake instead of stuffing herself with the whole thing. A glass of juice instead of the entire carton. No food was off limits, but Emma was only allowed a certain amount of calories a day, so she had to choose wisely. She liked the fact she had control over what she ate. She actually enjoyed the discipline and it had suited her down to the ground. That was how she began blogging.

Emma had never really been happy working at the accountancy firm in London. It paid the bills, but she never really enjoyed the job. She always had that Sunday night dread, a twisted, uneasy feeling when she thought about going back to work the next day. Her job simply hadn't fulfilled her; in fact, it had been nothing but boring and the only thing Emma had liked was socializing with her work colleagues; London nightlife had appealed to her immensely. Emma had always wanted to try something different, but she honestly didn't know what she wanted to do. She never had. She hadn't planned to be a lifestyle blogger and she never realized how much money she could make doing something so simple. After losing a stone, Emma had decided to take a before and after photo and post it on her Instagram page. She'd glammed herself up a bit for her after photo, and took the image on her father's professional Canon camera. It was only a stone she'd lost, but the difference between her before and after looked amazing and she'd even braved it by wearing a bikini in each picture. She just looked so much happier and healthier in the second image and her body was starting to take shape. She remembered taking a deep breath before posting the image. She'd just been on the way to the gym for the first time, the one Suzie had recommended, when she did it, and she'd left her phone in her locker for an hour while she did a yoga class.

Emma had been confused at first when she saw a dozen notifications on her phone, wondering what it was all about. But as she clicked on her Instagram page, she was startled by the huge response she'd had to her post. She'd had one hundred and twenty likes, with so many people complimenting her.

Well done, Em! You look incredible!

Wow! Such great results.

Where is your bikini from Emma? Love the colour on you.

She'd even had a couple of private messages.

Hi Emma. Do you mind telling me what diet you're doing? one had asked. *Do you have any tips for me?* another girl had asked.

The messages and huge response had given Emma a buzz of excitement she'd never felt before. She felt important somehow. Special even. She loved the fact that she might actually help people and even inspire them to go on a health kick too. A few days after she'd posted her weight-loss image, she decided to go back to the gym, this time to meet Charlie for a personal training session. The yoga class had given her the boost she needed. Emma had really enjoyed it; no-one was judging her like she thought they would, and everyone had seemed really friendly. There were women of all shapes and sizes there and she decided to overcome her fears and go for a one-on-one session. Emma had still been nervous, especially when she noticed how perfect Charlie looked. But he'd made her feel at ease right away. Charlie was a fantastic trainer and always made Emma feel comfortable, encouraging her to do that extra push-up or extra minute on the treadmill, pushing her just that little bit further than she thought she'd ever be able to go. In between breaks, they spoke about themselves. Charlie was interesting, and he seemed to want to get to know more about her too; he wasn't someone who just spoke about himself all the time. Emma discovered he was trying to get into fitness modelling, but was working as a personal trainer until he got his break. Emma had started to look forward to their chats; Charlie asked her general things such as what she was doing the weekend, what she did for work etc. It was during one of these chats after having a few sessions with Charlie that she mentioned that she was posting blogs about her journey on Instagram.

'Oh yeah?' he asked interestedly, 'what's your account name? I'll follow you too,' he said.

Emma had felt a little flustered as she told him, knowing he'd be able to see her 'before' bikini image, but Charlie had been nothing but supportive and impressed. 'Wow, you've got quite a lot of followers, you know,' he'd said admirably. 'You should keep going. Make sure you post something every day. People are clearly interested. Some people make a fortune from Instagram; it's worth a shot, hey?'

'It's hard to believe people really want to follow me,' Emma said modestly.

'Why would they not?' Charlie had asked her. 'You shouldn't be so hard on yourself. You're an attractive girl, Emma, and you're doing something that shows willpower and determination. I bet there're loads of girls who follow you that would love to lose weight or just shape up a bit. They want to know how you did it and if you're encouraging people to live a healthier lifestyle, then good for you. Don't underestimate yourself.'

Emma had held his penetrating gaze. She felt a surge of encouragement. He was right – why wouldn't people want to follow her? So she posted another image straight after their session to show people her continuing changing body. She gained extra followers immediately and she couldn't wait to post something else. It became addictive. She began to take an interest in other successful Instagram accounts. She looked at what they were posting and the type of photos that seemed to attract more followers. Before Emma knew it, she was buying new clothes to suit her slimmer shape and taking selfies. Gradually, her Instagram stopped being just about her weight-loss journey and her everyday life. It had been Charlie's idea to start tagging brands in her images to get their attention. Emma began to realize it wasn't the only attention she was getting. Charlie had begun to message her privately on her Instagram account. At first, it was just about training. Helpful tips and some low-fat recipes he'd tried. But not long afterwards, his messages began to get a bit more flirtatious and before Emma knew it, she began to like Charlie as more than just a trainer. It was clear he felt the same too. She'd always thought that someone like him was out of her league.

'I got a message from a gym-wear company asking if they could send me some outfits for free if I tag them on my page,' she'd told Charlie on their first date at a restaurant. 'It all feels so strange receiving things for free.'

'That's great,' he'd said passionately. 'I've got some great ideas how you can get other things too. The more followers you have, the easier it is and you seem to just continue to get more and more.'

'Really?' Emma didn't have any idea where to even start.

'Of course. I'll help you if you want? I like you, Emma,' he told her without hesitation, taking her hand across the table. 'Ever since I met you, I've started to fall for you.'

Emma felt her face suffuse with colour and her heart thump wildly in her chest. 'I feel the same,' she replied timidly.

After that first date, they became a couple. Emma would join Charlie on his morning workouts and they would train together. They met after work and spent any free time they had as well as the weekends together. Usually they were training, cooking healthy meals or visiting new places, always taking images for Emma's Instagram. Charlie created a new email account for her page, and he dealt with any queries when Emma was too busy.

Emma began to earn good money. The first thing she was asked to do was promote a clothing brand. She was given her own code, so her followers could receive a discount and Emma got a percentage every time someone made an order using her code. It had been the easiest way Emma had ever made money, and she decided to treat Charlie to their first holiday together to Bali. It was the least she could do seeing as he'd helped her achieve so much, both with her figure and career. Charlie had taken tons of photos: one of Emma pretending to meditate in front of Mount Agung, a volcano, one of her in front of a waterfall laughing, one of her with her back to the camera by an infinity pool. The responses continued to come flooding in.

Oh my God, I love your dress. Where is it from?

Can I ask what foundation you use?

Where did you get your bag? I need this!

Posting to her Instagram became a daily ritual. Even if Emma was only going for a coffee she'd get a photo, a fake image of her scanning the menu or a sultry pout looking into the distance as she shopped in London. Her inbox was always full of people wanting to know what camera she used or what her favourite highlighter was. It became so crazy that Charlie suggested Emma start an online blog which she linked to her Instagram page. Before she knew it, she had more and more freebies starting to come her way. She was constantly being sent free make-up, clothes and swimwear. So long as she posted about it, companies wanted her to use their products. Emma became obsessed with social media, gaining more followers and likes. Trips away started to become about taking photos, rather than actually enjoying herself and there had been times when Emma had to remind herself why she was doing it. When she became a bit too obsessed with it, Emma gave herself a few days off. Charlie was always enthusiastic to start with, taking selfies of the two of them and suggesting she posted a bit about their relationship to see if they could get any free weekend trips away. Charlie became a part of her account and her followers were always telling Emma how they were the perfect match. Their first freebie was a trip to Paris and Emma had to pinch herself over how well she was doing.

'Hopefully this is the start of many more,' Charlie had laughed, clinking champagne classes with her on the Eurostar as Emma filmed it for her latest story.

Despite what people must have thought when they looked on her Instagram page, Emma didn't want to appear like she was showing off, but she knew that in order to get the brand deals she had to be able to influence others. People had to want to buy her latest outfit, watch or lipstick she was wearing; it was the way she made her money. So she had to make herself look the best she possibly could. Emma just hoped that people would see past her flawless newsfeed, and understand that beneath it all she was just a normal, ordinary girl. She hated people who thought too highly of themselves, which was why she liked to sometimes post before and after images to show how far she had come. Emma hadn't always been someone to envy or desire; Emma had once been a size eighteen woman, who was very self-conscious and insecure. Despite now being a trim size eight, Emma certainly didn't love herself and she was very aware of how superficial and shallow social media could be. It was a fabricated world; Emma knew this. She wasn't completely ignorant.

Emma was brought back to the present when Charlie opened the bathroom door with a towel around his waist. Eyeing her up and down, he narrowed his eyes and his lips curved slightly upwards. 'You look nice. Trying to impress someone?'

'Haha, very funny. You're the only person I need to impress, and you've agreed to marry me,' Emma replied light-heartedly. 'When you're dressed do you mind…'

'Taking a photo of you?' Charlie interjected abruptly. 'Of course.'

'Thanks,' Emma smiled gratefully. She knew how much her photos had begun to annoy him. What he found so interesting at first, he now found tedious and dull. He didn't mind as much when it was of the two of them; Charlie seemed to love the limelight, especially if he was sent free things. But it was mainly Emma who was earning good money through her lifestyle blogging, not only through the advertising on her website, but she was now signed up to several apps where she advertised the outfits she was wearing. She was doing better than she ever dreamed of and she was getting fed up with reminding Charlie that she wasn't just taking photos because she enjoyed it. It was all part of her job and one that he had insisted she did when they'd first met. A job that he used to find fascinating.

Emma stood on the balcony, looking out into the distance of the strip moments later; she knew the lighting was perfect and angled her head in a way she knew would look flattering on camera.

'Done,' Charlie said dryly, after a couple of clicks.

'Do you mind just doing a few more please?' Emma asked him politely. He knew as well as she did she usually needed lots of images to pick from. She sometimes took over a hundred, just to get that one special shot. Not that she was expecting him to take that many at that present moment. She knew she had no chance from the way he rolled his eyes.

He sighed loudly as he took some more. 'You may have to stop all this once we're married you know,' he stated moodily. 'I'm not certain I can put up with sharing you with the world forever.'

Emma ignored him and did her best pose.

Emma felt in good spirits an hour later when they met their friends at the bar in their hotel. She shot Holly a huge smile and hugged her as they met.

'You look lovely. Is Kim too tired?' she asked, noticing she wasn't with her.

Holly nodded. 'All dressed in her pyjamas and ready for bed. I'm sure it's just for tonight. By tomorrow she'll be out and enjoying herself, especially seeing as it's your hen night,' Holly said enthusiastically, looking around the bar. 'Wow, this place looks nice and so do you, Em. I love that dress,' she complimented her. 'I still cannot believe how much weight you've lost – you look incredible!'

'Thanks,' Emma replied, feeling a flush of embarrassment yet again. She would never get used to compliments, no matter how hard she tried. 'I was going to ask if you and Kim wanted to come to look at the flowers with me tomorrow?'

'We'd love to. Just text us the time and place and we'll be there.'

'I will, and don't worry, I won't make it too early seeing as we're drinking tonight. Speaking of which, shall we get some drinks? There's more people out tonight for you to meet who weren't at the pool today.' Her eyes swivelled to Charlie's cousin, Frankie, who was walking through a crowd of people staring at her. He shot her a smile, and Emma felt glad he was there as she wanted to talk to him about the car he was arranging for their wedding day. Frankie was so helpful like that; he was continuously offering Emma help to take the pressure off as Charlie hadn't seemed to do much apart from arranging as much free stuff as possible. Emma was grateful for this, of course; it was fantastic that they were in such a lucky, privileged position to be gifted so many things, but it would have been nice if he was interested in helping organize some other things too. Frankie was always asking if there was anything he could do; Charlie was lucky to have such a thoughtful best man. 'Hi,' she mouthed to him, as Charlie slapped him hello on the back.

'Let me get a photo of the bride and groom to be,' Jason, one of Charlie's friends, suggested over the music a few seconds later.

'Here, take one on my camera,' Emma offered, knowing her phone took great images, perfect for Instagram. She could do with updating her stories on Instagram; so many of her followers were keen to see her Vegas trip. They loved the photos she posted of her and Charlie. She was often seeing people write things under her images like #couplegoals. They really did think that she had the most perfect relationship.

Charlie was more than happy to oblige and he stood next to her, placing his hand protectively on her lower back and gripping her just a little too tightly as they smiled into the lens. 'That dress is actually a bit low, don't you think?' he muttered quietly. 'You look like you're flashing to everyone.'

As usual, Emma pushed the comment aside and focused on the photo they were taking, knowing how happy she and Charlie

28

would look together. Her followers would swoon, believing that Emma was really lucky in love and was about to marry her dream man.

That was the thing about social media: it was all one big, fat lie.

Chapter 4

Holly

Holly sipped her white wine, passing back Emma her gin and tonic after she'd taken her photo with Charlie.

'Let me introduce you to the people you don't know,' Emma said kindly, tapping two women on the shoulder who were standing next to them. 'This is Jenny and Stephanie who I used to work with.'

Holly smiled hello at them as Emma pointed at a group of four people by the bar. 'The one in pink is my cousin, Gill, her husband, Doug, and I think you've met my friend Michelle and her boyfriend Peter at my thirtieth birthday drinks, didn't you? I'm not sure if I told you that my parents won't be coming?' she smiled, but her eyes were shiny.

'Oh no. Why not?' Holly wondered. She felt sorry for her friend getting married without her parents there to watch, but she couldn't say she was that surprised. Emma's father was a stern man and her mother had always seemed cold and unaffectionate.

'Dad's arthritis is playing up badly, my mum told me; it would have been a bit much for them to fly all the way out here.'

It was a lame excuse and they both knew it. Holly remembered Emma complaining once that her parents had a different excuse every time Emma mentioned them returning to the UK to visit her. Arthritis was one of the usual excuses, but Emma often pointed out that her dad was always posting photos of himself playing golf with his friends on Facebook, so it couldn't have been that bad.

'That's a shame, but like I said, anything you need help with, just ask. You're right; I think I do recognize a few people here,' Holly nodded, happy to see some more familiar faces.

'Danni and Fran should be here soon,' Emma explained as two men walked over and kissed her hello. Holly didn't see them properly at first. 'Do you remember Callum and Max from college too? Max is also a personal trainer and we've become great friends. Charlie works with him and Callum is their boss; he owns the gym they work at.'

Holly had to look twice at them before it actually dawned on her who these two were. They had been in the year above them at college and Holly hadn't seen either of them since they left all those years ago. Max immediately caught her eye with his fierce smile, light brown eyes, dark hair and olive skin. He looked like he had impressive biceps underneath his tight fitted black shirt and she could only imagine his athletic body underneath. He was absolutely gorgeous and she instantly felt self-conscious in a way she hadn't felt in a very long time. Callum was extremely attractive too, but with bright green eyes with fair hair, he wasn't her usual type. Holly had always gone for tall, dark and handsome. They certainly hadn't been as striking when they'd been at college as they were now. They'd both grown up. They were men now instead of lanky teenagers.

'Hi,' Max smiled, revealing immaculate teeth, 'I think I remember you. Holly, right?' he asked her confidently. 'I vaguely recall you trying to set me up with your friend Kim once,' he gave a light laugh, 'but it never happened.'

'Ah yes, I think I remember,' Holly said amicably. It was coming back to her now. It must have been one of the few times she'd ever spoken to Max. Kim had been going out with some idiot, Lee, who had been cheating on her. Holly had been in their local club and when she'd bumped into Max and they started chatting, she told him she was going to set him up with Kim. Kim hadn't been there and it had just been an idea to attempt to separate her from Lee. It hadn't happened though, because the next time Holly had spoken to Kim, she had told her she wasn't interested in anyone else. She wanted to give Lee another chance. Their rocky relationship lasted about another six months after that and Max had been forgotten about.

'Long time ago,' Max noted. 'Can I get you another drink?' he offered, touching her shoulder lightly.

Holly felt a fluttery feeling in her stomach. She had forgotten what it felt like. It both scared and enthralled her. This was a man she was interested in getting to know a bit more. This was a man she was attracted to. This rarely ever happened. Apart from when she'd first met Rob, Holly couldn't think of the last time she'd actually fancied someone. 'Yes please. A white wine please,' she requested timidly, 'if that's okay.'

'My pleasure,' Max grinned, before turning to Callum to take his order. It was at this point that Holly glanced at Max's ring finger. It was bare, much to her delight. No news of a wife to disappoint her. That didn't rule him out of being in a relationship of course. She decided to get some information about Max from Callum. He was clearly the quieter, more laid-back of the two, but he had a friendly, warm face.

'So, are you both here with your girlfriends?' Holly enquired in a nonchalant tone.

'No, we're both single,' Callum replied. 'We've both recently split with partners,' he told her. He looked up at her inquisitively. 'What about yourself?'

'Also single,' Holly told him, flicking her hair behind her

shoulders. 'I split with my boyfriend about eight months ago. We have two children though.'

'Boys or girls?' Callum asked, looking genuinely interested.

'One of each,' Holly replied, glancing over to Max who was just being served their drinks. She wondered if the fact she had children would put Max off. After all, it wasn't just *her* now. Then again, perhaps he was a father too?

'I have a five-year-old girl called Eva,' Callum told her, smiling with pride.

'Oh really? I'm hoping the tantrums stop by five?' Holly laughed.

'I hate to disappoint you,' Callum said, a light laugh escaping his lips, 'but no, not yet. In fact, I think they get worse. But maybe that's just Eva.'

'Does Max have children too?' Holly asked, her brow furrowing.

Callum looked at Holly as though the thought amused him. 'No, not Max. Max doesn't have any children yet.'

Holly didn't know whether this was a good or bad thing. She was glad Max was single, but perhaps he wouldn't consider someone with children if he didn't have any of his own? Holly came as a package. It was always going to be her plus two. Would it be hard to find someone willing to take on the three of them? Lottie was a handful at times and Jacob was still only a baby. Why was Holly even thinking about this when it had never bothered her before that men may be put off by extra baggage? She was perfectly fine on her own and had actually sworn to herself she didn't ever want to rely on a man again, but she was starting to question whether she really did want to be single forever. Would she be lonely in years to come? Just seeing how happy Rob and Nikki were was making her question things. Her mother was always telling her that one day her children would grow up. One day they wouldn't need her to clean their faces and brush their hair. They would know exactly what *they* wanted to wear. They wouldn't want their mother to drive them places. What was she

33

going to do then? Perhaps Holly had believed she was okay all alone because she'd never met anyone else she actually liked and had feelings for?

'One white wine.' Max shot Holly a devastating smile as he handed her the drink. 'The barman was so slow, I actually ordered us all two drinks each,' he explained, heading back over to get the other three.

'Thanks.' Holly's lips turned upwards as he walked back.

'So, where we off to next?' Max asked, gazing round the bar.

'There's a club here in the hotel, I think; Charlie mentioned we were going there earlier. I'm certainly up for it; I've heard Vegas clubs are amazing.'

'Sounds good to me,' Max replied enthusiastically, licking his drink from his lips. His brown eyes met Holly's and her insides turned to jelly. He was just so sexy. She couldn't believe she hardly knew him and he was having such an effect on her. Holly made her way to the ladies' after twenty minutes of chatting to Max and Callum and bumped into Emma again.

'Having fun?' Emma asked curiously, looking as though she knew Holly's secret. She was smirking as she asked the question.

'He's gorgeous.' Holly couldn't help herself.

'Which one? They both are!' Emma giggled. 'Slightly improved since college, haven't they?'

'Yes, they really have. They're both good looking but I was talking about Max though. What's the deal with him?' Holly asked as she washed her hands.

'He's just split up with his ex-girlfriend, Carmen,' Emma revealed, applying some lipstick in the mirror. 'He was with her about five months; I never knew him to have a girlfriend before that, and I've known him ever since I started going to the gym about two years ago. He gets tons of attention from women, not surprisingly. I think he's a bit of a charmer, to be honest.'

'Yes, I can imagine,' Holly replied, brushing her hair. 'He's so lovely though.'

'He likes you too,' Emma smiled widely, giving Holly a reassuring smile.

Holly felt a slight colour coming to her cheeks. She felt so silly and childish. *Clubbing. Having a little crush. Finding out he liked her back from her friend.* She was reminded of her past when this kind of thing was a regular occurrence. It had been so normal back then. 'What? How do you know?'

'I just asked where you'd gone and they told me. Then they both said they thought you were really nice and Max gave a cheeky laugh saying he hoped you weren't long as he was hoping to get to know you even better.'

Holly's tummy did another somersault. 'He just said that?' She adopted a tone of surprise.

'Yep,' Emma grinned. 'I think you could have yourself a little summer romance here in Vegas.'

Holly couldn't wipe the smile off her face. 'We'll see,' she said, as they left the ladies' room.

Thirty minutes later, Holly was entering the dark nightclub, following behind Emma. A small group of them had decided to go on, including Max and Callum, while a few of the others had decided to call it a night. The nightclub was absolutely huge, the music was blaring and there were tables full with gigantic bottles of champagne and vodka. Half-clothed waitresses were parading round with trays of shots. It felt crazy to Holly that she was actually here. Once again, she was taken back to the time before she'd had children when she used to go out with Kim. This environment had been her life at one point (not that the local clubs at home were even a fraction as good) and Holly remembered sometimes actually getting a little bored with it. Some nights she didn't always want to go to a club; it was the thing they did every weekend and it could sometimes get a little dull seeing the same faces and going to exactly the same places. Holly couldn't imagine ever finding Vegas dull. She was having the time of her life so far, enjoying every single second. She was going to make the most of her little trip, of that she was certain. She was in no rush to get back to the hotel room and go to sleep; all previous thoughts of being jet-lagged and tired had completely disappeared now she was out enjoying herself.

Max took her hand, pulling her backwards as Callum and Emma walked ahead, following a pretty waitress to their table.

'What's up?' Holly asked, confused.

Max didn't say anything, he just smirked amusedly before pulling her closer towards him, his hands around her waist.

Holly's heart raced as she gazed into his blazing eyes and without thinking, she leaned in for a kiss.

'I've been wanting to do that since I first saw you,' he told her with a wicked grin, before walking ahead assertively still holding her hand.

Holly caught her breath as she followed him, unable to believe what had just happened. Kissing Max had felt like the most natural thing to do and her stomach bubbled with anticipation. Max was rugged, confident and intriguing, exactly the type of man she found attractive.

Holly was hooked.

Chapter 5

Kim

Kim woke up and immediately sat up in a panic. *Why weren't the children awake yet?* It took her a few seconds to realize everything was okay. She wasn't at home. There were no children here. She was in Vegas, with Holly lying in the bed beside her.

She took a deep breath, stretching out in bed as she noticed the time on the clock by the television. She'd slept for over thirteen hours, only waking once in the night to notice that Holly wasn't yet back. Thirteen hours of pure, uninterrupted peace; she couldn't remember the last time she'd been able to do that. One of her children always woke her. If not in the middle of the night, then at the crack of dawn. They were such early risers and Kim found it difficult to think of the last time she'd slept past seven o'clock. Seven was *late* for her nowadays. If one of the kids woke and she saw seven anything on her clock she felt like it was an achievement, that she was winning at life and she would give herself a pat on the back in triumph.

Kim glanced over at Holly's bed, pleased to see her friend was now sleeping soundly. She hadn't heard Holly come in, but she knew it must have been very late because when Kim had woken at three, Holly still wasn't back. She honestly didn't know how Holly did it. Kim had been really looking forward to their summer trip away, but she had to admit she planned on relaxing as much as possible. She needed to relax a lot more than she needed to party. She completely understood that Holly was single and probably more interested in going out drinking than nice dinners and shows; luckily there were other people Holly could go out with if Kim felt like having a chilled one.

Kim reached across the side of the bed for her Kindle. She would have a nice few hours in bed reading before Holly woke up; this was what holidays were all about.

'Morning,' Holly stretched out, yawning loudly an hour and fifteen minutes later.

'Hey,' Kim smiled. 'How was your evening?'

'I met up with Emma and the others,' Holly told her. 'We went to a bar and then onto a club; it was such a good night, Kim. You should have come.'

'And miss out on the best night sleep I've had in years?' Kim gave a little laugh. 'No chance. Were there a big group of you?'

'In the bar there was, but only a small group of us went on to the club. There's a few people here we know. Danni and Fran from college are out here and do you remember me trying to set you up with someone called Max from the year above us when you were with that guy called Lee who cheated on you?'

'Vaguely,' Kim said frowning as she racked her brains. She didn't have the best memory. She was forever forgetting people's names and events that happened years ago. She wasn't even great at remembering to pack important things when she went out, like baby wipes and Willow's dummy. It was well known that Kim was a bit of a nightmare. Luckily she always had someone else around her that had the particular thing she needed on them. Someone super-organized and on the ball like Holly.

'Well they're here too. They're really nice guys. It was amazing,'

Holly said, shutting her eyes briefly. 'Honestly Kim. The clubs here are so good. It's so much fun; you're going to love it. I had so much to drink; I'm so glad I feel okay today. God knows what time I came back.'

'Did you have to come back alone?' Kim asked, feeling guilty she'd left her friend to fend for herself in a foreign place.

Holly bit her lip, trying not to smile. 'Actually I didn't. Max and Callum brought me back. They just wanted to check I got home safely, which was nice of them.'

'What's that smile for?' Kim asked her quickly, knowing her friend well enough to know she was hiding something. 'Which one of them do you like?' She asked wisely with a smile.

Holly laughed gaily. 'Is it that obvious?' There was a pause. 'I had a little kiss with Max, that's all.'

'Oh my goodness. I can't believe I've missed only one night and you've already been kissing people!' Kim clicked her tongue in mock-outrage. It was most unlike Holly to meet people she liked enough to kiss. She'd never really been the kind to kiss in a club, even when they were younger. That was usually Kim's job. She was the one who kissed people and then woke up the next morning with absolutely no memory of doing it. Holly would have been mortified if it had been her, but Kim couldn't have cared less. It was only a kiss. It seemed so bizarre that Holly was still single, stealing kisses in nightclubs with someone who was practically a stranger. The thought of doing anything like that seemed like a lifetime ago to Kim. She was married with two children. She only ever kissed Andy, and she was glad about that. It had been fun when she was younger, dating various men and not knowing what was going to happen, but Kim realized she was actually far happier now she was grown up, in a loving relationship with a family of her own. She'd had her fun and hung up her boots. Since becoming a mother she had transformed into the person she'd always swore she didn't want to be. She used to think being a housewife and taking care of children would be so boring and dull, so nothing stunned her more than when she got pregnant by accident, enjoying every second of being a mother when Mylo was born.

It had been extremely worrying at the start; Mylo had been born prematurely at thirty-three weeks weighing only three pound ten. She remembered staring at this delicate little baby in the incubator, terrified of taking him home in case she did something wrong. Seeing him so vulnerable and fragile made Kim promise herself she would be the best mother she possibly could. She didn't expect to love taking care of little people and protecting them, catering for their every need, but she discovered it wasn't boring at all. In fact, she loved it. She needed it. She loved feeling essential, with two tiny little people constantly climbing all over her, lying on her lap and resting their heads on her chest.

She couldn't believe how quickly Mylo and Willow had already grown; time seemed to be flying past and Kim wanted to relish every moment with her babies. The thought of going out like she used to just didn't appeal to her any more. She didn't mind the odd dinner here and there, it was always nice to catch up with people, but generally speaking, she didn't *want* to go out and get drunk, feeling ill all the next day. She had a family to look after and it just wasn't worth it. She had grown up. She was happy with her life now. When they'd first got the invitation to go Vegas, Kim had immediately thought there was no way she was travelling over ten hours away without her family. She knew how happy Holly would be if she went; Holly's excitement had been obvious the minute she'd seen the invite, but she'd wanted Kim to go too, and Kim just wasn't sure if she could just up and leave being a mother to two young children. They came first.

Kim thought back to how Andy had come home that evening, Mylo and Willow fast asleep upstairs, Kim just dishing up dinner.

'Good day at work?' she'd asked, like she did every day.

Andy was a PE teacher at their local secondary school. Rugby was his thing, and he also did rugby coaching on Sundays. He lived and breathed it, though Kim still didn't have the foggiest ideas what the rules were.

'Yeah, it was good thanks. Lily and I were just trying to organize sports day for most of the day. She's got some great ideas, I'll give her that.'

Kim's brow creased. 'Lily? Remind me who that is?' she asked. She thought she'd heard something about a Lily the week before, but Mylo had come downstairs saying he wanted a drink and Kim had been distracted.

'She's just a new PE teacher at the school,' Andy had told her vaguely, pouring them both a glass of orange juice.

'Oh right. What's she like? Young? Old?'

'She's twenty-eight, slim, long dark hair,' Andy said nonchalantly as he reached for two coasters before placing the drinks on the table.

'What about your day? Did you see Holly like you planned?' Andy asked as she sat in front of him, handing over his plate.

'Yes,' Kim had replied. 'We just took the kids to the park, that's all.'

'The one near the newsagents? I think Lily lives near there. She was telling me earlier today that they do a great summer fair in that park; perhaps we should check it out? Oh, I've been meaning to ask if you fancied a night out soon? Tony and Leah have asked if we wanted to go to their house for dinner. My mum said she'd babysit.'

Tony was Andy's oldest friend from school. He'd been best man at their wedding and Andy had been his when he'd married Leah. Though Kim knew they hadn't met up in quite some time, the prospect of spending an evening with them didn't exactly sound enthralling. Tony and Leah didn't have any children and Kim knew they would constantly be topping up their wine glasses, convincing them to stay for 'just one more'. They would most likely end up getting home in the early hours, and with Mylo and Willow being such early risers, Kim couldn't think of anything worse. She knew Andy would be keen to stay late and it would be Kim appearing like the boring one, battling to get him to leave.

'I'd rather not if I'm honest,' Kim told him.

'Why?' Andy turned to her, his brow knitted.

Kim sighed reluctantly. 'It will end up a late one, Andy. I don't want to feel rough the next day when we have such young kids. Maybe another time, eh?'

He sighed heavily and nodded, looking disappointed, knowing there was no point in pushing things further. When Kim made her mind up, she rarely changed it.

Kim was keen to change the subject. 'We've been invited to Emma Langford's wedding in Vegas. Shame it's so far away or we could have gone, but there's no way we could ask either of our mums to have the kids for so long, is there? I wouldn't feel comfortable leaving them either. I know Holly is really eager to go though.'

'Why don't you just go, Kim?' Andy suggested, running his hand through his beard, which needed a trim. 'Go and have fun with Holly. Just because we have kids doesn't mean we have to miss out on everything, does it? One of our mums can have the kids for a few days when I'm working and then I'll take care of them over the weekend. Come on, treat yourself. Once upon a time you would have jumped at the chance of going to Vegas.'

Kim shook her head, not feeling entirely comfortable with the idea. Kim was their *mother*. As much as Andy was a great father, he didn't do things like Kim did. He didn't know that Kim had to pretend to sprinkle sugar on Mylo's cornflakes to keep him happy in the morning or the way Willow had to be rocked to sleep if she woke up in the night. 'Yes, but things are different now, aren't they? I have responsibilities. No, honestly. Thanks Andy, but I don't think I should be leaving them.'

Andy shrugged with an unreadable expression before sitting at the dinner table and gazing out into the garden. 'I'm going to mow the lawn after dinner,' he said.

Half an hour later Kim was watching him roam up and down the lawn with a determined look on his face. Andy saw their garden as a serious business. He was often asking her opinions on the flowerbeds or if she liked the lines he'd made in the grass.

She'd always thought of Andy as her rugged bear: he was tall at six foot two, and being a rugby player, he was solid and brawny, but with kind, gentle features.

Andy's phone vibrated, which he'd left on the table and Kim picked it up, about to pass it to him before she noticed it was a message from Lily.

Hey hot stuff. What you up to?

Kim swallowed hard as she read the message again, an unsettled feeling washing over her immediately. *Hot stuff*? What on earth was all that about? It wasn't exactly the appropriate thing to write to a married man, was it? But perhaps it was just in a friendly way, Kim told herself. Harmless banter between two work colleagues. Kim didn't want to be suspicious and she knew she should just put the phone down, but her eyes flicked up at Andy who was in a world of his own in the garden, and she clicked on the message so she could see the rest of the thread.

The blood rushed to Kim's ears and she felt she had something lodged in her throat as she looked through their other messages, which had been going on over the past few weeks.

Lily: *Where are you eating lunch today? Want some company?*
Andy: *Sure! I'll come find you now.*
Lily: *Can't stop thinking about what you said earlier. I keep laughing!*
Andy: *Yep. Funny as well as good looking. Told you I was perfect!*
Lily: *Maybe you're right :)*
Lily: *Fancy a drink after work Friday night? I want to prove that I can drink you under the table ;)*

Andy: *Maybe. I'll see if I can make it.*

Lily: *Been thinking of you today. Missing me?*

Andy: *Like a hole in the head!*

Lily: *Ha. I know that's a lie. Of course you are x*

Andy: *Maybe a little bit. Could do with an extra set of hands here. How's the sickness bug?x*

Lily: *Getting better, but still a bit fragile so you'll need to look after me when I'm back. Wait on me hand and foot, that kind of thing ha. Hopefully I'll be back with you tomorrow xxx*

Andy: *Fingers crossed! Hope you feel better asap. It's not the same without you x*

Kim felt as though her heart was thumping at a million miles per hour. Was she overreacting to this? Kim couldn't help but notice that their messages were very flirtatious. Why was Andy entertaining this? She racked her brains looking at the date Lily had texted him about going out on the Friday night. They'd had her parents over that Friday evening she was talking about because it had been the day before Kim's dad's birthday. Andy had been home with her. She breathed a sigh of relief. Had he asked what their plans were that week to check if he was free? Kim couldn't recall it now. She was always bathing the kids when he arrived home or attempting to get Mylo to stop coming downstairs and reading him his fifth bedtime story of the night to make him go to sleep. There were always so many other things to think about that she rarely took much notice of Andy any more. Her hands were trembling as she nibbled the nail of her index finger. The thought of not taking much notice of her husband any more troubled her.

She looked up to see Andy strolling in looking pleased with himself. 'Grass looks nice, doesn't it?' He turned back round to view his masterpiece.

'Yes, well done,' Kim said, after waiting a moment to compose herself. She should say something. Kim knew she ought to bring it up, right there and then. She had to tell Andy she wasn't too happy with these messages and they had to stop. But she hadn't said a thing. It was as though the words were just stuck in her throat. Andy was right, she had changed. Kim used to be a bit of a wild child, always up for going out and getting into mischief. It was one of the things Andy had always told her he loved about her. As soon as she'd had Mylo, that had all changed. But didn't that happen to the majority of mothers? Was Andy getting bored of her? Was she pushing him into the arms of Lily, the twenty-eight-year-old, child-free colleague who thought her husband was 'hot stuff'? Kim took a deep breath. She needed time to process all of this.

'Andy, I've been thinking,' she managed. 'Maybe I'll take you up on that offer to Vegas after all.'

The memories of that evening disappeared as Kim heard Holly's soft giggle. 'I wouldn't have called it a proper kiss,' she pointed out, 'more like a little peck. I shouldn't have even told you. Now come on, shall we get ready and go get some breakfast? I'm starving,' she said as she jumped out of bed.

'Are we just going to a pool today? I can't wait to sunbathe without a single interruption.' Hopefully it would also give her time to think about her marriage too. She had wanted this time to come away and escape, forgetting about her troubles back home, but Kim couldn't help but feel she'd only brought them with her. Even last night she'd struggled to get asleep due to the worry, despite being exhausted.

'Yes. I said we'd meet the others there at oneish. It's somewhere called Encore; I can't remember the hotel though,' she said, before disappearing to have a shower.

After a delicious breakfast of pancakes drenched in maple syrup, the girls were making their way to the swimming pool.

'We must be the first to arrive,' Holly noted, looking round for the others. It was a huge place but was fairly quiet so far, with just the odd few sunbathers. Holly imagined it would get busier later on. She glanced at her watch. 'It's only twelve though, so I'm sure they'll be here soon enough.'

'Is lover boy coming?' Kim teased.

Holly rolled her eyes. 'Hey enough of that,' she laughed. 'I told you it was only one quick kiss and yes, I think he said he was.'

'Peace, quiet, sunshine and my Kindle,' Kim sighed loudly. 'This is the life. It's absolute bliss; I'm so pleased that I came away. I really do appreciate the break. I can't believe we once got to do this whenever we felt like it.'

The sunshine was blazing and Kim couldn't wait to try to relax. As she took a deep breath, she smiled as she realized it smelt like holiday: a mixture of coconut, chlorine and sun lotion.

Feeling a sudden wave of guilt that she was enjoying herself so much, she pulled her mobile out to call Andy, just to check everything at home was okay with the children. She'd never been away from them before, and despite telling herself she needed to switch off, she was struggling. It went straight through to voice-mail and Kim frowned.

'Calling Andy?' Holly asked, squinting at Kim in the bright sunshine.

'Yes. Just got his voicemail,' Kim said, an uneasy feeling creeping up on her.

'Perhaps he's working late.'

'It's about nine o'clock. at home. He wouldn't be working now,' Kim replied sighing heavily.

'I wouldn't worry; he's just probably a bit busy. He'll call back.'

Kim nodded. She knew she was overreacting, worrying for absolutely no reason at all. He could be in the shower or he could have left his phone upstairs; there were a million reasons why he may not be able to answer her phone call straight away. Her mum was watching the children until he got home from work, but Kim assumed she would be home by now, but she tried her phone anyway, anxious when she didn't answer either. Kim's mum was terrible with her mobile. Half of the time it was on silent and the other half of the time she left it at home. She couldn't stand not knowing what was going on. A thought dawned on her then and it was one she didn't like at all.

Had Andy wanted her to go to Vegas so he could spend time with Lily?

Chapter 6

Holly

'Fancy a cocktail?' Holly asked hopefully. 'I may get a Cosmopolitan.' Holly hadn't brought a book like Kim had. She had tried to explain to Kim how busy it would get; Vegas pool parties were hardly the place for reading. Kim hadn't taken much notice though and staying true to her new, sensible self, she'd pulled out a sun hat and Factor 50 cream. Gone were the days when Kim would sunbathe topless, lathering on Factor 2 oil.

As the minutes went by, it started to become more and more lively, with crowds of people walking through the entrance, security guards checking the ID of everyone coming through and it was clear they were in the right place. Holly knew Emma wouldn't disappoint with her plans and she was glad she'd worn her best swimsuit. Her plain, boring mumsy ones just weren't going to cut it here, she thought amusedly. The girls who had started to walk in were certainly dressed to impress, many having a full face of make-up on and freshly tonged hair. They oozed glamour and sex appeal, many laughing and appearing buoyant, ready to have a good time. The music started to become louder and Holly heard Kim exhale in frustration.

'No, I'll just get a Diet Coke I think. It's loud in here, don't you think?'

'I think this is just what a pool party is supposed to be like,' Holly explained.

She was hoping that Kim would come out of her shell and be a bit more positive and upbeat today. 'Honestly, take my advice and just enjoy it before it's over. Try not to worry about home at all. We're not going to be here long! We're all the way in Vegas now, so let's just have a good time,' Holly told her brightly. 'Anyway, I'm going to get a cocktail. Diet Coke, was it?'

'Please,' Kim said as she bent down to search her bag for her sunglasses. 'I can't really drink in the daytime any more; just goes straight to my head.'

Holly knew she had to accept Kim had changed in the past few years, but she knew her fun side was in there somewhere. She was no longer a daytime drinker and preferred to sleep rather than go out. Since when would Kim not have a cocktail round a swimming pool? They were on *holiday.* If you couldn't drink in the daytime on holiday, then when could you? Holly was determined to bring her out of her shell.

It was getting louder at the pool party and now there was a DJ standing in the booth. Holly was elated to spot Emma, Charlie and a few others walking through the entrance. She waved her hands wildly as though they were going to miss her, beaming with joy as they walked over. She quickly scanned the small group of them, feeling a little gutted that Max hadn't yet arrived. She was really looking forward to seeing him, even though she felt a little nervous about it.

'Drinks?' Holly offered, as Emma danced over with the broadest smile on her face.

Emma hugged her. 'How cool is it here? Let's do a whip, shall we? We can buy a few jugs of cocktails and loads of beers for the boys so we don't have to keep coming and ordering.' She looked round. 'Where are you sitting? Did Kim make it out today?'

As Holly's gaze landed on Kim, she tried to contain her laughter. She was lying down, reading her book with a huge sunhat on, as girls around her flounced around in tiny two pieces, drinking, dancing and splashing in the water. 'She's just over there.'

'Come, let's leave Charlie to take our order and we'll sort the money out in a bit. Let's go see Kim,' she said happily.

'Just a Diet Coke too, Charlie, if that's okay? For Kim,' Holly added hastily.

Emma gasped in mock-offence. 'Diet Coke? Charlie, just pretend you didn't hear that. She's not drinking a Diet Coke when she's out with us,' she said cheekily, pulling Holly along behind her.

'Kim!' Emma practically jumped on top of her, making her scream.

'Em, you frightened the life out of me!' Kim said in a high-pitched voice with a smile on her face, looking pleased to see her. 'How are you?'

'I'm good. Amazing. About to get married, can you believe? Thank you so much for coming all the way out here. I honestly feel so lucky to have people to make such an effort for me,' Emma told them graciously, sitting on the edge of Kim's sun lounger.

'Ah, I'm so pleased to be here,' Kim gushed. 'I can't wait to see your dress. You're looking tiny by the way,' she commented, pointing and admiring Emma's toned figure through her white kaftan. 'Holly mentioned that we were coming to help you with flowers or something? What time are we going?'

'We'll stay here for about an hour and a half and then get a taxi there. Thanks for agreeing to come.'

'Is that Charlie over there?' Kim questioned. 'I've only ever seen him on your Instagram. He looks lovely. I bet you can't wait to get married; you two literally look like the dream couple.'

'Definitely can't wait,' Emma replied in a shrilly voice. 'I'm so lucky. I can't wait to start trying for a baby like you girls. I'll be

50

coming to you both soon for lots of advice I hope. Then I can join you on your kids' days out.'

'Don't get too excited,' Holly laughed heartily. 'I'd happily never see another baby group again, but seriously, we can't wait for you to join us either. Are you going to start trying straight away?' Holly asked curiously.

'That's the plan,' Emma said cheerfully. 'Hopefully I'll be pregnant by the end of the summer…' she tailed off.

'How exciting,' Kim replied, her eyes glittery.

'Oh look, there's Max and Callum,' Emma announced, looking over to the entrance.

Holly felt her heart gallop at the sight of Max and Callum as she narrowed her eyes trying to make them out.

'Oh my God,' Kim said, her eyes widening and mouth forming an 'o' shape. 'They're hot. Wait, *that's* the guy you tried to set me up with?' she asked Holly. 'The dark-haired one? Jeez. If I'd known he'd turn out like that I would have ditched Lee in a heartbeat,' she giggled girlishly.

'Yes, that's him,' Holly replied, wishing Kim would stop staring. It was so obvious they were discussing him. Not cool in the slightest. 'He didn't exactly look like that at college though.'

'What exactly happened between you two last night anyway?' Emma asked, grinning.

Holly flapped her hand dismissively, feeling her face growing hotter. 'It was nothing, honestly. Nothing at all.' She didn't want to admit how much she liked him already. Holly had always kept her cards close to her chest where men were concerned. She hardly knew Max and she didn't even know if he liked her back yet. He may go around kissing everyone for all she knew. She remembered once at her school prom when she told everyone she really liked a boy called Matt Renshaw. She'd been spending quite a bit of time with him, and he'd hinted a few times he liked her as more than a friend. Everyone had teased her about it for ages, but Holly had never admitted it, too afraid of rejection. All girl friends got so excited when one night she finally said she did have feelings for him, trying to persuade her to go over to him to chat. When Holly finally gathered the courage to walk over to him, Matt started kissing a girl called Sarah Bentley. There had been tongues and everything and Holly had felt humiliated as she gazed at her friends' pitying glances. She'd left it too late. Matt had got bored of waiting for her and was moving on. She'd have much preferred to never have said she liked him in the first place. That way, no-one would have been any the wiser over how sad she'd felt about the whole thing. For months Holly felt embarrassed every time she spotted Matt and Sarah together. The last she heard, Matt was still with Sarah and they had two little boys together so it all worked out for the best in the end.

Charlie walked over with their drinks and Emma poured them out their cocktails. Holly noticed that Kim introduced herself straight away, taking a cocktail without even questioning where her Diet Coke was, much to Holly's surprise. Then she noticed Kim put away her sun hat and take her shorts off, looking round at what everyone else was wearing.

'I kind of wish I'd made a bit more effort with my swimwear now,' Holly heard Kim say to Emma. 'I've had this costume for years. I really should have gone shopping before coming here.'

Emma shook her head dismissively. 'You look great. I hope I look as good as you after two children,' she said sweetly. 'Besides, there's tons of shops in Vegas if you want to go shopping.'

'That would be great – maybe we could go after the flowers or something?' Kim said hopefully. 'I may just go and freshen up a bit in the ladies,' she told her. She glanced in Holly's direction. 'Need to go?'

'No, I'm okay,' Holly replied.

Kim seemed to be more up for it now since the others had arrived and Holly was glad.

Max and Callum walked over to where they were standing.

'Hey,' Max said in a friendly voice. 'What's everyone drinking?'

Charlie signalled to the table of drinks. 'Beers are here mate,' he pointed out, 'just join the whip and help yourself.'

'Cheers,' Max replied, peeling off his white t-shirt to reveal the most stunning body Holly had ever seen. He was muscular, but not too big, with several tattoos on his chest and a sleeve tattoo on his right arm. Holly wasn't really into guys with huge muscles like some personal trainers, so the fact he had just the right amount made him even more perfect. If someone asked her to draw her dream man, she'd be drawing Max. His skin was bronzed already, smooth and flawless. She felt her heart skip a beat when he looked in her direction with a smoldering gaze.

'Hi Holly,' he smiled, leaning over and kissing her cheek. She could see his eyes roaming up and down her body through his sunglasses. 'How you feeling this morning?' he asked.

He was so confident and charming, and without a doubt the most handsome man she'd ever kissed. Holly wasn't shallow and she knew looks weren't everything, but she couldn't recall a time she'd been so drawn to someone. She couldn't recall ever fantasizing about someone the way she had done the past morning about Max. She'd found Rob attractive when they first met, but it was his personality that had made him more appealing the longer they'd dated. With Max, she could just stare at him all day. He was literally her type to a 'T', and so far, he seemed to have the personality to match.

'Hey,' Callum smiled in her direction and Holly couldn't help but notice he was in amazing shape too. Being a gym owner, she guessed it was part and parcel of the job to look good. He literally had no excuse not to go. She felt slightly guilty looking at their sculpted bodies. She hadn't gone to the gym in years. Firstly she didn't have time having the children and secondly, even if she did, she knew she wouldn't pick the gym over shopping and getting a manicure. It just wasn't a priority of hers at all, but with Max being a personal trainer, she was starting to think about taking more of an interest. Then again, she wasn't ever going to be a tiny size six parading around in a bikini and she was okay with that. Bikinis were now out of the window; her two children had seen to that. Being a size ten/twelve, Holly wasn't exactly big in any way, but her skin was a bit crinkled on her lower stomach and she had a few silver stretch marks, something she tried to view in a positive light. They were marks to show she'd made it through childbirth and was lucky enough to have delivered two healthy, beautiful babies; Marks she was proud of, but not quite brave enough to show to the world.

Max sat next to Holly on the sun lounger. 'Wow, it's hot today,' he said, running his fingers through his hair.

She could smell his aftershave as he lifted his arm – a mixture of earthy patchouli and rosewood. 'You're not wrong there,' Holly replied, leaning back, closing her eyes and putting her face into the sunlight. 'Heatwave at home and now we're here. I don't think I can remember a hotter summer.'

He half smiled. 'Fancy taking your drink into the pool? I think I need to cool down.'

Holly didn't need to be asked twice and she followed him, watching the other admiring glances from females as they walked past. They were looking at Holly as though she was lucky, and at that point in time she honestly felt it. Being with someone like Max made her feel special. There was just something about him and the way he looked at her that made Holly feel important.

They sat on the edge of the pool and Max put his arm round her. Her skin tingled and she felt herself weaken at his touch. She needed to get a grip, she told herself sternly. She hardly knew him.

'Last night was fun,' he smirked, as he glanced around at the other people in the pool, which was becoming more crowded by the second. The music was even louder now too.

'Yes, I had such a good night,' Holly told him.

'Do you go out much at home?' Max asked, cocking his head to the side.

Holly shook her head. 'Not any more. I have two children,' she explained. She wanted him to know this sooner rather than later. If Max had an issue with it, then it was never going to work out anyway. The quicker Holly knew this, the better. 'I don't get the chance to get out as much as I used to.'

'So are you still with the father of your children?' Max asked cautiously. His brow furrowed and he looked a little worried and surprised.

'No, no.' Holly couldn't reply quick enough to put him at ease. She may not have been happy with Rob, but she certainly wasn't the type to cheat. 'Rob and I split up about eight months ago. He has a new girlfriend now. He told me just before I came out here. We're still friends.'

Max nodded. 'Glad to hear it,' he said, an unreadable expression on his face.

'I love kids,' Max added, 'can't wait to have my own one day.'

Holly knew this was his way of saying he wasn't put off by the fact she was a mum and she felt herself relax.

'Hi!' Holly heard Kim's merry tones behind her. She turned round in surprise to see Kim emerge from the crowd, having glammed herself up in the ladies. She was even wearing lip-gloss now and her blonde hair, which had been up in a messy bun, was now cascading down her shoulders. She sat next to Max and put her hand out. 'Sorry, I don't think we've met. I'm Kim.' She shot him her biggest smile. 'So nice to meet you.'

'Ah yes, I've heard about you. You made it out today then?' he asked, splashing his legs about in the pool.

'Yes, I'm fresh and ready for the day. The sleep did me the world of good,' Kim replied, shooting him another bright smile. 'So I hear we were supposed to go on a date years ago?' She giggled, raising one eyebrow.

'Indeed we were,' Max replied. 'I think you blew me out though,' he smiled, looking more handsome than ever.

'I'm sure you were heartbroken,' Kim responded, laughing gaily.

55

'Shall I get some more drinks?' Holly offered, standing up to get out the pool.

'Go on then,' Kim grinned, downing the last bit of her cocktail and handing Holly the glass.

Emma was in deep conversation with Frankie when Holly walked back over to their sun beds.

'Sorry,' Holly apologized, as she walked past and leant over to pick up the cocktail jug.

'Don't be silly,' Emma replied. 'Frankie was just telling me their stag do plans tonight. He's promised me he'll look after Charlie,' she laughed good-naturedly. 'Charlie has a bit of a habit of getting a bit too drunk.'

'Understatement of the year,' Frankie grinned. 'Do you remember that time we had to find him when he'd fallen asleep outside at Helen's wedding?'

Emma laughed vigorously with Frankie. 'That was so funny. I'd forgotten about that.'

'I see you've been with Max again,' Emma said to Holly, with a suggestive glint in her eye.

Holly blushed. 'Yes. He's a nice guy,' she said in a non-committal tone.

'Where is he now?' Emma turned round and noticed him in the pool. 'Oh yes, he's over there with Kim.'

'Let's get a photo,' Holly suggested, taking her phone out of her bag. She usually forgot to take pictures on holidays and nights out and relied on other people to take them. She took a selfie of them together and then Holly flicked through her Facebook newsfeed because she had a notification.

'Right, we'd best leave in about fifteen minutes and then perhaps we'll go shopping quickly afterwards,' Emma explained, going on to tell Holly the plans for her hen do that evening. 'Holly, are you even listening to me?'

Holly shook her head as though she was in a daydream. 'Yes, yes. You were talking about tonight,' she said, her eyes flicking back to her phone. Rob had added some new images of himself and Nikki and Holly couldn't help but flick through them nosily. There was one photo of them both laughing and it reminded Holly that she hadn't seen Rob look so happy in a very long time. Had they once laughed like that? They certainly hadn't at the end of their relationship. It had been constant huffing and eye-rolling. Was it possible to be happy for someone but also feel a stab of envy? She noticed Rob's mother, Judy, comment underneath the photo.

Lovely couple, it read.

Holly swallowed hard, feeling a pang of betrayal towards Judy. She'd always got on well with her, but wasn't liking the feeling of being replaced so easily. Didn't they realize it wasn't easy for her to see things like this?

'Are you okay? You seem to be in another world,' Emma asked caringly.

'No, I'm fine, honestly.' Holly attempted a light laugh. She did her best to listen to the rest of what Emma was saying, but the truth was Holly felt a bit empty inside. *We weren't right together,* Holly reminded herself over and over as Emma continued to chat away. She had been the one who had made the decision that they should go their separate ways. Despite wanting a perfect family for her children, she knew it couldn't go on as it was, so why did it all feel so final now Rob had moved on? She didn't *want* to find this difficult. She'd been adamant that she and Rob would remain friends on social media as well as in real life because everything was cool between them. There wasn't anything to get upset about. She couldn't very well delete him now, could she? He would wonder what he'd done wrong.

She looked back down at the laughing photo. No, Holly wouldn't delete him. But she sure as hell was going to unfollow him so she didn't have to look at photos like that ever again.

She looked over at Max, who caught her eye and put on her most seductive smile.

Chapter 7

Emma

Emma pulled her phone out to get some videos of the pool party to upload to her Instagram. She knew she would be inundated with messages asking where she got her beautiful white bikini from (a freebie from a new swimwear company) or people asking for advice about Vegas and where to go. Posting on Instagram was addictive. Emma honestly couldn't remember the last day she hadn't posted something. She'd been ill the previous year and had felt guilty for not posting as much as usual after spending nearly a week holed up with tonsillitis. She had even created a video just to apologize to people who liked being updated with her new make-up routine or what new outfit she was wearing. People were actually messaging her and asking where she was, as if it was the end of the world that she hadn't posted in a while. As though they *needed* their Emma fix. It was crazy, but it had become normal life for Emma. The amount of people wishing her well that week had been incredible. Emma felt like some kind of celebrity. She felt like someone valued, special and important. She couldn't deny it boosted her ego and made her feel good in a way nothing else could. Watching as hundreds of people liked her photos, reading their lovely comments and receiving the private messages; many offers from various companies and brands wanting to send her freebies just so she advertised them in a post. Her numbers of followers just kept on rising and rising. The amount of likes she received continued to increase every week. Her business was growing at a rapid speed – Emma could hardly keep up. That's when Charlie reminded her how lucky she was to have him to help; he often dealt with lots of the enquiries. He often told her what she was doing and when.

She wanted to get a quick video before she had to leave to look at the flowers. Emma put her camera in selfie mode and smiled, whilst waving her hand in time to the music. She then turned it round in the direction of the others who waved and cheered. Everyone apart from Charlie, who pretty much rolled his eyes and turned the opposite way. It hadn't gone unnoticed to Emma.

'Does it ever get exhausting always having to update your fans?' Frankie asked, standing beside her with a grin as Emma tapped away on her phone adding the location of where they were to her video story.

'Sometimes,' Emma answered truthfully. She'd never really admitted that before. Charlie had recently been making snide comments, especially if she was posting something in which he wasn't included. He was always fine accepting the free trips and gifts she got from companies that included *him*. If he was in the photo, he always seemed more than happy to pose. It just seemed that recently, he'd been putting Emma's job down and making her feel as though she should be doing something normal like working in an office or cutting people's hair. He made her feel as though she was vain for constantly taking photos. She constantly had to remind him that it had all been *his* idea in the first place. Emma had actually asked herself the same question on many occasions: did it make her narcissistic indulging in so many selfies, even though it was her job?

'Certainly not a bad job though, is it?' Frankie said encouragingly to reassure her he wasn't putting it down. 'I guess it's just one you never really get a break from. Still, not your typical nine to five. I think it's great. I know I'd happily be a blogger over working in finance,' he admitted.

He was certainly right that Emma never really got a break from it. If she was really honest, there were some times where she felt like she wasn't actually *living* these moments she was capturing on camera and showing the world. The trip to the Maldives was an example. She'd gone with Charlie for the New Year and every time she saw a beautiful setting, she just couldn't help but think, *this will make a great photo.* Had she truly appreciated it or just admired it through a lens?

'Why don't we just go out as we are tonight?' she remembered Charlie saying one evening. They'd been on a boat and for a swim in the sea. Emma looked like a drowned rat with her tangled wet hair and her face free of make-up. She was only wearing a cheap, plain kaftan too.

'No,' she recalled protesting, 'I want a shower and to get ready. I want to wash my hair and freshen up.'

Had she really wanted to do that though? Or was it just because she wanted to take the stunning photo they got that evening of them in front of a sunset on the beach? Emma had wanted to look nice in the image so she could post it. There wasn't any room for 'normal' on her Instagram feed. She wanted to keep up the pretence that she had the perfect, magical life and just so happened to always look amazing twenty-four hours a day. She and Charlie had argued that evening and she remembered going to bed without even saying goodnight. That certainly hadn't made it onto her Instagram feed.

Then there were the horrible comments from the trolls. It was funny, the name 'troll', a term used for people who made nasty remarks anonymously from behind a computer screen, but it was a perfect really. When Emma thought of that word, she thought of a little green goblin kind of person, cowardice and ugly on the inside. Emma could never quite get her head around the fact that people could be so mean to someone they'd never even met. Someone they didn't know. Luckily she didn't get too many horrible comments, but just like anyone who had a lot of followers, it came hand in hand with the game.

You've airbrushed your photo. So pathetic, she clearly recalled someone writing once. (She hadn't actually 'airbrushed' anything, didn't have a clue how to Photoshop, but she couldn't pretend she didn't pick the most flattering filter and adjust the lighting and saturation of her images. But *everyone* did that, didn't they?)

Your forehead is sooooo big another had said. (Emma was looking in the mirror at every chance she got that day and even measured it and Googled average forehead size. Hers was completely in range.)

You're way too skinny. I preferred you when you were bigger. Time to stop the dieting now. She would never get over how people felt they could tell her what she should and shouldn't be doing when it came to her weight. It was up to her, surely?

Not as pretty as you think.

Some comments stung. They really, really hurt and there were days when Emma felt like she'd had enough of it all. Couldn't take another malicious remark. They got her down and made her feel rubbish about herself. Worthless and insecure. It didn't matter how many nice and lovely comments she received, it was always the bad ones that stuck. It was always these ones that would whirl around her mind all day long and make her wonder if that person was actually right.

Emma was brought back to the present and turned to Frankie. 'There's pros and cons I guess. It's not as easy as it seems sometimes. It takes over my life a bit.'

'Still, you get free stuff as well as holidays though, don't you? I know Charlie was chuffed when you both got sent all that sportswear recently. He was saying how he managed to convince the company to send him some too,' he laughed. 'Always manages to wrap people round his little finger, that one.'

Emma forced a laugh, but she felt a little rattled by the comment. She wasn't aware that Charlie had persuaded the company to send him clothes too. He'd told her that they'd offered and she rarely checked her emails; she had always trusted everything that Charlie told her.

Frankie continued, oblivious to Emma's troubled expression. 'When people click your links and purchase the same outfits you wore, you get money for it, when essentially all you've had to do is post a photo. It's pretty cool,' Frankie reminded her. 'And it's far more interesting than a lot of people's jobs.'

Emma nodded and smiled warmly at him. Frankie was always so upbeat and complimentary. They had always got on from the first day they'd met. Emma felt truly comfortable around Frankie as soon as they'd been introduced and could honestly say he was one of the nicest guys she knew. A great friend. He was a couple of years younger than Charlie, being twenty-eight, but he and Charlie were really close. She was pleased Frankie was going to be part of the ceremony; it wouldn't have felt right without him being involved somehow. Especially seeing as he was such a great help and support with the wedding. Charlie often told Emma how much Frankie looked up to him. He was the closest cousin Charlie had, and Frankie had sadly lost his father to cancer when he was only twelve. Charlie thought he was the older male relative Frankie needed in his life, though he sometimes made unpleasant remarks about Frankie being like an annoying little brother, which Emma ignored.

'So things didn't work out with you and Marie then?' Emma enquired in a gentle voice.

Frankie cleared his throat and shook his head. 'Nah. I wasn't ever really sure about her if you know what I mean?' He paused for a moment. 'She was a bit too materialistic for my liking. Always hinting for me to buy her some designer bag or another and telling me what her friends' boyfriends were buying them. I felt like she wanted to be with me for all the wrong reasons. It was never a serious relationship and I called it a day. She was impressed that you were marrying my cousin,' he let out a little laugh. 'I think she follows you on Instagram and is one of your fans. Said something about a lovely bag you had or something once.'

Emma closed her eyes for a moment, feeling embarrassed. She struggled to hear people use the word 'fans' and always found herself feeling so awkward. 'Oh god. Yes, sorry, maybe I'm to blame for some of the bags she likes,' she chortled. 'I always tag my bags in the photos I post. I get sent some for free, but my expensive designer ones I saved up for myself. Everyone is allowed a little treat from time to time, aren't they? I'd never expect Charlie to fork out for them though; if I want anything I make sure I buy it myself. I've just always been like that.'

'You're a hard worker. Independent, and I admire you for that. I guess that's where you and Marie were very different.'

'She was very pretty,' Emma recalled, thinking of her beautiful long red hair and bright blue eyes.

'Yes, but looks aren't enough, are they? When you like someone and have a real connection, you just know don't you?' His hazel eyes burned into hers and feeling the atmosphere shift slightly, Emma looked away quickly. She wasn't even sure why.

It took her back to a time when Charlie disappeared on a night out. They were together in a group and Frankie had been there too. There had been a few other couples as well as some of Charlie's single mates. They'd been drinking in a London bar and after a few hours, the other couples had left.

'You don't mind if me and the boys go on to a club, do you Em?' Charlie had asked. His voice was slurring and Emma knew it was going to be difficult to reason with him. They were an hour and a half from home. Emma had to get up early the next morning to be bridesmaid at her friend's wedding, which he was supposed to be accompanying her to. They hadn't planned for a heavy night and Emma really didn't like the thought of getting the train back all alone.

'Charlie,' she said in her sweetest, most placatory voice, 'we need to be up early. Are you actually going to leave me to get back home all on my own? I don't want to ruin your fun…'

'Then don't,' Charlie had glared at her. 'Come with us,' he suggested.

He knew she wouldn't. He was fully aware that she wasn't going to go to a nightclub until the early hours when she had to get up early the next day to get to the wedding venue. She didn't want to be tired and hungover. They'd been together for nearly a year and though Charlie had started out being the most attentive and considerate boyfriend in the world, he had slowly started to change as he became more comfortable in their relationship. Not for the good either.

'It's okay, I'm heading back,' Frankie had butted in, overhearing the conversation. 'I'll come back with you, Em,' he'd offered sweetly.

'Are you sure you don't want to go out with the others?' Emma had repeatedly asked him before they'd left. 'Please don't come back just because of me. I'd hate for you to miss out.'

'I really don't fancy waking up with a hangover, honestly. I'm more than happy to go back. I'm using you as a bit of an excuse,' he'd told her, 'you're actually doing me a favour.'

'I can't believe Charlie wanted to just leave me to get home on my own,' Emma had tutted when they'd sat in the empty carriage on the train. 'I really do wonder about him sometimes.' They were already engaged. Emma wasn't blind to Charlie's faults, but she did love him, regardless. He had helped become the successful influencer she now was, and she would always be so thankful for that. At this stage in her life she couldn't flit from one man to the next like she used to anyway. She needed to grow up and settle down if she ever wanted a family. She'd always told herself that her standards were too high. No man was perfect.

'He wouldn't have left you if you hadn't had gone with him and I wasn't coming back,' Frankie said, but she could tell by his doubtful and concerned expression that he wasn't actually sure about that. Emma hadn't believed him either. 'He's a good guy, Emma. I know he can be a bit moody at times, and probably difficult to live with, but he really does love you,' he told her seriously. 'He's lucky to have you and he knows that.'

Frankie had looked at her in such a way that made Emma felt slightly vulnerable and shy at that point, and she remembered looking out of the train window , unable to look him in the eye a moment longer. Frankie didn't know the Charlie that Emma did, but she didn't want to tell him that.

Emma blinked several times as the flashback disappeared, her eyes focusing on Charlie walking over holding the cocktail jug and pouring Emma another drink.

'God, it's sweltering in this heat, isn't it?' he said, wiping his forehead with the back of his hand. 'Can you put some suncream on my back, Em?' he asked.

'Sure,' Emma replied, putting down her drink. 'Having fun?' she asked him in a cheery voice.

'I'm going to have a look at the food menu,' Frankie said, walking off.

'Yes, it's great, isn't it? I'm so glad we decided to get married here. It was a good choice,' he pointed out. 'Where you off for your hen night tonight?'

Emma rubbed cream into his hot skin. 'I'm not entirely sure; Fran and Danni have arranged it all and made sure with Frankie that we won't be bumping into each other.'

He turned around and kissed her. 'Perfect. Can't be meeting up on our last night of freedom, can we?'

'Wow, when you say it like that it seems so hard to believe, doesn't it?' Emma replied, it suddenly dawning on her that she wasn't going to be Emma Langford for much longer. In four days' time she would be Emma Quinton.

'Not long Emma and you're all mine,' Charlie remarked. It wasn't said in a particularly jokey kind of way though and Emma was unsure what to say back to him.

Just like the bad comments on her Instagram feed that she focused on, it didn't matter how nice Charlie could be at times, how lovely he looked in front of other people, Emma was nervous. After all, Charlie had another side to him that only she knew about. A side where he wasn't the perfect, loving gentleman that he liked the rest of the world to believe him to be. That was the side of him that she couldn't get out of her head.

Chapter 8

Kim

Kim was enjoying herself. She was actually having *fun* and even though she wasn't certain if she was drunk yet, she knew she was definitely on her way. It was a foreign feeling. It felt *good*. What was it about the summer sun that made alcohol go straight to your head? It was either that or she really had turned into a lightweight like Holly often teased. This would hardly be surprising seeing as she never really drank any more. It was all about the kids, and having a few drinks, then getting woken up at the crack of dawn, or worse, in the middle of the night, just wasn't worth it. The dry mouth, splitting headache and irritable mood she had after drinking was twice as bad when you had a teething baby and demanding toddler to take care of. It was bad enough in her child-free days; Kim never really did get away lightly. Not like Holly had always seemed to, waking up brightly and chatting away like there was no tomorrow.

'How do you manage it?' Kim recalled saying croakily one morning when they were on holiday after a heavy night out.

'What?' Holly asked, mystified, applying a full face of make-up. 'How do I manage what?' She looked stupefied.

'To just act so full of energy and life,' Kim had groaned. 'You even look nice. I feel like death and I'm certain I look it too. You just don't get hangovers like I do.'

Today though, she could drink until her heart was content. Sod it. Her only plans were looking at flowers and going on a hen do. It wouldn't matter if Kim woke up with a hangover tomorrow. For the first time since booking her summer trip, Kim was actually relaxing and getting into the Vegas spirit. There were no children to wake her up the next day and if she wanted to stay in bed until four o'clock tomorrow, then so be it. Seeing the others show up had made her realize that she should be making an effort to get more involved. She didn't want to be seen as the boring, sensible one of the group Who knew when or if she would ever get to visit Vegas again? Everyone seemed so free and excited; it reminded Kim of her younger years, when she, Holly and Emma used to go on girls' holidays together. She needed to make the most of it before she went home and became 'mum' again. Being here in Vegas was only highlighting how much Kim had altered since having Mylo and Willow. Kim and Andy had only been married for six months when she accidently fell pregnant – they'd had so many other plans.

'I want to travel,' Kim had told him, wrapping her arms him and kissing him on the neck. 'Come on Andy, let's go everywhere. Australia, New Zealand, Bali; there's so many places we need to see.'

'What about work? What about money? I thought we were going to save to buy a house?' Andy had questioned. They were currently living in a one-bedroom apartment, but the dream was to buy a house with a garden. Andy's lips had been curving at the edges when he spoke, and Kim had known he liked the idea of going away and that she could have easily persuaded him. She could see the rebellious glint in his eye.

'There will be others schools you can work at when you get back!' Kim had told him energetically. 'We will save after our trip. We should book some flights; the sooner we leave this cold weather the better. It will be the trip of a lifetime.'

Andy had kissed her on the lips. 'The thought of some sun does sound good,' he'd agreed dreamily. 'Let me see what I can do.'

Kim had squealed in delight. But only a month or so after, not long after Holly announced she was having a baby, Kim's period was late and she had started to feel nauseous. She'd put it down to drinking too much and late nights after work, but when the feeling wouldn't shift, Kim began to worry.

It was a well-known fact that Kim could be negligent and unorganized and she knew she didn't always manage to remember to take her pill every day. She'd always seemed to get away with it though. She never thought it would happen to her. Seeing the two blue lines appear when she took the test just to rule it out had made Kim feel even more sick. They didn't want a baby at that point in their lives, and she felt an incredible sense of guilt and disappointment that she'd messed it all up. Such a simple mistake, with *huge* consequences. She pictured Andy's uncomfortable expression when she'd told him the news.

'How has this happened?' he'd asked in disbelief, before pointing out, 'you're on the pill.'

Kim had clenched her teeth, wondering how to tell him she'd slipped up. It was her fault that their amazing travel plans were going to be ruined. She'd really hoped that Andy would be happy with the news. So they weren't going to travel the world, but they were going to have their own little adventure! They were going to be *parents*! It made it all the more fun that Holly was pregnant too; their children would be friends. 'I guess I missed one or two pills last month,' she explained helplessly. 'It's easily done, Andy.' She saw him throw his eyes upwards, as though it was so typical of her. She guessed it was really. It was only the month before that he'd commented how careless she was when she hadn't paid a parking fine within the timeframe allocated and the price had doubled. 'Say something then,' she pleaded. 'Are you angry?'

Andy had walked over to her slowly and took her in his arms. She rested her head on his chest. Her big, cuddly bear. 'Of course I'm not angry,' he said slowly. 'Just shocked, that's all. We're not ready for this. It will be fine though,' he exhaled. 'Of course everything will be fine.'

As soon as she'd got over the shock, Kim had started to become excited about the prospect of being a mother. She'd beamed in amazement when she felt the first kicks, rushing to wherever Andy was in the house to let him feel it.

'Isn't that just the most *incredible* thing, Andy?'

He'd give a little nod, not quite sharing her enthusiasm. 'Yeah. I'm not too sure I felt it though.'

Kim could have sworn Mylo deliberately stopped moving the moment Andy felt her stomach.

Andy did perk up about it towards the end of her pregnancy, but Kim always felt a sense of blame because if she'd remembered to take her pill, they would have had their baby when the time was right and he was ready. But who knew when the time would ever be right? They loved each other deeply and they were married, so what did it matter if it had happened earlier than planned?

Kim told herself that she was going to be the best mother there was. She wanted to breastfeed and smother her baby with love. She would be the one getting up when he or she cried. She was going to make sure that Andy didn't need to worry about any of those things.

When Kim had experienced some sharp pains in her stomach one evening, she'd gone straight to the doctors the following morning. Her doctor hadn't seemed alarmed in the slightest when Kim told him she was still feeling the baby move, and he put it down to Braxton Hicks.

He'd smiled warmly at her, looking amused, as though it was sweet this little first-time mother was concerned about such an everyday, trivial thing like Braxton Hicks.

'Just rest as much as you can before your baby gets here!' he'd advised.

Andy had also been insistent that she put her feet up as much as possible but Kim just hadn't been able to sit still. When she hadn't been going up to London to work in her admin job, she was tidying and clearing things out. Just after that doctor's appointment, they'd purchased a new cot. Andy had been in a rush to meet his friends and he left it in the boot of the car telling Kim he would get it out in the morning and put it together. But Kim had another idea: she wanted to attempt to make the cot as a surprise. She'd always been quite good at DIY. She actually enjoyed it. So she'd watched Andy drive away in the taxi and opened the car boot to get the cot out. It had been heavier than she thought, and she did remember thinking when she got it halfway up the stairs to their apartment that she probably shouldn't have been carrying it so heavily pregnant. But she'd never wanted to feel like being pregnant was a big deal. She wasn't ill after all.

When Kim had felt the water trickling down her leg as she carried it over the last step, she recalled the feeling of horror that pulsed through her: *What have I done?* She'd been thirty-three weeks' pregnant. This was too early.

She could hardly breathe and steadied herself against the wall as she pushed their apartment door open, searching for her mobile to call the ambulance as well as Andy.

On the way to the hospital, Kim couldn't help but blame herself for her premature labour. Had she been doing too much? She should never have attempted to carry that cot, and despite everyone telling her it hadn't brought on the early labour, she had always felt tremendous guilt. She hadn't listened. She wasn't resting. Had she made this happen?

'Will the baby be okay?' She had tried to sound calm when she was introduced to the midwife on arrival at the hospital, but her voice wobbled out of control.

Mylo was born only two hours later, and Kim had given him

the quickest of glances and pecks on the head before he was whisked off to the newborn intensive care unit. It had been her worst nightmare, terrifying and shocking, and her whole world had revolved around Mylo from that very day.

Kim splashed her legs in the water of the pool as a new song started. She hadn't mentioned seeing Lily's text messages to Andy before she left, and she was starting to think it wasn't the best idea to have left it the way she had. She'd thought she would come away and forget all about it. Out of sight out of mind. But it wasn't working in the slightest.

Kim splashed some water in Max and Callum's direction, letting out a giggle as she tried to push thoughts of her marriage to the back of her mind. 'Come on you boring two, come in the pool,' she attempted to persuade them. They were sitting on the edge looking at her amusedly. They were both so handsome. So grown up from the two boys she vaguely remembered at college. Max, the louder of the two, was the kind of guy that she would have gone for when she was single, though she could imagine that Callum was better husband material; someone you could depend on and trust. She guessed it was Max's confidence and flirtatious personality that she found so attractive; Kim could see why Holly liked him.

'Hols!' she screeched over the loud music when she spotted her. 'come in the pool!'

'You okay?' Kim asked. 'This pool party is absolutely incredible. I can't actually believe I'm here.'

'Let's cheers to that,' Holly grinned broadly. 'You seem to be enjoying yourself now the others have turned up.'

Holly's tone sounded pleased about this, but Kim suddenly felt guilty that she may be taking it personally that she was making more of an effort just because the others had arrived.

'I don't know,' Kim said gingerly. 'I guess I just suddenly thought I should join in and get into the spirit. When do we get to go out at home? It just dawned on me that I'm on holiday in

Vegas. We have the summer sun, alcohol, great music, clubs, a wedding to attend – what's not to love?' she said in a merry voice.

'I'm so glad you've finally caught up with the way I'm feeling,' Holly announced, looking elated. 'Emma said to take it a little easy today as she wants us out tonight for the hen, so maybe let's not go too crazy as we need to leave in a sec to look at flowers.'

'Cool. Let's get out and get dressed in a minute then,' Kim replied. 'Shall we get some drink for the room when we're getting ready afterwards?' Kim suggested with a cheeky look in her eye. Now she had the taste of alcohol, she wanted more. That had always been Kim's problem when she used to go out; she never quite knew when to stop; most likely why her hangovers were so bad the next day. She just didn't have that voice inside her like most people did, the one that said, *That's enough now, Kim. One more drink is going to be going a step too far.*

'Good idea,' Holly smirked back, always willing to join her. 'Hey, what did you think of Max and Callum? I noticed you were chatting quite a bit to them earlier.'

'They're nice,' Kim replied hesitantly, choosing her words carefully. 'Both lovely guys. So… do you really like Max then?'

'He's good-looking, isn't he? But I hardly know him,' Holly brushed her comment away, timidly. 'Hey, did you hear from Andy?'

'Not the last time I checked. I'm sure everything is fine though,' Kim said, probably trying to convince herself more than Holly.

'Of course it will be. Did you still want to try for baby number three soon? Honestly Kim, I just don't know how on earth you do it. I don't know how you survive on such little sleep. You seem to do everything too; I don't know how you don't ever ask Andy to help.'

Kim shrugged. 'I guess I'm just used to it. We haven't spoken about having another for a while,' she admitted. 'I'm not entirely sure. When the time is right, I guess.'

As soon as Mylo had been born and back home after spending

four weeks at hospital, Kim wanted another baby. Not at that very moment, but she knew she didn't want a big age gap. She had been mesmerized by this tiny little person that they had made and she couldn't bear to be apart from him. She'd been obsessed and always turned down anyone who offered to watch the baby for a while so she could get some rest. He was her baby and she loved being with him. Kim hadn't wanted a break. Andy had wanted to wait a bit longer until they had Willow, but Kim had kept on about how it was best to not to wait, seeing as they were going through the baby/toddler stage anyway. Besides, it was nice for siblings to be close in age. Even though Willow had only just turned one, Kim wanted to try for a third baby. She hadn't mentioned to Holly that the last time she'd spoken about it with Andy, he'd been dead set against it.

'You *are* kidding me, Kim?' He looked at her as though she had two heads. 'Don't you think we have enough on our plates with Mylo and Willow? We don't have enough room as it is.'

Kim had tutted loudly, deciding to wait until he was in a better mood to bring it up again. *She* did all the work anyway; Andy was the one who went to work and got to escape the chaos. She did everything where the children were concerned because that's the way she wanted it. Andy worked hard and she didn't want him feeling as though he was working at home too. Looking back, Kim guessed she'd taken over to a degree.

'I bet Andy is loving some alone time with the kids. Probably spoiling them rotten,' Holly chuckled. 'Has he ever had them on his own before?'

Kim was about to laugh and say that of course he had, what a ridiculous question! He was their *father*. But as she dipped her chest into the cool water of the swimming pool, racking her brains, she came to the conclusion that she had always been there. Even in the past when she'd gone out for the odd dinner, Kim had always put the children to bed before she left. She remembered once when she'd been about to leave the house when Mylo had started screaming upstairs in the bathroom with Andy. He'd only been around ten months at the time.

'Doesn't seem to like his bath tonight, do you little man?' Andy said, planting kisses on his head and attempting to console him.

Kim had felt the temperature of the bath water. 'Andy, that's far too hot for him!' she screeched irritably, before taking Mylo out of his arms. Okay, so it hadn't actually been that hot, but it had been too hot for Mylo. It hadn't really been Andy's fault, thinking about it now, because Kim had never given him a chance to run the bath before. She had never thought it would something he would want to do, so automatically, it just became another one of her jobs.

'You're right,' Kim said, staring into space thoughtfully. 'It's actually Andy's first time alone with them.'

'Wow, that's crazy,' Holly pointed out. 'Then this is a well-deserved break for you.'

Kim forced a smile, but the thought disturbed her deeply. Had she spent so much time focusing on their children and being the best mother possible that she'd forgotten all about Andy in the process? She'd hardly been the best wife the past few years. Now Andy was getting attention elsewhere, could she really blame him for entertaining it? Yet equally, Kim couldn't help but feel as though Andy should have spoken to her if he was feeling neglected. They had always been honest with each other, or so Kim had thought. Reading his messages to Lily were like reading messages from a stranger; they just didn't sound like Andy. He had so much to lose, so what on earth was he doing?

Chapter 9

Holly

Holly, Kim and Emma said goodbye to the others and jumped in a taxi to the florists, which was about a ten-minute drive away.

Holly could see why Emma needed help selecting what she wanted; as they walked through the sea of lilies, tulips and peonies, she couldn't help but feel overwhelmed. How on earth did people decide what they wanted?

'Wow,' Kim commented, 'smells lovely. Do you already know what you're going to have?' she asked.

Emma had her phone out and was busy filming the shop for her news feed. 'They're offering me a massive discount,' she whispered, 'so long as I promote them and yes, I sent images of the kind of thing I'm after. Tara is just showing me some options today and I wanted your opinions.'

'Are you going for pinks?' Holly wondered, knowing the theme of Emma's wedding was rose gold.

'Yes. Tara sent some images of these beautiful rose-gold tall vases with the most amazing flower arrangements. I can't wait to see them.'

Tara was a lady in her fifties with clipped back, bleached blonde hair and bright red lipstick. She was wearing a blue and white, short-sleeved polka dot blouse covered by a white frilly apron.

'Emma? So pleased to meet you,' she said enthusiastically. 'How are you liking Vegas so far? Are these your bridesmaids?' she asked, with a huge grin.

'I'm loving it,' Emma replied with a gracious smile. 'These are my friends, Holly and Kim. I decided not to have any adult bridesmaids as I have so many younger flower girls. We will be needing seven flower girl hearts that you sent me images of, if that's okay? They're so cute,' Emma said dreamily, twisting round to Holly and Kim. 'They're these heart-shape floral arrangements, which they can hold onto. They're for all my cousin's daughters; we seem to have all girls in our family.'

'Ah, how sweet,' Tara replied, cocking her head to the side as she spoke to her. 'It sounds perfect. Let me just show you some of the flowers I was telling you about.' She walked away behind several tall plants and came back moments later holding some flowers. 'We have the cotton candy pink hydrangeas, blush white roses, pink and cream garden roses, angel leaves, rose-gold gems, gold baby's breath, and a touch of soft gray lamb's ears. What do you think?'

Emma's eyes widened and her face split into a huge smile. 'Oh wow. They're gorgeous; they're even prettier in real life!'

Holly agreed; they really were the most stunning flowers and they were going to suit her colour scheme beautifully.

'I *love* them,' Kim told her earnestly.

'I'm so glad,' Tara's face stretched into a smile, looking delighted. She lowered her voice a little, just addressing Emma. 'Also I just wanted to mention that we got your email about giving you a bigger discount and we're happy to go ahead,' she nodded.

Emma stared at Tara in bafflement. 'I'm sorry, what email?' she asked, looking blank.

'The one sent to us last week. I'm so sorry for not having a moment to reply, but the bigger discount is fine for the extra couple of posts.' Tara shot Emma a satisfied smile. 'Now let me show you those hearts I was telling you about. One moment, I'll just go find one.'

Holly gazed at Emma's concerned expression. 'Everything okay, Emma?'

'I'm just a bit confused, that's all,' Emma murmured, looking at her phone. She began to click away, eyes fixed on the screen before she quietly clicked her tongue. 'It was Charlie. I wish he'd said something before I came here. We were already being offered a big discount.'

'What's he done?' Kim probed in a gentle voice.

'Nothing, it's fine,' Emma replied lightly without looking up, continuing to tap away. 'He's just asked for another discount behind my back so they're giving us even more money off now.'

'I'm confused,' Holly said slowly, unable to prevent her frown. 'Charlie has access to your work emails? He actually answers people for you?'

'Yes,' she replied breezily. 'I couldn't always answer enquiries when I still worked in London, as I didn't always have the time, so Charlie kindly responded for me. Ever since then he just seems to have helped with the liaising with brands. I did tell him he doesn't need to any more; it can get confusing with the two of us doing it and I wouldn't have felt comfortable asking for even more money off – they were doing me a great deal to start with.'

'I didn't realize he was *that* involved in your work,' Kim said, a concerned expression on her face. 'Doesn't he discuss everything with you first before he replies?'

Emma bit her nails, distracted by her phone. 'Not all the time, no. But I guess maybe he forgets. Oh well. I guess I can't complain having such a savvy fiancé, can I?' She gave a hollow laugh. 'I guess Charlie just knows an opportunity when he sees one, and at least we're saving even more money.' Emma raised a meagre smile.

'Maybe just tell him how you feel if you don't need him to help any more?' Kim suggested, shooting Holly an odd look without Emma seeing. She clearly thought Charlie sounded a bit controlling, but perhaps he really was just being helpful. Taking the load off Emma when she had such a big day to plan? After all, they didn't know Charlie.

'Oh no, there's no need for that,' Emma said dismissively, 'Charlie just looks out for me, that's all. He has done since day one. He only wants the best for my career, even though, in all honestly, he's getting slightly fed up with me always taking videos and photos. I do understand where he's coming from though,' she said before letting out a little laugh, 'I always want him to take about a hundred and it does take up so much of my time.'

'Yes, but that's your job,' Kim reminded her. 'He has to understand that it's the way you make a living now; you're not just doing it for fun.'

'He does understand that,' Emma said brightly, flashing them both a smile. 'Now let me know what you think of these hearts when she brings them out. Then we'd better be off so we can start getting ready for my hen do tonight. I can't wait!'

Chapter 10

Emma

A few hours later and the girls had met up at Center Bar in the Hard Rock Hotel.

'Oh wow, we have a full three hundred and sixty-degree view of Vegas,' Kim said, her eyes glittering and her face lighting up.

Emma was filming a story for Instagram, her phone on selfie mode as she told her followers where they were and what they were up to.

'So as you can see,' she smiled broadly, 'I'm here at Center Bar for my hen do with my sash on and flashing tiara. I mean, just look at that amazing view, guys,' she aimed her camera at the glass windows. 'I'm so looking forward to celebrate with my closest friends,' she gushed. 'Say hello girls,' she sang, turning her phone round to the group as they all waved at the camera. She then switched it off.

'We have a surprise for you, Emma,' Fran announced mischievously.

She pulled a face. 'Is it strippers?'

When Fran and Danni giggled, she knew her suspicions were

correct. Emma didn't really mind though; it was all part of the fun on a hen do. She wasn't particularly up for being the centre of attention with half-naked men as she found it cringing, but she wasn't going to be a spoilsport. She'd get involved with a good heart, even though she couldn't think of anything worse.

The group followed Danni and Fran in taxis and they ended up outside somewhere called Hunk House.

'I can't believe it,' she giggled, getting her phone out to film the outside for her Instagram. Anything worth filming was instantly uploaded.

Look where I've ended up! #helpme #hendo

She posted the video to her story, following the others inside.

It was dark and dingy inside and there were already several groups of girls sitting down, waiting for the strippers to come on.

Emma frowned when her phone started vibrating in her bag and she spotted Charlie's name flashing on the screen.

She wanted to ignore it. She knew, by the feeling in the pit of her stomach, that it wasn't good news. But it was as though her thumb had a mind of its own as she clicked on the answer button.

'Hello?' She raised her voice over the noise in the room and the loud music playing.

She could hear his muffled voice and she wanted just to put the phone down and ignore him. Pretend he wasn't really there. But obediently she went outside, signalling to the others she just needed to take the call. She could just imagine how angry she would make him if she hung up the phone. He would be seething and it was this thought that forced her to go somewhere quiet so she could speak to him.

'Hello?' she said again, when she reached the entrance.

'So you're at a strip club?'

The malice in his voice made her flinch.

'Yes, so what?' she said, feeling tired and drained. She was exhausted by his mood swings. So fed up not knowing what to expect. She'd been to a male strip show before for her friend Moira's hen do; he hadn't bat an eyelid then. When she showed him the photos he'd even laughed. So why on earth was this any different?

'Are you actually joking?' he retorted, his voice as sharp as a knife. 'Are you purposely trying to show me up or something?'

'Oh for God's sake, Charlie,' Emma groaned. 'It's my *hen* do and you're on your stag do. I'm marrying you in a few days. It's just a bit of fun. Why are you even checking my Instagram? Besides, you didn't mind when I went before,' she told him, feeling confused.

'I was messaging someone with an opportunity the other day and I forgot to reply so I just logged into your account,' he spat. 'I'm doing you a *favour*. I couldn't exactly miss the strip show video you've just posted on there for the whole world to see,' he sulked.

'Which person was it who had messaged? I told you before, just leave it to me. I'll get back to all my messages as soon as I can.'

'With all due respect, Emma, you're hardly capable of managing your messages. I couldn't count how many times I've found messages you've taken far too long to respond to or ones you've simply missed,' he said curtly. 'You *need* me and don't forget that. Perhaps you should think of that next time you want to show me up on your page. I helped to grow you to be as big as you are. *Me.*'

'I know, Charlie. You know I'm grateful for your help, really I am. But I don't expect you to do any of it.'

'I do it because I love you.' He had calmed down now and his tone had changed. 'Come to the club afterwards and meet us.'

'But it's our stag and hen nights,' Emma said, feeling as though it was a bad omen or something. 'Shouldn't we just see each other in the morning when we wake up? I thought we were meant to spend it apart.'

'I don't care about all the rules, Em. I want to be with you.'

There was silence for a few moments and Emma thought about how quickly Charlie could turn from angry to nice.

'I'll text you where we're going and see you there, okay?' he said.

It was more of an order than an invite and Emma sighed inwardly, telling herself it was normal for a man to get jealous if his fiancée was at a strip club. It was nice that he wanted to see her. She tried to pretend it wasn't Charlie being controlling at all.

Chapter 11

Holly

'Right girls, we're off to Tryst at The Wynn now,' Fran told them excitedly.

The strip show was over and Holly was looking forward to a change of scene.

'Actually girls,' Emma said, biting her lip hesitantly, 'I told Charlie we would meet up with them. They're at The Bank at the Bellagio Hotel. I hope you don't mind?'

'Really? I had sorted it with a promoter that we would go to The Wynn though? Shouldn't you two have at least this one night apart?' Danni said, looking disappointed.

'No, I've told him we will go there now,' Emma replied, an unreadable expression on her face.

'Okay,' Fran shrugged helplessly. 'It's your hen do, so we'll go where you want.'

'He's got a table there for us all. It will be fun,' Emma told them.

They jumped into several taxis and Holly noticed Rob had sent a message earlier on that she hadn't read. She opened it, pleased to see it was some photos of the children. She ignored the fact that Lottie was wearing a t-shirt from last year, clearly too small for her (where had he even found that? She'd organized all their clothes for each day and realized he must have had it at his place.). She also choose to turn a blind eye to the fact they had food smeared round their chubby little smiling faces and their hair desperately needed brushing. She'd been so keen to have a break away, but now she was seeing their innocent happy faces, she wanted nothing more to kiss and hold them. She missed them and her heart burst with pride as she stared at the image. They looked like they were having fun whatever they were up to. She felt grateful that Rob kept her up to date with what they were doing. She tapped a message back.

Give them a big kiss from me and tell them I love them xx

Twenty minutes later, after standing in the queue for the club, they were let in, escorted by a man when they told him they were on Charlie's table. The nightclub was rammed.

'Wow, don't they look handsome?' Kim spoke loudly into Holly's ear, looking into the distance to the table where Max and Callum were facing them. Charlie, Frankie and a few others were on the other side of the table.

Holly followed Kim's gaze, her stomach full of butterflies as she noticed them. She couldn't answer. All Holly could do was stare. Max was wearing dark blue jeans and a tight fitted white shirt showing off his tanned skin. He flashed them a wide smile as he walked over, which made Holly feel weak inside. Callum looked gorgeous too and Holly realized she actually found his kind features and friendly smile rather endearing; he wasn't as flash or confident as Max, and he seemed more mature somehow, as though he was a few years older. Perhaps it was because he was a father, Holly decided. She imagined him to be a good dad too, from the way he'd spoken about his daughter, Eva. The type of dad who cooked homemade meals instead of lazily running to McDonalds at the last minute. The type of dad who played with his child and gave them attention, helping with their homework and watching them perform in their school assembly. He just gave that impression.

'Hey girls. You've scrubbed up well,' Max winked as he made room for them to sit down. He let Holly in first and she felt pleased she was the one to be sitting next to him. It would have been a bit difficult to chat otherwise. 'You're both looking beautiful,' he said to them, but his eyes were mainly on her. It made her cheeks begin to flush, as though she was still in the warm sunshine.

'Thanks,' Kim replied, taking a glass of champagne that the waitress handed her. They clinked glasses and Holly could sense Max's gaze was still on her. It made her feel giddy with anticipation. She wondered if he had plans to kiss her again that evening – she hoped so. She felt like a teenager with her first crush.

Kim pretty much necked her champagne in one, holding out her glass for the waitress to refill it.

'Wow Kim, maybe slow down a little,' Holly encouraged in a hushed tone. Kim hadn't been hungry when Holly had ordered room service before they went out for the night and she didn't drink much any more; she really didn't want her to get too ill from all the booze. Or embarrass herself and fall over or something.

'I'll be fine,' Kim shot back, lifting her chin. 'Honestly, stop worrying about me.'

Holly knew Kim couldn't really handle her drink and would most likely end up going overboard, but wasn't this what she wanted? Kim to be fun again? How could she moan that Kim was now having *too* much fun? Kim was a good mother and she was always with her children. She never got a break. Holly had told her before she needed to ask Andy to help more often, but Kim would have none of it.

'I like things done my way where the children are concerned,' she'd explained. 'They're my job.'

Holly had wondered if Andy *wanted* to be more involved. She thought her friend should have given him the chance, but she'd kept silent, not wanting to get involved. Perhaps that was the way it worked for them? Holly was always grateful to have Rob there whenever she needed him. She certainly wasn't keen on doing *everything* herself.

Holly picked up her drink and clinked glasses with Kim. They were going to have a great night, Holly told herself, the sour bubbles of her champagne fizzing in her mouth as she sipped it.

'I love this dress you're wearing,' Max complimented Holly as his eyes roamed her body as though he was undressing her.

'Thanks,' Holly replied shyly. 'You look nice too.'

Holly couldn't help but notice Max flash the pretty waitress a grin as he ordered some more drinks. The waitress fluttered her lashes at him, welcoming the attention. Holly could tell Max loved girls. He knew he was good-looking and aware of the effect he had on women. He lapped it up. He was just one of those guys who couldn't help but adore the opposite sex. He was charming and sexy. Whether or not he behaved differently when he was in a relationship was something Holly was unsure of. He was the type of man Holly's mother would tell her to steer clear of.

'Too good-looking for his own good, that one,' Holly remembered her mother saying once about an ex-boyfriend, when he'd treated her badly. He'd been the most popular boy in their school. 'The problem is, he's always had girls throwing themselves at him. He's never had to make an effort for anyone.'

She'd been right. Edna was always right about everything.

The drinks were constantly being poured and thirty minutes later, Holly could tell that Kim was a little drunk by the way she was swaying to the music and slurring her words.

'Shall we dance?' Kim asked enthusiastically.

'Sure,' Holly said, walking over to the dance floor with her friend. A group of American men came over to them and Holly chatted away to them politely, unable to help but notice that Max was watching them from the table. It was good for him to see that other men were interested. It certainly wouldn't hurt. They were standing close to the DJ booth and Holly could hardly hear what the men were saying over the music, and eventually they made their excuses and walked back to the table.

'Who are your new friends?' Max asked, raising an eyebrow.

'Oh you know, just some of our *many* admirers,' Holly replied dead-pan, enjoying the fact he was so interested. He was obviously bothered by it.

'Oh really?' he answered, enjoying the game. 'How many others do you have then? Sounds like I have competition,' he said, pretending to be worried.

Kim tapped Max's shoulder and began to chat to him and Callum turned to Holly. 'How long are you staying in Vegas for?'

'We're leaving two days after the wedding. What about you?'

'Same.' He paused. 'It's nice to have a break away but I'm looking forward to seeing Eva, I've got to say,' Callum admitted. 'I didn't see her the week before I left as it wasn't my turn with her and I've missed her. It's not easy when you can't see your children as much as you'd like. Do you and your ex-partner get on?'

'We do,' Holly replied, thinking of Lottie and Jacob again and feeling a wave of love. 'It's the one thing I've tried to make sure of. We split amicably though so I guess we're very lucky. He has a new girlfriend now. In fact, my children will probably be meeting her tomorrow for the first time.'

'How do you feel about that?' Callum asked.

Holly paused thoughtfully. 'It was a huge shock when he first told me. I know it sounds ridiculous, but I kind of felt betrayed or something, which doesn't make sense because we're no longer together.'

Callum nodded, looking as though he understood. 'Eva's mum, Hayley, has a new boyfriend. He also has a little boy who's three who Eva has started to call her brother. It's complicated when you have a child together; I found it really hard too when Hayley announced she was with someone else.'

'I've met her though, his new girlfriend, and she's actually really nice. I'm happy for them. At the end of the day, Rob and I just didn't work together, but that doesn't mean I don't want him to find love with someone else.'

'What went wrong with the pair of you?' he asked. 'Why didn't it work?'

Holly sipped her drink. 'Before kids, I used to love how laid-back Rob was. Nothing really fazed him and I used to wish I were more like him. I mean, don't get me wrong, I would have liked him to help around the house a bit more,' she rolled her eyes with a smile, 'I'm organized and he's the opposite, but I think once the children came along, all the things I used to love about him really started to annoy me.'

'Like what?' Callum asked.

'I feel bad saying it, because he is a good dad, but we just always seemed to argue about little things,' Holly said. 'I like to keep on top of things in the house, but when Lottie and Jacob came along it just became more of a struggle for me to keep up to date with the washing and tidying up. It never used to bother Rob, he was always saying I should relax more, but I felt like I needed more help from him. He would think I was being over the top worrying about the house and the truth is, we were just different. He's so laid-back with the children too and I had to always be the disciplinarian; I always felt like the bad cop. We just had different ways, I don't know,' she shrugged, deep in thought. 'I remember once when we went to a farm and went into the café for lunch, when I came out of the toilet, Lottie was crawling round on the dirty floor while he just sat there on his phone. She was filthy, but he just told me I was making a big deal over nothing. He seemed to *always* be on his phone and it drove me crazy. I wanted to enjoy some rare family time together at times, but I just felt like I enjoyed the children more when I was alone. You probably just think I'm coming across like a bit of a nag…' she broke off with a little laugh, hating the way she sounded.

'Not at all,' Callum told her seriously. 'Things change when you have children. Your whole relationship changes and sometimes it's not for the better. Sometimes you can be better parents apart.'

'Exactly,' Holly agreed. 'Rob adores our children and I know he spoils them rotten when he sees them. They love being with him. He's just more relaxed than me on the whole, I guess, and we clashed when parenting. Suddenly, what were once odd arguments were happening continuously. I knew it wasn't healthy for our children to be around it.'

They sat chatting away about their children and drinking and Holly could feel herself getting drunk. It was so easy to get carried away when there was a waitress constantly topping up your drink. So easy to forget you needed to stop. Callum made her feel comfortable too, and she was opening up about things she hadn't really spoken about before. He was so down to earth and open. They actually had lots in common. Callum pulled out his phone and showed Holly a photo of Eva. She looked adorable with a mop of blonde hair and had his green eyes.

'She's gorgeous,' Holly said honestly.

'Takes after her mum,' Callum said modestly.

But Holly could see she looked just like her father.

Max interrupted them moments later. 'Hey, I think she needs to get home,' he told them, nodding to Kim who was now falling asleep at the table.

Holly shook Kim gently and she opened her eyes, looking confused as she squinted at her.

'Come on, shall we go back?' Holly said gently.

A frown crinkled Kim's brow. 'No, I'm fine here,' she responded mulishly. 'I don't want to go back yet.'

Holly sighed, knowing how stubborn her friend could be. When Kim was enjoying herself, she never wanted to go home. She'd always been the same. Holly had completely forgotten this side to her.

'Just tell her we're going back to your hotel room for drinks,' Max suggested.

It was a good idea and one that worked. As soon as the four of them got into the taxi, Kim had fallen asleep.

'How are we going to get her into the hotel room?' Holly giggled.

They managed somehow to carry her to the lift, before she woke up, leaning on them for support as they walked her to their hotel room. As soon as they got Kim onto the bed she was fast asleep again. Holly tucked her in and pulled the covers up, knowing there was no way she was going to be able to get Kim undressed while she was in such a state.

'There's no point in you going to bed as well,' Max declared, a faint smile on his lips. 'We're staying on the floor above; why don't you just come up to ours for a few drinks? We've got some vodka and gin in the fridge.'

Holly hesitated. It would probably be best if she just went to bed now seeing as she was back in her room. But as she glanced at Max's handsome face, she knew she couldn't resist spending more time with him. 'Okay,' she said, making sure she had a room key, 'maybe just one.'

When they made their way up to the room, Max turned to Callum. 'You're going to meet the others, aren't you?'

Callum looked puzzled as he squinted his eyes. 'Yeah,' he answered slowly. 'That's right.'

Holly could tell Max had just made that up. She knew by the look on Callum's face that Max just wanted him gone. He wanted to be all alone with Holly. She wasn't silly. She wasn't some young teenager, completely naïve to what Max's intentions were.

'Night, Holly,' Callum smiled at her.

Holly watched Callum walk away, wondering whether she should go with him instead, to where there were other people. To where it was safe from her doing anything she might regret. She knew for certain she wasn't going to able to resist him if he made a move. She wanted him; she hadn't felt so in lust in a very long time. There was nothing she wanted more than to be with

Max, but it was ridiculously soon, wasn't it? She couldn't stop her thoughts turning to Rob; Holly had made sure she waited at least a month when they'd first started dating. She hadn't wanted to jump straight into bed with him and for it to become a casual fling, and she thought it would just complicate things when they had been going so well. Why was she even thinking about him now? She had moved on just as much as he had, but she couldn't help but acknowledge that she hadn't been with another man since him. Her eyes flicked over to Callum as she watched him strolling towards the lift. She could just catch up with him if she walked away now.

'Coming in?' Max asked, opening the door.

Holly smiled sensuously. She deserved some fun. She followed behind him, closing the door.

Chapter 12

Emma

Emma woke up with a headache. She wondered how many calories she'd consumed last night in alcohol alone. Not that it mattered that much; she was down to her target weight, getting married in two days and she was on holiday. She'd been so good in the lead up to Vegas, eating healthily and exercising constantly in the gym, that she was allowed a break. What was the point in living otherwise? You needed to treat yourself occasionally. After the wedding she was going back to being good though. She had to in order to maintain her figure, and she knew Charlie would be put off if she put weight on. When she'd shown her some old photos a few weeks back he had an expression on his face that read *yikes*.

'Were you really that size when I first started training you?' he said, turning his nose up in revulsion. 'I did a bloody good job getting you down to the size you are now, didn't I? Lucky you met me and I agreed to marry you!' He'd guffawed, leaving her feeling hurt. She knew he liked her looking after herself and keeping herself trim. She'd just told herself it was because it was Charlie's job, which was why he was so health-obsessed and body-conscious.

Emma rubbed her temples, her head fudgy from the previous evening. She'd had too much to drink. She couldn't recall getting home. She was wearing her silky pyjamas, she noticed as she looked down – had she put those on? Or had Charlie dressed her? She had a feeling of dread in the pit of her stomach that she'd upset him. She had that feeling every time she drunk alcohol and couldn't really remember the previous evening. In fact, even when she didn't drink she felt that way. Her first thought most mornings was: *Is Charlie speaking to me?*

Charlie began to stir and Emma's heart hammered in her chest. Was it normal to feel this way about your husband-to-be? She brushed that thought quickly under the carpet, reminding herself that no relationship was perfect. It was just one of Charlie's flaws that she had to accept. She had her own flaws too, didn't she? She cleared her throat. 'Good morning,' she said gently, leaning over to him and resting her head on her shoulder.

When he just lay there with his back to her, she knew it wasn't good news. Charlie was a master at ignoring her. He was the most stubborn person that Emma had ever met. If he had a problem with something she'd done (no matter how small), he could blank her for days on end. It drove Emma crazy and he knew it. She could never be bothered to argue and keep up the silent treatment. When Emma was angry with something he'd done, she was of the belief that she would end up talking to him anyway, so the best thing to do was talk about their issue straight away and move forward. It was a much more productive, healthy way of dealing with things. She wasn't one to drag it on and on. She wondered how long it would last this time? It couldn't be too long or the wedding wouldn't go ahead. He could hardly stand there at the altar remaining silent when the vicar asked him, 'Do you take Emma Langford to be your lawfully wedded wife?' Just imagine.

Emma lay with her head on his shoulder even though she *knew* he was in one of his moods. If only she knew what had happened so she could attempt to make things right again. Charlie's moods were draining. They could be scary too.

'Everything okay?' she asked gently, finding his hand under the covers and squeezing it.

He ripped his hand away, making her flinch and he got out of the bed, stomping to the bathroom.

Silence.

Emma's heart sank and she picked up her phone as a distraction, noticing that Frankie had texted her.

Morning Em. You okay? Hope you're not feeling too worse for wear this morning. Just checking we're still meeting at one. by the pool? Xx

Emma sighed. If she did go out today, there was no way she was drinking. She questioned, not for the first time, whether it would be better for her in the long run to just not drink any more. That way she wouldn't upset Charlie as often. That way, she'd remember exactly what had gone on and wouldn't have to feel like this.

Charlie marched out of the bathroom in only a white towel around his waist. Despite the fact he wasn't talking to her, it never failed to amaze her how attracted she was to him. As she gazed at his perfectly toned abs and broad shoulders wet from the shower, she still wanted him. That was the problem. The sex they had was mind-blowing, the make-up sex even better. It almost made it worth arguing just to rip each other's clothes off afterwards. *Almost*, she thought, feeling downbeat. His moods were getting more and more frequent. The way he treated her was getting more and more concerning.

'Charlie,' Emma started, hating how desperate she sounded, 'what's wrong? What have I done to upset you? Just tell me. *Please*,' she begged. Her voice was small and pathetic, exactly how she felt.

He sprayed his deodorant without a care in the world.

'Please Charlie,' she continued, unable to face the day if they were on bad terms. They were going to be around their friends and family all day and she really didn't want it to be frosty between them. It was be awkward and obvious to everyone else that there was an atmosphere. Couldn't he just put it to the side just for once and talk about it? Couldn't he just grow up for once?

He started to brush his hair in the mirror.

'Don't ignore me,' she said tiredly. 'We have people who have travelled a long way to be here for us. If you can't do it for me, then do it for them.'

She could see his jaw clenching and she knew he was thinking about what she was saying.

She exhaled loudly. 'What exactly have I done wrong? How am I supposed to even apologize if you won't even speak to me?'

He turned to her with a flinty stare. 'You're an embarrassment,' he spat. 'That's why I'm not talking to you.'

He'd spoken and she felt a wave of relief. This was going to be sorted out quicker than it usually was. Emma held her breath, racking her brains. She knew he would be overreacting. He always did. She actually tried to not go out with him any more because it only ever ended up in an argument. She'd really hoped it would be different in Vegas. After all, they were getting married. Surely he knew how much she loved him if she was going to be his wife? Surely his insecurities would go away after that? She thought back to when they went out to dinner once and he ignored her the entire time because he thought she'd fancied a man sitting behind him.

'What are you talking about?' Emma had asked in bafflement. She hadn't even been sure which man he was talking about as it had been really busy. There were lots of other couples all around them.

He'd looked the other way, anywhere but at her, and blanked the question.

'I don't fancy anyone except you, Charlie. When are you going to get that into your head?' She had been looking forward to the meal as it was a new Italian restaurant in their area, and Emma recalled looking round with envy at the other normal couples chatting away. Why couldn't they be like that? Why couldn't they just have a night out without something upsetting him? She was so disappointed he was ruining their night out. So frustrated by his jealousy that she wanted to scream. When Charlie was nice, he was lovely. He honestly made her feel like the most special, loved person in the world. But when he was like this it was like thinking you'd won the lottery, only to double-check and find one of the numbers was wrong. He just made her feel so disappointed that he had this side to him.

She took a deep breath. 'Look, I'm sorry for whatever it is I've done to embarrass you. I really am. But you need to snap out of it, Charlie. We're getting married. You can't keep behaving like this.' She closed her eyes, exhausted with constantly trying to reason with him.

'You spoke to me like an idiot,' he retorted furiously, 'in front of *everyone*.' He was glaring at her looking exasperated. 'After everything I do for you, Emma! Do you know how much I've actually helped you get to where you are with your career? *Do you?* Half these free things we're getting given are because of *me*.' He jabbed his chest violently.

'I'm sorry, Charlie, and you know how grateful I am for everything you've done. I'm so sorry for whatever it was I said,' Emma replied, hating that her voice was scratchy with nerves. 'I would never do anything to make you look stupid. I'd had too much to drink; you have to accept my apology so we can just meet everyone today and have a good time.'

When he just ignored her, she tried again.

'What was it that I said?' she ventured wanly.

'You were trying to control me,' he responded hotly, his face darkening. 'Telling me I'd had enough to drink and trying to make me look bad because I wasn't willing to take you home when *you* decided you wanted to leave,' he fumed with a grimace. 'I was enjoying myself with my mates. I don't appreciate you telling me what I can and can't do.'

Emma shook her head, wishing this were all over. Hoping he was going to forgive her quickly this time. She hated arguing. She'd never seen her parents argue once; they spoke to each other calmly, with respect. Emma didn't know what she'd done to deserve to be spoken to the way Charlie did. Even if she'd tried to get him to go home when he was with his mates, was that such a bad thing? Was that *really* trying to control him? She'd most likely needed him to get her back and look after her, like any normal fiancé would. He was the one who had wanted to meet up on their stag and hen nights too, not the other way around. Not that she would dare to say that; it just wasn't worth another row. Then there was the fact he kept bringing up how much he did for her. Emma was confused; he'd always wanted to get involved in her brand deals, give them a once-over to make sure she was given as much as he felt she should be. Whenever she suggested she was capable of managing her own life, he was quick to tell her how much she needed him, but then constantly threw it back in her face.

The sooner she agreed with him, the sooner it would be done. She got out of bed and stood behind him, looking at his face as he dressed in the mirror. She walked up closely behind him and put her arms around his waist.

'Please, Charlie. I'm sorry, okay? I won't tell you what to do ever again. I swear it.' She knew she shouldn't even be apologizing. She was aware she was allowing him to control *her*, not the other way around, which he was trying to imply. But Emma just wanted an easy life. She just wanted to get on and see the nice Charlie again.

She kissed the back of his neck, trying with all her power to wash away his agitation. Her eyes flicked to his softening expression in the mirror and she knew it was working. He turned around and kissed her roughly, just like she knew he would. His hands reached for her bra as he unhooked it hungrily, pushing her back on the bed. Emma wished she didn't want him the way she did. Their relationship wasn't healthy and at times, Emma had to admit, she didn't actually like Charlie. He was like a spoilt child, petulant and unreasonable, but as he tugged at her underwear, Emma couldn't help but crave every inch of him. She despised his tantrums, but when he finally forgave her for whatever little thing she'd done, when she finally managed to turn him round, it was always such a turn-on for her. As he pressed his body up against her and she arched her back longingly, she wondered if she could honestly put up with this for the rest of her life. You were meant to take someone for better or worse, but what if the worse was clearly starting to outweigh the better?

Later as they lay in bed watching television, Charlie's phone rang.

'You alright, mate?' he answered.

Emma attempted to listen to who was speaking but the voice on the other end of the line was muffled.

'Yeah, one o'clock, that's right. It was a good night, wasn't it? Where did you end up going in the end?' Charlie grinned and let out a loud, excitable laugh. 'No way! Trust you,' he said.

Emma sat there frowning, wondering who it was and what they were talking about.

'Okay, mate. I'll see you soon,' Charlie said before putting the phone down.

'Who was that?' Emma enquired curiously. 'What were they talking about?'

'That was Max, just wondering where we were going,' he answered with a slight smile. Charlie and Max had become good friends since meeting at Callum's gym several years ago. Charlie had kept talking about his friend Max from work, singing his praises, and it had been a coincidence when Emma realized she already knew him from college. Callum didn't seem to go out with them as much and Emma guessed it was probably because he owned the gym and perhaps didn't want to always mix business with pleasure.

'Right,' Emma said slowly, 'and what else did he say?' she asked.

'You'll never guess what he ended up doing last night? Or should I say, who he ended up doing,' he chuckled.

Emma knew before he even told her, but she felt annoyed for her friend. Why was Max blurting out what had happened to Charlie like an ignorant loudmouth? 'He slept with Holly?' she guessed.

'Yep,' Charlie was smiling. A typical man, impressed by his friend's antics.

'I don't think he should be telling you that,' Emma responded, lines creasing her forehead. She knew she wouldn't be happy if she were in Holly's position. It was as though Max couldn't wait to blab about it. It was immature and boastful. Holly wasn't just some girl he'd met on a night out; she was Emma's friend attending her wedding. She felt disappointed he didn't have a little more respect. It was different when she heard about him bragging about someone she didn't know.

'Oh lighten up,' Charlie brushed away her comment. 'He told me not to say anything. It's hardly a big deal, is it?'

'It probably is to Holly,' she said pointedly. She paused for a moment, deep in thought. 'If you didn't bring me home last night, who did?' she asked him interestedly. She genuinely had no idea.

'What?' Charlie asked, confused now she'd changed the subject.

'You didn't want to come back last night, you said earlier. Did you end up coming back in the end or did someone else get me home?' she asked.

'Oh, it was Frankie who brought you back. Anyway, we'd better start getting ready,' he said, turning to her and looking at her lovingly. He kissed her on the nose. 'I love you, Em. So bloody much.'

He was Jeckyl and Hyde. He blew hot and then cold. Emma never knew where she stood. She was always walking on eggshells. Skating on thin ice. She nodded, wondering if she was strong enough to do this for the rest of her life. What on earth was she signing up for?

Chapter 13

Kim

Kim clicked off the cute image that Emma had just posted on her Instagram of her and Charlie smiling in bed together, thinking what a cute couple they made, and turned to Holly who was talking about the previous night.

'It doesn't matter, Holly,' Kim said calmly, trying to hide her surprise. 'You obviously really like him.'

Holly had just announced that she'd slept with Max the previous evening. She appeared a little apprehensive and sheepish, unsure if she had done the right thing. Holly was single and she'd had a rough year after splitting up with Rob. She was thirty-two and she'd slept with a guy she clearly liked more than she was letting on. Holly never normally had one-night stands. It just seemed like something from the past. Kim never imagined she'd be talking about this kind of thing again with Holly when they both had children, yet here she was, trying to make her friend know that the situation was okay. She'd stayed the night in Max's room and was worried she was going to regret it. She was scared she was going to feel awkward around him and it would change things between them.

'I don't know what came over me,' Holly said looking a little guilty. 'He's just so good-looking and charming. I guess I just want to move on from Rob. You know what they say...'

'You only get over someone by getting under another?' Kim raised her eyebrow. 'You did what you wanted to do at the time, good for you,' Kim replied. 'Being single and having sex with someone you fancy is hardly a crime, is it? You're just enjoying yourself and you're entitled to. Don't beat yourself up about it.'

'Yes, I know,' Holly sighed. 'But I like him. Well I think I do. If I'm honest, he's probably not as down to earth as I'd usually go for and I hate the fact that he stares at every woman that walks past,' she said rolling her eyes, 'but I just don't want things to feel uncomfortable between us now.'

'What was it like anyway?' Kim asked her, her eyes twinkling as she waited for some details. This was interesting stuff and it made Kim feel like a teenager again.

Holly's face split into a grin. 'Amazing,' she gushed, 'honestly, *so* good. I've been so used to sleeping with the same man that I completely forgot what it was like to be with someone else. It was so much more exciting. Max was unfamiliar and new. The sex between Rob and I became such a routine in the end I knew exactly what was going to happen and when. Do you know what I mean?' She asked. 'Oh, actually you probably don't. You and Andy have such a strong relationship,' she added.

Kim forced a smile. Of course she *knew* what Holly meant. It was exactly the same for Kim and Andy. They tended to do the same thing every time; Sunday morning was their day, and if Kim was honest, once it was over with she'd feel a bit relieved she could relax for another week. Though as she sat there thinking about it, she doubted it was even every week any more. When *was* the last time they'd had sex? The thought startled her and hit her like a fever. It couldn't have been too recently because Kim would remember. They'd once been so *passionate*, kissing at every opportunity and able to have sex when they felt like it. Kim even used to dress up for him! Once upon a time they would do role-play and games. It was always fun and always exhilarating. She just simply couldn't imagine having the time and energy to do that now. Her whole day was filled up with jobs: feed the children, get them washed and dressed, brush their teeth, make a packed lunch, get them out of the house, meet the other mothers, do the food shopping, make the dinner, clean the kitchen, put on the washing. At the end of it all, when the children finally went to bed, Kim just wanted to unwind. She wanted to put her feet up and watch television with a cup of tea – was that really so bad? She hated to say it, but sex now felt a little like another job to do on her never-ending list. She was just always so tired, usually having been up in the night with the children. She rarely felt sexy any more, never having the time to make an effort with her appearance like she once had. She viewed sex with her husband like she did going to the gym: she wasn't always overly keen at thought of it, but doing it was never as bad as she thought it would be, and she always felt much better afterwards, as though it brought them closer together. It wasn't as though she didn't enjoy it when it happened, because she did, but it had become a bit mundane and predictable. 'It's nice to feel comfortable and relaxed with someone you know though,' Kim said, perhaps trying to convince herself. 'It's nice to be in love with the person you're doing it with.'

Holly nodded slowly. 'Yes, I know all of that, but it's much more enthralling to be in lust,' she smirked, 'and honestly, Max was incredible. We did it five times.'

Now she was just showing off, Kim thought. '*Five?*' she squawked.

Holly laughed gaily. 'Yep.'

Kim couldn't help but feel envious. There was her not even having sex five times in a month and Holly had done it five times in one night. She couldn't deny there was a part of her that was envious of the fact her friend was single and could have fun with whoever she liked. She had no-one to answer to. She could be with whoever she wanted. It felt like a lifetime ago that Kim had been in that position. It had been years since she'd been all over Andy, in that stage where you just couldn't get enough of each other. That feeling when you first met someone, and the infatuation and electricity you felt every time they so much as touched you, could never come back again. It was a bit like lighting a sparkler. It started off so strong and powerful, bright and alive, before slowly and quietly fizzling out. When the spark had gone, it simply couldn't be lit up again. Or could it? Kim knew that her marriage needed work in more ways than one. She could see that now. Her marriage had taken a backseat since having children; it was something she just assumed was working, while she was getting on with her busy life and putting all her time and attention into the kids. Since the messages from Lily, now Kim wasn't so sure. She turned her thoughts back to Holly. 'Were you careful?' Kim asked Holly seriously. She wasn't deliberately trying to put a downer on the situation, but she thought it was an important thing to ask.

'Yes, of course,' Holly replied as though it was obvious. 'I'm not stupid.'

'I was just checking,' Kim replied.

Holly's phone beeped and her face broke into a beaming smile. 'That's Max now actually. Just checking that we're going to the pool party at one.'

'See, nothing to worry about is there?' Kim said brightly, 'he's messaging you already.' Again, a small part of her wished she could go back to the days where text messages were exciting and made you grin from ear to ear. Kim remembered when she'd first met Andy. Every time she even saw his name on the screen her heart would flip over. Even if he was only asking how her day was going, she would feel her spirits lift and would have a spring in her step. He'd genuinely had the power to make her feel like the happiest person alive. Now it was just normal seeing his name flash on

105

the screen. He'd be asking what they were having for dinner or informing her he was coming home from the school a little late, that kind of thing. Just usual, everyday stuff. There was rarely anything that made her smile like Holly was doing right at that moment. Kim knew this was normal too, no spark remained the same forever, but she couldn't help but realize that she actually missed it. Why had she turned Andy down all those times he'd tried to take her out for dinner since the children had been born? Kim always had an excuse: she didn't want to put either of their mothers out coming over to babysit, she didn't have anything to wear, she was too tired or she just didn't feel like it. Why wasn't she still trying to make effort with their marriage? Kim often felt because Andy hadn't exactly been overjoyed when she'd accidently fallen pregnant with Mylo, she should be the one always dealing with him when he cried or needed feeding. She knew it was ludicrous, but she'd also blamed herself for Mylo being born early, questioning whether it was something she had done, even though she'd been told dozens of times it was just 'one of those things'. Had the shock and fright of Mylo's early birth turned Kim into a control freak where the children were concerned? She hadn't enjoyed her pregnancy with Willow one little bit. She'd rested as much as possible, terrified an early labour was going to happen again. She only finally relaxed when she got to thirty-seven weeks' pregnant and felt even more thrilled when Willow had been born a week after her due date at eight pounds seven.

She remembered Andy once clicking his tongue when she re-dressed Willow before they went out for the day to meet family.

'What?' she'd asked. 'I just think it may be cold out; she should be wearing something warmer.'

'There's just no point in me getting them dressed, is there?' Andy had mumbled.

Kim ignored him, thinking he was being silly. She just couldn't help herself. She always thought she could do things better; but how did this make Andy feel? Why was she only thinking about it now she was worried about his relationship with Lily? It was as though she'd been blinded and could now finally see the error of her ways. She'd only ever meant well though; she certainly hadn't meant to ignore her husband and make him feel inferior. Kim couldn't wait to see Andy again and talk to him. Communication was such an important part in a relationship – everyone knew that. So why had she felt the need to run away when she'd seen those messages? Why had she fallen silent? *Fear*. The word popped into her head, uninvited. She was afraid of what Andy was going to tell her. Kim didn't want this to be it. She loved Andy more than anything, and even though she was upset that he'd even replied to those inappropriate, flirty messages, a tiny little part of her felt she hadn't helped matters over the years by behaving the way she did. Not that this excused his behaviour in any way whatsoever; she was furious at him as well as being hurt. She would never have been chatting like that with another man, even if they were just friends. A line had been crossed in her opinion, and Kim wouldn't ever betray Andy like that. Andy often joked that he felt like a spare part, unwanted. But was he really joking though? Kim wanted to get to the bottom of why this was happening and if possible, make it all better again. Seeing Holly trying to cope with life as a single mother and having to deal with Rob being in a new relationship made Kim determined to save her family in any way she could. She would be devastated if their family was torn apart. Kim had always told herself that once she'd settled down, that would be it. No-one said a marriage was easy and Kim was willing to work at it. She didn't want to be sending one-word messages to Andy, arranging days for him to have the children and being introduced to his new partner; it just didn't bear thinking about.

She clicked on Andy's Instagram account to see if he'd posted anything new lately. He didn't use it much and was more just someone who browsed it occasionally than someone who posted his own images and liked people's photos. Kim couldn't recall a time she'd ever checked up on him, but after thinking about their relationship, she was intrigued. His latest post was a selfie; he was flashing an enormous smile at the camera wearing his rugby kit on the school field. It was odd seeing Andy take a selfie, as though she was looking at a stranger. He was the least vain person she knew and didn't really rate himself as attractive as such (something which, ironically, Kim had always found so attractive). She clicked on the image, immediately noticing the comment underneath:

@Lily.Anderson28- Great pic xx

Kim couldn't hear anything against the thrumming of her ears. Her throat was tight and she couldn't swallow. So this was Lily? Kim clicked on Lily's page, both pleased and frightened that it wasn't private. Did Andy write comments underneath her photos too? She was fuming. Lily's account seemed fairly new, with just the odd selfie, photo on a night out with friends of a Jack Russell called Rex. Kim exhaled slowly, relieved there were no comments from Andy when she checked all her images. It was so ridiculous she was even doing such a thing! Kim hated to think of herself as a snoop, but it was impossible not to. She clicked on the latest selfie, looking inscrutably at Lily with her shoulder-length auburn hair, striking almond eyes and English rose, flawless skin; she looked nothing like Kim.

Just as she was about to click off the image and get on with the rest of her day, her finger froze, as she noticed something underneath the selfie: Andy had liked her photo.

Chapter 14

Holly

'You okay? You seem a little quiet,' Holly asked Kim as they walked through the entrance to the pool.

'Yes, course,' Kim said, looking as though she was in a world of her own. 'Why wouldn't I be?'

'You're not worried about the children at home, are you? They're going to be fine with Andy. We don't have long left – let's just enjoy our time here,' she enthused.

Kim nodded. 'I'm not even going to think about home at all,' she turned her head and smiled.

Holly nodded and smiled back, not entirely convinced as she searched for the others. She spotted Max, sitting on the large round sun lounger and waving. Everything was going to be just fine between them; last night wouldn't change a thing, she told herself. She needed to remain her usual positive self and stop worrying.

Max was sitting with Callum and she suddenly felt a little ill at ease, despite telling herself she shouldn't, knowing that he'd probably told him about what had happened between them. She felt self-conscious, as though all eyes were on her. She felt like she had a flashing sign above her head saying, *Look at me.*

Emma was looking sensational in a red swimsuit, taking a selfie in front of a large bottle of champagne. She looked every bit suited to a glamourous Vegas pool party. Her long, thick hair was wavy from the humidity; anyone would guess she had hair extensions, but it was all natural. She'd always had the most beautiful hair, Holly thought. Emma was obviously posting to her Instagram again; Holly had seen lots of posts pop up on her timeline since she'd been in Vegas, many that she hadn't even realized Emma had filmed. She wondered how Emma could always be bothered to do it; weren't there ever times when she just wanted to turn her phone off and not check her messages? But she always had her phone in her hand, posing for some picture or another, tagging the location and brands. She respected her though. It was amazing to think she only had to so much as post a video or photo to get paid. There was no alarm clock waking her up at 6 a.m. each day. No boss to answer to. No train to catch. It did seem that Charlie had more to do with Emma's Instagram than Holly first realized and she wondered why Emma seemed to believe she *needed* Charlie's input. Emma was a smart, intelligent woman; Holly just wished she could see this.

'Hey everyone,' Kim said chirpily. 'You all okay?'

'Hi,' Holly smiled, sitting down next to Callum where there was room.

Kim peeled off her pretty white summer dress, revealing a bright orange, cut-out swimsuit; she looked really lovely, Holly thought. She was more curvy now than before she'd had children, her bust obviously not as pert as it once had been, but she still looked great.

'How was your night, Holly?' Charlie asked, his mouth twitching as though he was holding back a grin, raising one eyebrow.

Holly felt her face getting hotter and she slid her sunglasses from her head down onto her nose. She was irritated with herself for reacting to his comment, but couldn't help it. She really hadn't expected anyone to say anything. So Max had already told Charlie? She felt a hint of annoyance, but also felt more let down than angry. How old was he? It was so *immature*.

'Fine, thank you. Yourself?' she responded, more boldly than she felt.

'I'm great,' he grinned, looking as though he wanted to laugh, 'just fine.'

Idiot, Holly thought sourly. She didn't know Charlie that well, but the more she got to know him, the more she thought he wasn't as nice as he first seemed. There was something about the way he looked at Emma, like she was his property and he owned her. Something about his tone of voice at times that made her think something was off key.

'How you doing?' Emma asked in a shrill tone. 'I was wondering if you both fancied coming with me a bit later on to a wedding shop here in Vegas? They've offered to give me some bridal accessories for free in exchange for promoting them,' she explained. 'Then perhaps we can do a hair trial tomorrow, Holly, if that's okay? I honestly can't wait for you to work your magic,' she smiled broadly.

'That's so cool,' Kim replied enthusiastically. 'I can't believe you get so much free stuff; you're so lucky. We'll definitely come, won't we, Holly?'

Emma smiled proudly, but Holly noticed that she looked distracted somehow, as though she had something on her mind.

'You'll love it when Holly does your hair; she's amazing,' Kim added, her face filled with awe.

'Is that what you do then?' Callum asked, listening to their conversation. 'Wedding hair?'

'Yes,' Holly replied. 'I specialize in bridal hairstyles so it makes perfect sense for me to do Emma's.' Holly was pleased she would be saving Emma some money as she knew the prices for bridal hair and make-up in Vegas certainly weren't cheap.

'I guess it's the perfect job to have when you have kids; you can pick and choose when you work,' Callum replied, leaning back on the sun lounger.

It was impossible not to notice his perfect body, and Holly cleared her throat, forcing herself to look away.

'It really is,' she told him.

Emma looked grateful. 'Thanks so much, Holly. I still don't know what I want yet, so I'll have a look on Pinterest for some inspiration.'

'Come on girls, let's get some drinks and go in the pool,' Kim suggested, looking over at the crowds laughing and splashing in the water.

'How can you seriously be up for drinking again after last night?' Emma asked in amazement.

'Hair of the dog,' Kim giggled. 'It's the only way to cure yourself.'

Holly nodded and shot her a natural smile. Kim really had seemed to enjoy herself over the past few days; Holly could just about keep up with her. She seemed distracted though, as if she was drinking to block out something else on her mind and Holly reminded herself to ask her about it when they were alone.

'Fancy coming in the pool?' She turned to Max and Callum.

Callum looked at Max with a slight shrug of his shoulders as though he would go if Max were up for it.

'Maybe in a bit,' Max replied casually, lying back and closing his eyes. 'I want to just chill for a bit and catch some sun.'

Holly swallowed down her disappointment, but told herself she was reading too much into things. The man was allowed to sunbathe if that's what he wanted to do. She wouldn't have thought anything of it if he'd said the same thing yesterday. He hadn't though. He'd constantly been beside her, showing interest. Refusing to feel insecure and needy, Holly turned her thoughts to having a good time with her friends.

'Let's go,' she said, beginning to sing along to a song.

Moments later they were saying 'Cheers', clinking together glasses of Prosecco. Holly honestly couldn't believe she was drinking again, but if Kim was encouraging her, then she felt obliged to follow suit.

'I'm just going over to the others quickly to say hello,' Emma told them, glancing over to some of the others who had just turned up. "I'll be back in a bit.'

Kim began to chat to two men who told them they were from Canada. Holly chatted to Chad from Toronto, secretly hoping that Max would notice. He didn't seem too fussed about spending time with her today and had barely even said hello to her. It was good for him to see that she had options; despite being a mother of two in her thirties, she was certainly still desirable.

Holly laughed at Chad's jokes and politely answered his questions even though if she was honest, he was starting to bore her a little, droning on about his job in IT. She couldn't help but stare at his ridiculously white teeth (clearly veneers) and was losing track of what he was saying. As she looked over at Max, her heart sank when she spotted him and Callum chatting to a group of girls. Max was throwing his head back, chuckling at something one of the girls had said, and Holly couldn't help but feel irritated. She knew she was doing exactly the same thing and it was hypocritical, but now the doubts about how much he actually liked her were starting to set in. She'd done the exact same thing when she was younger on a holiday to Portugal. Liam had been her first (and only) one-night stand. Holly just hadn't been able to resist his charm and promises. She'd fallen for everything. No sooner had she slept with him, he lost interest. He'd been straight onto the next girl and Holly had felt foolish when she saw him leave the bar the following evening with a girl with long dark hair. He most likely used the same lines on everyone. That was the last time she'd ever slept with somebody so soon.

This time, Holly had told herself, she could handle it. After all, she'd wanted it to happen, but now she was watching Max flirt with other girls, the same feelings she'd had all those years ago in Portugal were starting to come back to her. A feeling of being used and discarded, and she realized then that she probably wasn't strong enough to have casual flings. She cared too much, even though she didn't really know how she felt about him. Such a typical girl, she thought, irritated with herself. When she'd met Rob, she had hoped that was it. No more game-playing. No more awkward first dates. But it wasn't meant to be. Now here she was, single in Vegas, while he was playing happy families with his new girlfriend and their children. It made her want to be home with her babies. She suddenly wanted to cuddle them. To snuggle up on the sofa and watch a Disney movie, their three bodies tangled up under the blanket. That was most likely what she'd be doing about now, she realized. Her children always made her feel loved, content and safe. When she was with them, she didn't need anyone else in the world. They made her happier than they would ever know.

'Don't worry about him,' Kim said caringly, her eyes flicking over to Max who now had his arm around one of the girl's waists.

'I'm not,' Holly lied. She didn't want to admit it, even to Kim.

'You can't fool me, Hols,' Kim replied tenderly, 'I know you. I'm looking at your face now and you look shocked at his behaviour.'

Holly nodded, watching Max's every move intently. He was loving every second being around those other girls. *Onto the next one.* Just like Liam in Portugal. As much as she didn't want to care, she knew she was upset at his change of behaviour. Nobody around this pool could have imagined the things he'd been whispering in her ear not so many hours ago, all the promises he most likely never planned to keep. He knew all the right things to say. Her mind wandered elsewhere as she noticed Charlie's expression as he was talking to Emma. His eyes were as thin as slits and he looked angry, as though he was hissing at her.

Kim squeezed her shoulder gently. 'Max is only talking to that girl. I'm sure it's harmless flirting. Maybe go and talk to him?'

'Yes, maybe,' Holly agreed, to keep her quiet.

She wasn't thinking about Max any more though. At that moment, he didn't matter one little bit. There was something else Holly was concerned about.

'Come on then,' Kim said with enthusiasm, 'let's go and chat to the others. Forget about those girls,' she said.

Kim continued to talk but Holly wasn't listening. Her eyes wouldn't budge. They were still focused on the way Charlie seemed to be speaking to Emma, who was standing there with her head bowed, looking meek and remorseful. What on earth had happened? They seemed to be arguing about something.

Suddenly, Emma spun round waving a mobile phone.

'Someone's phone is ringing,' she shouted, walking nearer to the pool.

'It's mine,' Holly replied, moving closer so she could hand it over. It was Rob calling and Holly's forehead creased as she answered it.

'Hello, Rob?'

'Holly, hi. Me and your mum were trying to call you earlier, but it wouldn't go through.' He then spoke to whoever he was with. 'I've got through to her, she's on the phone.'

'What's wrong?' Holly panicked, her heart hammering in her chest. She just knew something had happened.

'It's Lottie. Now, don't worry, she's okay,' he informed her gravely. 'She fell off the bed earlier and has been taken to hospital. They think she's fractured her arm.'

Holly couldn't breathe. 'Oh my God,' she gasped, a million questions going through her mind. She felt the guilt, worry and anxiety coming off her in waves. 'What do you mean she fell off the bed? *How*, Rob? Has she been asking for me? Is she in pain? I cannot believe this has happened when I'm away.'

'It was just an accident. She was jumping on the bed this morning and just fell off,' he explained.

'What the hell, Rob? Why weren't you watching her?' The shock of the situation was making Holly feel angry with him, despite knowing he was a good father and would never put his children in any harm. Holly couldn't help but think this wouldn't have happened if she had been in charge though. She would have told Lottie to get off the bed at once. Holly could always see the dangers, whereas Rob could only see his child having fun.

'I was with Nikki…' Rob began.

'Nikki?' Holly interjected furiously. 'Oh my God, Rob, you've got to be kidding me,' she snapped hotly, feeling enraged. 'If you can't look after your own children now you have a new girlfriend, if you can't be bothered to *watch* them and they're now just one big inconvenience to you, then maybe you shouldn't even have them when you're with her!' Holly was exasperated. This was the first big accident that Lottie had ever had and she wasn't there. Her children had never been to A & E before. Not once. Yet now Rob was busy with Nikki, the first time her kids had even met her, and this had happened. Her poor little Lottie. Holly felt horrendous that she hadn't been there to comfort her.

Rob sighed heavily. 'If you let me explain…'

'No, Rob, you let *me* explain. When you have the children, they are *your* priority, not Nikki's. Do you understand that?' Her tone was scathing.

'For Christ's sake, Holly, let me speak!' Rob demanded.

'I want to speak to Lottie,' Holly told him firmly, cutting in again.

'Your mum is on her way home with her now. I'll get her to call as soon as she's back.'

'What are you talking about – my mum?' Holly was baffled. 'I thought the children were with you?'

Rob exhaled slowly. 'No, Holly. That's what I was trying to tell you. They were at your mum's this morning. Lottie fell off your mum's bed when she was getting Jacob out of the bath. I was on my way round there with Nikki to collect them. When I arrived, your mum had called the ambulance. She went to the hospital with Lottie and Nikki and I stayed to look after Jacob.'

Holly grimaced, cringing with embarrassment.

Well, that was just perfect.

Chapter 15

Kim

Kim could tell something was wrong with Lottie and couldn't wait for Holly to get off the phone. She watched her suddenly pulling a mortified expression, apologizing profusely to Rob. What on earth had happened?

'What's up with Lottie?' she asked as soon as Holly hung up.

Holly explained the situation.

'Oh dear,' Kim wrinkled her nose. 'Is she okay though? It's just an accident that's easily done. Mylo fell off the bed when he was a baby, do you remember? Luckily it wasn't bad enough for hospital, but it was so scary. He had such a big bump.'

'Apparently she's not in any pain now,' Holly said, 'but she has her arm in a sling and stuff. She has to be really careful and go back to the hospital for a check-up. I feel awful that I'm not there.' Holly looked crestfallen as she spoke. 'I *should* be there. And what I just said to Rob, too, wow.' She clenched her teeth in humiliation. 'He must hate me. I went so over the top at him and he hadn't even done anything wrong. I was so scared that I just lost it with him. I guess I'm just feeling a bit unsettled today, what with what happened with Max last night and I guess you're right, Kim, it's not a nice feeling to see him chatting up other girls right in front of me. I think I must have taken it out on Rob. I don't know, maybe I'm not finding this as easy as I thought,' she finally confessed with a sigh. 'Once upon a time everything was so simple. Not in our relationship, but just the fact that Rob and I were together with the children.'

Kim shook her head. 'Rob will understand you were just worried and in shock, don't worry. He'll get over it,' Kim tried to reassure her. 'I really wouldn't beat yourself up about the fact it's taking time to get used to the new set-up. You're bound to feel a little strange and uneasy about it all to start with.'

'Maybe. I think sometimes I just feel a little sad that things didn't work out, you know? There's nothing more I would have loved than a family that remained together, especially for the children. It's something I'd always wished for as a child when my parents split up.'

'You weren't happy with Rob, Holly. Don't forget that. Your happiness is more important than staying together. The kids would have picked up on it eventually and it wouldn't have been healthy to stay together just for their sake.'

'I know, I know.' Holly swallowed hard. 'I should never have spoken to him like that though. Rob didn't deserve that. I can't wait to speak to Lottie.' She glanced at her phone.

'I bet,' Kim answered sympathetically. She would be feeling exactly the same if she was in Holly's shoes. It was always complicated when people split up and they had children together, even when they were breaking up amicably. It was another reminder that Kim didn't want this to be her and Andy one day. 'Come on, let's go back to where Emma is sitting.'

Kim walked over to the others with Holly behind her, pleased when the group of girls Callum and Max were chatting to said their goodbyes and walked away. Who on earth did Max think he was? It seemed obvious now that he was a player, someone who just wanted a good time and not a relationship. She was worried that Holly had got the wrong impression and she was annoyed for her friend if she'd been led on in any way. Yes, Max was good-looking and charming, but no-one was going to upset her best friend. Especially now she was feeling in even lower spirits because of Lottie's fall.

Apart from the thoughts of her marriage issues constantly popping into her mind, Kim was doing her best to enjoy the break away. Thinking of home, she realized she hadn't replied to Andy's latest message asking her if she was having a good time. She quickly tapped back a reply to tell him she was, and that she hoped the children were all okay. Listening to what had happened to Lottie was a reminder to Kim that she should be checking in more often to see how they were.

'What's up?' Callum asked, noticing Holly appeared distressed.

She explained what had happened to Lottie.

'Oh no,' Callum's face fell, 'I can imagine just how you're feeling. I'm sure your mum will be spoiling her though and giving her tons of attention. I swear Eva enjoys being ill sometimes as I let her sleep in my bed,' he told her kindly, trying to put her at ease.

'Yeah, you're probably right,' Holly replied, her eyes glassy. 'I just feel terrible for not being there.'

'Can't be helped.' Max said in a tone that implied he clearly didn't share her concern.

'I'm sure she won't be in any pain any more,' Callum continued, with compassion in his eyes. 'They'll have given her medicine in the hospital, I'm certain of it.'

'Thanks, Callum,' Holly replied, biting a nail.

Max began to talk to Holly then, and Kim was pleased. The last thing she wanted was for Holly to be hurt by him. Kim just wanted to see Holly happy. If Max was the man to do that (womanizer or not), then so be it. Perhaps he wasn't as bad as Kim had thought? He was a single man on holiday. He wasn't exactly Holly's husband who had sworn an oath to only be with her.

Kim turned her attention to Callum, who seemed to have caught the sun on his face, bringing out the stunning green colour of his eyes.

'Did you have a good time last night?' she asked in a friendly voice.

'Probably not as good as you, judging by your state at the end of the night,' he chuckled light-heartedly. 'But yes, it was a great night.'

'You've not been married, have you?' Kim asked curiously.

Callum seemed like such a nice guy. The type to instantly make you feel comfortable. He was a catch and Kim couldn't see how he was still single, unless it was by choice.

'No, my ex and I never got that far in the end. We were engaged, but things fell apart after we had our little girl. I'd love to get married one day though. Have a few more kids, the whole shebang.'

'I'm sure you will,' Kim said earnestly. She turned to Holly mouthing, 'You okay?'

Holly nodded as she chatted to Max, quickly glancing at her phone again.

'Fancy getting some shots in with me?' Callum asked Kim, raising an eyebrow.

'Why not?' Kim giggled, following him to the bar. 'Let's get some tequila!'

Kim had done tequila shots the first time she went on a date with Andy. She remembered it so well. He'd taken her to Umbertos, a beautiful little Italian in Colchester near where they went to university. She could tell he was quite taken with her from the beginning. It was the way he couldn't help but appear fascinated by everything she said. He seemed to want to know everything about her, and Kim had no trouble chatting about herself. She'd always been so full of life and confidence back then. He made her feel great about herself from the very start, even though at first she wasn't entirely sure he would be able to keep up with her.

121

'Dessert? Coffee?' Andy had asked, his eyes scanning the menu after their dinner.

'How about tequila?' Kim had said. She had planned to meet Holly and a few others in a club after her date and she didn't want to be behind on how many drinks they'd had.

'Tequila?' he said in bafflement, his eyes widening as though she'd suggested poison.

Kim had nodded, her expression serious. 'What's wrong with that?' she asked innocently. He was so tall and robust that if he couldn't handle shots, then he wasn't the man for her. She hoped he wasn't so into his sports that he was really health-conscious or anything like that. She wanted someone on her level. Someone who wanted to enjoy life and party. Life was for *living*.

Andy hesitated. 'Okay,' he'd replied slowly. It had sounded more like a question than answer. To him, drinking shots of tequila after a lovely meal on a date was the most alien thing in the world. 'You're not like most girls,' he'd commented, gazing at her as though he was trying to work her out.

'I'm not?'

'No, Kim. There's something about you,' he said, narrowing his eyes and taking her hand across the table. 'Something I want to know more about.'

Kim hadn't planned for Andy to be her boyfriend, even though she had always liked him and admired him from afar along with the other girls. Kim dated *a lot* back in those days at university, just for fun. She didn't really care if she could see a future with them or not. She had enjoyed being single. She loved the thrill of not knowing what was going to happen. She never felt the need to have a boyfriend like some of the girls she knew. When she'd met Andy, Holly hadn't long been in a relationship with Rob. The thought of double dates had seemed like a fun idea; they hadn't ever done that before. Thinking about it now, it was probably the reason that Kim gave Andy a chance to get to know her better. She was like a wild horse that couldn't be tamed. Not until she had decided to let someone tame her. Andy had been the right man at the right time. Timing, Kim realized, was so important.

Kim had still remained the same party girl even when she did get into a relationship with Andy. Whether it was out after work for drinks in London or going out to bars and clubs drinking at the weekends, she wasn't going to let having a boyfriend stop her doing what she enjoyed. She was only young once and Andy knew the score. In fact, he seemed to love that she was so free-spirited and lively.

'Life just feels more exciting with you in it,' he'd said to her in a little speech when he'd proposed in South Africa (it had been Kim's idea to go on a safari). 'I never know what's going to happen with you. I never know what your next plans are for us to do. I've never laughed and smiled so much with anybody. You're extraordinary, Kim.'

Despite being engaged, Kim had made sure she spent lots of time with her friends too. There was nothing Kim had hated more than girls who stopped seeing their friends when they got into a new relationship and she had sworn that would never be her. Andy went out with his own friends as well, just not as often as Kim did. He liked his nights at home, and was more than happy to have friends over for a few beers to watch the rugby or football rather than go out to pubs and bars. It was easy to give up being single to be with Andy. He was secure in their relationship; never once put off by the fact she was such a party girl. In fact, it was her wild side he found so attractive about her. Again, an uneasy feeling crept up on Kim. She was no longer the same carefree, crazy, tequila-loving woman he'd fallen in love with. She was so different now. Did Andy even recognize her any more? Did he still love her as he once did?

'Ready?' Callum asked, holding up a shot glass, making her memories drift away.

'As I'll ever be,' Kim giggled, sucking the lemon before downing her shot. She grimaced as she drunk it and then burst out laughing at Callum's face, crumpled up in displeasure before he licked the salt from his other hand.

'That was vile,' he laughed. 'Come on, let's give the rest to the others.'

Max looked up as they approached. 'You two look as though you're having fun. What's that?' he asked, looking at the tray in Callum's hand.

'Shots for you guys,' he said, handing them out.

'I want to speak to Lottie before I really start drinking,' Holly said worriedly, pushing hers aside towards Max who downed it in one. She was holding her mobile ready for the call when it came moments later.

The others downed their shots and Kim continued to talk to Callum, feeling really relaxed in his company. He was like a friend she'd known for years.

An hour or so later, Emma put on her kaftan. 'Girls, are you ready to come to the shop with me?' she asked. 'How was Lottie when you spoke to her?' she asked Holly.

'She seems fine,' Holly told her. 'She actually seems to think it's pretty cool she has a sling.' She attempted a laugh, but Kim knew how concerned she was. 'There's nothing I can do though, I wasn't there and she seemed happy enough to be spending the day with Rob and Nikki.'

'Ah, glad to hear she's okay,' Callum said.

'I do understand how you feel not being there, but at least you know she's perfectly happy and not in any pain,' Kim said to her. 'Come on, let's go and help Emma find her dream wedding accessories.'

'I'll see you a bit later,' Holly said to Max, kissing him on the cheek.

'See you,' Kim waved to Callum as she walked off with the others. 'Actually girls, I'm going to quickly nip to the loo. I'll meet you by the exit,' she said, pivoting round.

When Kim came out of the toilets, she was shocked to see Max standing there. It appeared as if he was waiting for her.

'Everything okay?' she asked him in wonderment.

Max had a strange, unreadable expression on his face. His eyes appeared glassy and a little bloodshot from the alcohol he'd been drinking.

'Yes, everything is fine,' he said, staring at her intently and making her feel uneasy. It was like he knew something she didn't, and Kim's first thoughts were about Holly.

'Holly is by the exit,' Kim told him, glancing over but unable to see her friends due to it being so busy. For some reason she couldn't look Max in the eye. They were all alone apart from a few strangers dancing close to the bar. 'Were you after her?'

'It's actually you I came to see,' he smirked.

He was so handsome it was ridiculous, and he knew it. There was something very off-putting about a man who knew how good he looked. He was the epitome of a bad boy with his cocky grin, carefree, confident nature and tattoos, but she wasn't really sure that he was actually a nice person.

Kim's brow furrowed, unsure what to say. She didn't really understand what any of this was about. 'What did you want?' she asked him, feeling baffled.

'You look like you were getting close to Callum earlier,' Max said in a smooth voice. His ran his fingers through his dark hair.

The lines on Kim's forehead deepened, bemused. 'What are you talking about? As friends, yes,' she stated firmly. What was he suggesting? She didn't like where the conversation was heading and really hoped Holly and Emma would come over and rescue her. Max was being so serious. He wasn't talking to her in his usual jokey way. Why did it concern him who she spoke to?

'Is that all it is then?' Max asked, cocking his head to one side and moving even closer towards her.

'Yes,' Kim replied indignantly. 'Why do you care?'

He squeezed her hand slightly, making her feel as though she'd had an electric shock and his mouth turned up at the edges. His eyes blazed into hers and Kim felt as though her face was on fire. Her heart began to race. This felt very wrong. What was he doing?

'You're with Holly,' Kim said timidly, unable to stop frowning as she gazed at him, searching for answers as to why he was behaving this way. Her head was a little blurred from drinking, but she was certain he was being inappropriate. Was he saying he was jealous that she had been talking to Callum?

'I've been with Holly for one night,' he said. Then he shot her a cheeky smile and let go of her head, muttering under his breath as he walked off, 'but I haven't been with you.'

Kim stood there, flabbergasted, unable to move from the spot. Did that really just happen? Had she heard him correctly over the loud music? As she walked over to the others who were chatting chatting about bridal veils and hair pieces, she wondered if she'd just imagined the whole thing.

Chapter 16

Emma

Emma wondered how Americans were always full of so much energy. It was like they never got tired or miserable in Vegas; the staff everywhere were always ebullient, energetic and bursting with enthusiasm. They couldn't do enough for you. Everything came with a smile. Emma had always thought it was the way it should be when you were served by a waitress or shopped in a store, but today, Taylor, the pretty lady standing in front of her, was too much. She was actually making Emma feel tired and drained of energy. She knew it was probably the late nights catching up with her, but as she stood there watching her get out all the accessories she might be interested in, Emma wished that Taylor would just calm the hell down.

'So how are you feeling about your big day?' Taylor asked in a high-pitched, shrilly voice. 'You're going to have the most amazing weather as it's been super-hot lately. I bet your dress is *gorgeous*. You have the most amazing figure.'

'Thanks,' Emma answered tiredly. 'I'm feeling good, I guess,' she forced herself to sound as happy as possible. She knew she should be feeling incredibly grateful for everything this store was offering her for free, but there was something bothering her and she couldn't put her finger on it. She was starting to feel trapped, knowing she was getting married in a few days' time. Like someone was smothering her and all she needed was a little air. She just needed to breathe a bit. She knew it was normal to be feeling this way, most people had cold feet before making such a big commitment, so she pushed her doubts away, focusing on the beautiful accessories being shown to her and reminding herself that she was lucky.

She took her phone out and shot a video to her Instagram, filming the shop and the lovely items they had. She would make sure she posted about them quite a bit as a thank you. It was the least she could do.

Thanks to @littlewhitedress for all the help today buying bridal accessories! #almosttimetosayido #vegaswedding

'So we have these gorgeous veils here we thought you may like,' Taylor began to explain. 'We have all different lengths and fabrics from lace to chiffon, organza or silk tulle. Or if you'd prefer a bridal hair comb, we have some gorgeous designs right here. Or how about a hair vine? We have the most beautiful pieces I'm about to show you.' Taylor was looking through a box like a child looking in their stocking on Christmas Day.

Emma snapped away taking images and tagging the shop on her social media, but she began to feel overwhelmed and despite the air-conditioning blasting down on her, she felt sweaty and hot. 'I don't know,' she mumbled helplessly. 'I don't know what to do. I just don't know what I want.' She turned to look at Holly and Kim. 'Help me, girls. I sent you a picture of the dress, didn't I? What should I have in my hair?' She purposely hadn't decided because she knew she'd be visiting this store. Was she crazy leaving it to the last minute?

They discussed some ideas and Emma was grateful to her

friends for helping. There had been so much organizing to do for this wedding and it was all beginning to seem so real now. It was only just dawning on her that this was really going to happen. Everything had suddenly got on top of her. When she'd picked her wedding dress ten months earlier, it had been fun and exciting. After all, her wedding had seemed so far away it felt like it was happening to someone else and she was just getting to buy a gorgeous dress. But now she was only days away, picking out all the final touches, she was feeling different about it somehow. She felt silly getting married. How was she doing something so grown up and serious?

'Why don't we try this hair vine?' Holly suggested helpfully. 'I'm just thinking it would look beautiful with your long hair, Emma. I could do some soft mermaid waves and it would give it a bohemian, whimsical look. I've done it on lots of brides recently and it looks beautiful. I think it would really go well with your floaty wedding dress.'

Emma felt herself nodding. Yes, that sounded perfect. She needed someone else to make the decisions for her; she just didn't feel strong enough at that moment to decide upon anything. She trusted Holly implicitly; she followed her bridal hair Instagram page and she honestly thought her friend was extremely talented. She was always fully booked, another good sign. Holly had done her hair for a night out before too, and she'd loved it; there was nobody better to help her decide.

But why was she feeling so anxious all of a sudden? She loved Charlie, didn't she? Everyone was always saying how the two of them were a match made in heaven. She wanted to spend the rest of her life with him. That's why she was there, in Vegas, surrounded by people she cared about.

'Can I have a drink of water?' Emma croaked, fanning herself with a bridal magazine on the coffee table in front of her.

'Absolutely,' Taylor replied hastily. 'I was just about to offer you three glasses of champagne. Would you like that?'

129

'Oh yes please,' Kim responded before Emma could get a word in. 'That sounds much better than water,' she chuckled. 'You have to have champagne in a wedding shop.'

Emma couldn't speak. She didn't want to sound like the boring one who just wanted a soft drink. She was the one who was supposed to be celebrating. She needed water though, just something to quench her thirst, but remained silent, concentrating on keeping herself cool. She walked over to the exact spot below the air-conditioning.

'Are you really that warm?' Holly asked in bewilderment. 'I think it's chilly in here.'

'I'm boiling,' Emma gasped, 'that feels lovely.' She held her arms out to let the cold air hit every part of her. She lifted her face upwards and relished the freezing blast whipping through her hair.

Emma felt her phone vibrate, signalling she had another email. She normally just got rid of the notification and let them all build up. Charlie would probably reply anyway, so she wouldn't need to worry about it, but this time, she decided to check who it was from.

She didn't recognize the name of the person who had sent it and clicked on the email curiously.

Dear Emma, thank you so much for contacting us. We would be delighted to use your fiancé in our next shoot for sportswear, but were hoping you would be able to join in too and collaborate with us? If this is okay, then we would be happy to use the both of you and would like to discuss a fee…

Emma felt perturbed as she read the email. She had no idea what it was about, and it was clear it was someone else Charlie had been chatting to behind her back, using her name. Her index finger hovered over the 'sent' items. She'd never checked them before and she was a little nervous as to what she was going to discover. Her hand started to shake as she read the tons of emails

Charlie had sent pretending to be her. She could see that every email sent would benefit him.

I was wondering if you would be interested in my fiancé modelling/being sent your products in exchange for promotion from both him and myself? As you can see from my page, I have over half a million followers…

What on earth? There were dozens of them and her mouth hung open. It was all about him. Why would he not have asked her first? She was more than happy to help him in his career, but this seemed a bit sneaky. What right did he have? She was furious. She wasn't comfortable with Charlie trying to use her to get to places without letting her know what his intentions were.

Taylor walked over with the champagne and Emma knew she should capture this moment for her Instagram. Maybe a Boomerang video of them clinking their glasses. She simply couldn't muster the energy to do it though.

'Thank you,' Emma said to Taylor, attempting a smile. She wasn't feeling right, especially after receiving that email, but didn't want to mention it to the others, too embarrassed by what they would probably say.

'You're so welcome,' Taylor said in a saccharine tone, practically bouncing over to the hair vines. 'Shall we?' she said, holding one up.

'This one is lovely,' Holly gushed, holding up a rose-gold floral vine. 'It would match your rose-gold theme perfectly too, wouldn't it? Here, let's try it on.'

'We have some great necklaces that would go with it too,' Taylor beamed excitedly. 'I'm not sure if you were planning on wearing jewellery, but this necklace here is absolutely gorgeous. It's new in.'

Emma nodded, trying to get into the mood. Trying to share their enthusiasm. Holly placed the vine in Emma's hair gently, adjusting it into the correct position.

'You have to remember that your hair will be wavy. We can

do a bit up here,' she said, holding some of her hair up as Emma gazed at herself in the mirror. 'What do you think?'

'I love that,' Kim said in admiration, sipping her champagne on the sofa.

'I think it really compliments your skin tone,' Taylor nodded encouragingly.

'Yes, I guess I like it,' Emma replied, feeling really unsure and indecisive. What did she want? She did like the hair vine, but she just felt really confused. She had been looking forward to visiting A Little White Dress and had felt really flattered that they were offering her something for free just for her promotion on her page. Yet now she was here, she felt like she would rather be anywhere else in the world. Emma wiped her brow.

'It's probably best to try a veil to compare,' Taylor suggested. 'I think a veil would look gorgeous on you.'

'I did try on one with my dress when I bought it,' Emma explained, 'but I wasn't a hundred per cent sure it was really me.'

'Perhaps try this beautiful one here,' Taylor continued, as if she hadn't heard her. 'This is waist-length, gathered with two tiers and has a beaded edge. It's ivory; you said over email your dress was ivory, didn't you? This will look beautiful.' She dragged the word 'beautiful', making her voice sound whiny.

Emma felt pressured into trying it on.

'Maybe just give us a few moments?' Holly said to Taylor delicately. 'I'm doing her hair so if it's okay, we will try on a few and see how we get on?'

'Of course,' Taylor smiled widely, but it didn't reach her eyes.

Clearly she wasn't used to being told to go away, but Emma was so thankful to Holly for realizing she needed space that she could have kissed her.

'Are you okay?' Holly whispered when Taylor was out of earshot.

Emma gulped. 'I'm fine, yes,' she lied, not wanting to make a fuss.

'Are you sure?' Holly probed. 'You look as though you're trembling.'

Emma glanced at Kim who was busy reading a magazine and drinking her champagne.

'Yes, I'm sure,' Emma told her in the most reassuring tone she could muster. She just wanted to pick what she wanted and leave. She needed to lay down or something and had a horrible feeling in the pit of her stomach.

Holly's eyes darted to Kim to check she wasn't paying attention and then back to Emma. 'Listen, Em, is everything okay with you? Not just now, in here, right now, but in general? You'd tell me if something was wrong, wouldn't you?'

Emma frowned. 'Why are you asking me that for?'

'I noticed the way Charlie was talking to you earlier. He looked furious about something. Is everything okay?' Holly asked quietly.

Emma folded her arms across her chest protectively. 'When?' she asked, feeling her face burn. She guessed it must have been at the pool when Charlie had been annoyed with her. An American guy who had been a club promotor had briefly stopped to chat to her about where she was going that evening and Charlie had accused Emma of trying to show him up by chatting to other men in front of him. She'd calmed him down eventually by explaining the man had just wanted to know where she was going because that was his *job* to get people into the club, and not for any other reason, but he'd seemed really enraged at one point. The tiniest little things were beginning to irritate him lately. Emma had thought he'd have behaved better in Vegas seeing as they were so close to getting married, but no such luck. Until now, no-one had ever seen Charlie behave any other way than lovely towards her. No-one had ever asked if everything was okay, and now Holly was standing before her, gazing at her suspiciously, Emma genuinely didn't know what to say.

'The conversation looked quite heated, that's all,' Holly said in a hushed voice.

'It was nothing.' Emma took a deep breath. She just needed a bit of air. Her heart began to beat faster until she could feel the blood rushing to her ears. Her vision was blurring and she could feel a tidal wave of panic hitting her.

'How are you getting on? I just found some beautiful tiaras out the back.'

Taylor was back now, with her sing-song, irritating voice.

'Emma? Are you alright?' Holly asked worriedly.

Something was in her throat. She had something lodged there and she couldn't swallow it down. She couldn't breathe. Her head felt like it was going to explode. She was burning hot. Her heart was thumping away violently and everything was starting to go black. Maybe she was dying? It sure felt that way.

'I think she's going to pass out,' Emma heard Taylor say in an astonished voice.

'Emma?'

The last thing Emma heard before she fell into Holly's arms was Kim.

'I think she's having a panic attack.'

Chapter 17

Holly

Holly had never had a panic attack before so she had no idea what it felt like. It looked truly terrifying, she thought, as rubbed Emma's back tenderly. Holly wondered if they needed to get medical attention. Emma was sitting on the sofa with her head in her hands, trembling all over. After a minute or two, she seemed to be over the worst of it and her breathing was returning to normal. Holly just hoped she wasn't responsible for bringing the attack on because she'd asked her why Charlie had seemed so cross with her earlier that day. She couldn't help but feel partly responsible and an uneasy feeling of guilt washed over her. She was only being a good friend checking that she was okay though, wasn't she? What type of friend would she be if she just ignored the fact that Emma might need help or needed to talk? Holly wasn't the kind of person to interfere with someone else's business. She was never one to gossip or to want to know all the details about someone's private life. Holly only wanted to know the things that people wanted to tell her. Kim was the opposite and it had always been something that Holly didn't understand.

'Don't you want to know why they broke up?' she remembered Kim asking after her brother announced he was splitting from his wife.

'Yes,' Holly had answered. 'But I'm sure he's going to tell me everything I need to know in his own time. I'm not going to ask him and put him on the spot.'

Kim would always look at her as though she was crazy. Kim was the type of girl to find out how much her brother-in-law's salary was when he seemed to be doing well for himself and treating her sister to designer shoes and bags (she researched how much solicitors earned and even made a few phone calls because she was *that* interested). She investigated things that she didn't feel comfortable asking people outright. She was the kind of girl to ask if someone was pregnant as soon as they ordered a soft drink. She just liked knowing things about people, it was as simple as that, whereas Holly wasn't fussed. She never wanted to interfere.

'Are you feeling better now, Emma?' Kim asked, looking really worried.

Taylor was standing over Emma with a glass of water, and Emma took it from her gratefully, downing several gulps.

'I think so,' Emma responded breathlessly. 'Sorry about this,' she said apologetically to Taylor, 'I honestly don't know what's come over me. This has never happened before.'

'Don't be silly,' Taylor said reassuringly, 'so long as you're okay, that's the main thing. Take as much time as you need.' She walked away to serve another customer who had just walked into the store.

'Sorry girls,' Emma said, swallowing hard and rolling her eyes. 'I'm so embarrassed. I'm starting to feel okay again now.'

'Don't be ridiculous,' Holly replied, placing her hand on her shoulder. 'Thank God you're feeling alright now. I was really concerned about you at one point. So you've never had a panic attack before then?'

'Nope,' Emma shook her head. 'It was horrible. I didn't even know what was happening to me. I wasn't even aware that it *was* a panic attack until I heard Kim say it. Maybe it's just the stress of the wedding.'

'Yes, of course,' Kim told her. 'The only reason I knew it was a panic attack is because a friend at university used to get them all the time. I could just tell it was the same thing.'

Emma nodded and attempted to stand up. Holly and Kim held their arms out for support.

'Thanks girls. I think I'm fine now. It's scary how it comes on so quickly and then goes, just like that,' Emma said thoughtfully. 'I think I'm just going to go ahead with that rose-gold vine for my hair. The sooner I get out of this place, the better.'

'You're sure?' Holly checked. She didn't want her to just be picking anything on such an important day because she wasn't feeling well. 'It will look lovely,' she told her sincerely.

'Yes, I'm sure. I'll just tell Taylor and then we can go and maybe grab something to eat. I think I just want to sit down and chill out. I'm sure the vine will be perfect and it's the right colour.'

An hour later and the girls were sitting down eating.

'This is delicious,' Holly said, spooning some pasta into her mouth. 'The food is here is so lovely. Every place we've eaten in has been amazing.'

'It's lovely, but I'm not sure I can eat much,' Emma explained, pushing the food around her plate.

'Are you okay, Emma?' Kim asked, caringly.

Holly noticed that Emma still looked weak and despite having a tan, she looked pale.

'You really don't seem yourself,' Kim continued.

Emma nodded. 'Of course. I have no idea why that just happened. I'm not panicking about getting married or anything,' she gave a nervous giggle. 'It's what I want.'

Holly eyed Kim, willing her to not ask anything else. It was obvious something was up with Emma, but she knew the more they pressed her about it, the more they were likely to push her away. Emma would tell them what she wanted to, and if she didn't want to confess her true feelings, then that was her choice and they needed to respect that.

Emma took a sip of water and a tiny bite of her burger. 'So Holly, how's things with Max? Do you really like him?' she asked, trying to change the subject.

Holly inhaled for a few seconds. 'I do, but we've only just met. I'm feeling a little cautious around him, especially after he couldn't wait to blab about last night to people,' she threw her eyes upwards. 'I don't want to get ahead of myself. I'm not really sure about it all,' she admitted, looking out of the window deep in thought.

Emma's mouth was a straight line. 'I think that's wise. I don't want to put you off him, he's the loveliest guy at times and I've always got on with him, but he doesn't seem to have the best track record with girlfriends. I just wanted to warn you. You never know though, perhaps he'll change? I'm certain he likes you.'

Holly's heart sank. She knew what Emma was saying was true. Holly had felt it from the start. She wasn't stupid; she could tell the kind of man Max was. She knew she needed to keep her guard up to protect her feelings. But what were those feelings? He had been irresistible the previous evening, but waking up with a clear mind she was beginning to question things.

Kim remained silent, looking a little uncomfortable as she moved the food around on her plate. She cleared her throat. 'I'm not sure he's right for you,' she stated, looking into the distance with a little shrug.

Holly was taken aback. This was certainly news. 'Why are you saying that suddenly?' she asked her. It was odd that Kim was making such a bold statement out of nowhere and she hadn't said that hours before when they'd been discussing the fact that Holly had slept with him.

'I just think you can do a lot better,' Kim responded sweetly. She hesitated. 'I don't know. There's something about Max that

I'm not sure about. He just seems like a player, that's all. He doesn't seem like boyfriend material. I can't imagine him wanting to play daddy anytime soon.'

Holly nodded, thinking the same thing. Still, she felt as though she owed him a chance at least.

'What was it like when you first met Rob?' Emma asked. 'I can't really remember ever discussing it with you before. When did you realize you were going to break up?'

'Everything felt right when we first met,' Holly told them, looking into the distance thoughtfully. 'There was no guessing if he liked me. I just knew. Our relationship just seemed to work and we rarely argued when it was just the two of us. I guess it was when we became parents that things just changed. I don't think being a parent is an easy job – it's tiring and can be stressful. It's like you've literally said goodbye to your old life as you once knew it. You have these little people relying on you for everything and we didn't cope well under the pressure. We began to argue. We just stopped seeing eye to eye any more. I like to be organized and I'm pretty strict with Lottie and Jacob's routine, whereas Rob was the opposite. We did try to make it work, for the children's sake, but I think we both knew we were kidding ourselves. You know in your heart when something isn't right,' she said, looking at Emma who was biting her lip.

'It's hard when you have children, but it's great that you both get on still,' Kim put in.

'Are things still good with you and Andy?' Emma enquired, looking up at Kim.

'Yes, perfect,' Kim replied quickly, pushing the hair back from her brow. 'Where did you say we were going tonight?' she asked.

Emma began to tell them the plans, but the way Kim had changed the subject didn't go unnoticed by Holly. She scrutinized her friend, trying to put her finger on what could be troubling her. In fact, Holly was sure that both Kim and Emma had things on their mind that they were keeping to themselves and she hoped if it was anything serious, rather than dealing with it alone, they knew they could confide in her.

Later that evening they were having drinks in the bar when Max bowled over to Holly, kissing her affectionately on the cheek.

'Evening gorgeous,' he said, 'you're looking stunning as always.'

Holly couldn't help but beam at his handsome face. When she was away from him, she questioned whether spending time with him was a good idea. But the moment she saw him she couldn't control the drumming of her heart just being near him. Every time she thought about the night before, she felt her heart flip over. It wasn't often she felt such a physical connection to someone, even though she knew deep in her heart it probably wasn't a good thing. Not with Max. That was the thing about meeting Rob that she'd told Emma and Kim earlier. Not only did she know he was keen on her and found her attractive, but straight away she could tell he was the type of man who wanted a relationship. She had felt safe from the very start. Rob had made his intentions clear. He wanted a girlfriend, someone who he would marry in future and have children with, and he wanted that girl to be Holly. It had been nice knowing where she stood. There hadn't been any games and that had suited her. She didn't want to be messed around – what girl did? With Max she didn't feel safe at all. It was like jumping out of an aeroplane and not being entirely sure that your parachute would work.

Max slid his arm around her waist. 'What can I get you to drink, girls?' he asked them.

'I'll get this one,' Callum said kindly, as they all requested a glass of wine.

'So, Em. You have two more evenings before you're married,' Max reminded her. 'How are you feeling?'

'Fine.' Emma attempted a casual tone, but her voice quavered.

Charlie came over at that point and starting chatting to Emma while Kim began to chat to his cousin, Frankie.

'So whereabouts do you live at home exactly?' Max asked Holly. 'You're not too far from me, are you?'

Holly explained where she lived, secretly pleased he was talking about home and his plans with her afterwards.

'I'll have to take you to the most amazing Thai restaurant in the world near me. Have you ever been to Thai River?'

'I haven't, but I've heard of it,' Holly answered.

'You'll love it if you like Thai food,' he said confidently.

Holly began to relax, thinking that perhaps it hadn't just been a one-night thing for him after all. He *did* want to meet up again after Vegas, but she still had a few doubts about him that she couldn't shake off, no matter how hard she tried.

'So,' Max said, lifting Holly's chin and kissing her on the lips, 'you going to the club with the others afterwards?' he asked interestedly.

Holly kissed him back, then shrugged her shoulders. 'I guess so.'

Max started to talk about how he'd been to the gym that morning, despite feeling hungover, but Holly couldn't help but hear the conversation going on behind her between Charlie and Emma. She didn't turn round as she didn't want to make it obvious she could hear.

'Please Charlie, not now. It's embarrassing,' she heard Emma hiss at him.

Callum came back from the bar and handed them their drinks, distracting Max, so Holly continued to listen to what was happening behind her.

'I have the right to check,' he retorted haughtily. 'I honestly don't know what on earth has got into you.'

'Just give it back,' Emma muttered, sounding vexed. 'I'll talk to you about it later. *Please.*'

Holly couldn't help but swivel round discreetly to see what was going on, just in time to see Emma prizing her mobile phone out of Charlie's grasp. His eyes flashed with a wicked gleam and Holly had to prevent herself from gasping when he shot Emma a vicious, flinty glare before storming over to his friends.

Emma was looking in the direction that Charlie had gone and hadn't seen Holly's gaze fixed on her, so Holly quickly span back round to the others as though she hadn't seen a thing.

Holly couldn't concentrate after that. It didn't matter where they were going or what they were doing that evening; that really was the least of her worries. She'd known that something wasn't right with Emma and Charlie. It was a gut instinct. Somehow, she had to stop Emma from marrying that dreadful man. She couldn't stand there and watch her friend make the biggest mistake of her life.

Chapter 18

Emma

Emma felt the familiar tingle in her nose and sniffed loudly. She would not cry in front of people. She wasn't going to allow people to see that Charlie had upset her. Maybe she was embarrassed by the fact that she put up with him? He always acted as though she deserved the way he treated her. Most of the time he made her feel like it was her fault and she often wondered if that was true. She didn't see other couples behaving the way that they did. He was much worse behind closed doors, but he seemed to care less and less about talking down to her in public. It was starting to unnerve her. She guessed he was feeling a lot safer to do as he pleased because she would soon be his wife. He nearly had her exactly where he wanted her. She remembered when she was younger watching a documentary about someone who had been abused for years by her husband, but kept going back to him. Emma just couldn't understand why the woman didn't just leave him. How could anyone put up with somebody treating them like that? She recalled the narrator on the programme saying that these situations were never as simple as they seemed; some of the women were afraid. Many had been controlled for years felt isolated because they didn't feel they had much support elsewhere, and they still loved their husbands, despite everything they did.

Emma had thought it all seemed ludicrous. In her opinion, if someone treated you poorly, you just walked away, changed your number and ignored them. It was simple. You moved on. So how on earth was she now standing here in Vegas probably feeling exactly like those women on the documentary? Was she afraid of Charlie? She didn't think so. It wasn't as though he had ever actually hit her. He was cruel at times and toyed with her emotions, but she'd never voiced her concerns that it wasn't right. He'd always convinced Emma to let him be some kind of manager to her, arranging her diary, negotiating deals with brands and answering her emails and she had always let him. It was the things he did behind her back that was starting to bother her. At first, she'd let it slide, but a few months back he'd organized a deal with a protein shake company for himself, all through her emails. The deal was that Emma had to be tagged in some of the images he posted as well as Emma posting a few from her account, which had more followers. Now she'd seen that that wasn't the only one; Charlie was trying to get as much work and money as he could, all through her name, and without being honest and upfront with her what he was doing. It just didn't sit right. When he finally told her about the protein shake deal, Emma had to explain that she couldn't promote it as she already had a deal with another protein company and it would be breaching the terms of her contract. Charlie had been exasperated, and though he still got the deal for himself, his commission dropped from thirty-five per cent to ten per cent when the company was told Emma wouldn't be involved too.

When she'd told Kim and Holly about Charlie managing her emails, they seemed to question why Charlie was involved any more, now it was Emma's full-time job. It had made her start to question if she really did *need* Charlie like he constantly told her, at all? Seeing all the messages he had been sending earlier that day only told her, that actually, he needed *her*. So she had changed her Instagram password and as soon as Charlie had tried to log in from his phone and had been logged out, he'd felt as though he had the right to grab Emma's phone and look on it anyway. She knew he would accuse her of all sorts of things if she didn't eventually tell him the password; there was no way he would let her get away with not telling him and it was beginning to ring alarm bells. She had always made excuses for him, telling herself that he only did things because he cared so much.

After first meeting Charlie, Emma had only seen his caring, loving side for months. He'd been everything she had ever wanted and she couldn't have been more elated that with every bit of weight she lost, her love for Charlie only grew. Emma couldn't believe how supportive and helpful Charlie had been, and never having been in a serious relationship before, she had nothing else to compare it to anyway. She just knew he made her feel good about herself when she had suffered from such low self-esteem.

Things had started to change when she'd agreed to live with him. It had started off with just the odd little comment at first, but as time went on, Emma was seeing more and more of Charlie's wicked side. The person he now was was almost unrecognizable from the man she'd fallen in love with.

Then today Emma had a panic attack. What was all that about? Was she panicking about the wedding more than she realized? When she'd told Charlie, he hadn't seem remotely bothered about it.

'Loads of people get them,' he'd said with an insouciant shrug when she'd got back to their hotel room. He'd been playing cards with Frankie on the balcony. 'They're no big deal. You just learn how to cope with them.' Frankie had seemed more concerned than him.

Emma didn't want to learn how to cope with them. She didn't want to ever experience one again, full stop. They were horrible and she felt hurt by his blasé attitude. There were no words of comfort or support like there would have been once upon a time. No attempts to reassure her that everything was okay. It was just brushed under the carpet as it was whenever she had a problem with anything. If it didn't involve Charlie, he was rarely interested.

She wasn't drinking alcohol tonight. Emma didn't want to wake up the next morning unsure if she and Charlie had argued or what had happened. She wanted to be on the ball, in control of everything she was doing and saying. She was getting married soon and she didn't want anything to jeopardize her big day, despite the fact the thought of getting married was now making her feel nauseous. She felt a huge responsibility to her guests; they had all flown out to Vegas to see her get married, so she would, no matter how scared she was beginning to feel. She had a gorgeous man who loved her and maybe he would change after the big day? That's what Emma hoped more than anything. Maybe once Charlie knew Emma was his wife and wasn't going anywhere he would relax a bit more. Loosen her reins a little.

Emma thought back to earlier that day and how stunned she'd been when Holly had asked why Charlie had been so cross with her. It had taken her by complete surprise. No-one had ever quizzed her before about anything, or had ever said anything other than positive things about their relationship. She was often told things such as how well they were suited, they would make beautiful babies and how nice Charlie was. She was constantly informed that she'd met 'a real catch'. She believed them too. Charlie was handsome, successful and funny. A little immature at times, but she could see why everyone thought she'd hit the jackpot when she'd met him. No-one knew how small and ashamed he managed to make her feel. Nobody saw him having a tantrum and ignoring her over some-thing pathetic. They didn't hear the nasty names he called her. She recalled how she'd almost told Frankie once what Charlie was like. She had wanted to hear someone else's take on him. He'd popped over after work one evening and Charlie hadn't yet arrived back.

'Do you and your girlfriend ever argue?' Emma had ventured.

She knew Frankie hadn't been with her for that long, but she was intrigued.

Frankie had narrowed his eyes a little, thinking. 'We have disagreements, yes. Everybody does. Sometimes I don't agree with things she does, but we always sort out our problems and talk them through in the end. Why do you ask?'

Emma was stirring the curry she'd made on the hob. 'Oh, I don't know. I just heard a couple rowing on the train the other day, that's all,' she lied. She stood there contemplating whether or not she should tell him. Would he tell her to leave Charlie? Would he end up disliking him? Emma didn't want either of those things to happen, though she did wonder whether Frankie would always take Charlie's side regardless. Emma wanted to be Charlie's wife and settle down. She didn't want to go back to square one and meet someone new all over again.

There was a pause before Frankie spoke again. 'I think respect is a very important thing in a relationship. Once the respect has gone, it rarely ever comes back.'

Emma thought of Frankie's wise words as she stood in the bar. Had the respect disappeared from their relationship as soon as they moved in together? But Charlie always apologized after he was nasty to her and Emma always made excuses for him. She always told herself she was partly to blame for his behaviour. He was constantly reminding her how much he had done for her and how appreciative she should be. It seemed that according to Charlie, Emma should forever be indebted to him.

Emma had a sudden urge to talk to someone before she committed the rest of her life to him. She longed for someone to tell her she was doing the right thing. She looked over at Holly who was busy chatting away to Max and made her way over.

'Holly, can I speak to you a moment?' she asked feebly.

Emma felt nervous to admit the truth out loud to somebody, but she knew she had to. She trusted Holly and knew she would give her good advice.

'Of course,' Holly replied, appearing puzzled. 'I won't be long, Max,' she told him as she followed Emma's lead.

Emma walked out of the bar and through the hotel. There was a seating area near to the casino, which looked fairly quiet, and she sat down on two empty seats. 'Sorry,' she started, her eyes downcast, 'I didn't mean to interrupt things between you and Max.'

'Don't be silly,' Holly told her, her brow furrowed. 'What's up? Are you okay?' she asked, concerned.

Emma inhaled slowly, looking at her nails; they were immaculate. Recently done for her big day free of charge by a salon at home in return for a few posts on her Instagram. 'I just wanted to talk to you about Charlie,' she began. 'I feel really awkward talking about this…' she tailed off.

'Is everything okay between you?' Holly asked, looking at her sympathetically.

Emma hesitated. Once she admitted the truth, it was out there. She'd never be able to take the words back and pretend everything was perfect again. 'Not really, no.'

'Does he hit you?' Holly asked delicately. 'I won't tell anyone. Whatever you tell me will be in the strictest confidence, I promise you.'

'No, no, nothing like that,' Emma said, attempting to sound surprised that Holly thought such a thing. He wasn't *that* bad. She wasn't one of those battered women who needed shelter at a women's refuge. She wasn't even sure if she was overreacting about the whole thing.

'Then what is it, Emma? Are you just not getting on? Has something happened?' Holly probed gently.

'He does this thing,' Emma said slowly, thinking how she should word it so Holly would understand. 'He gets upset over really little things, and sometimes, most of the time, he won't speak to me afterwards. I swear he's the most stubborn man on the planet,' she gave a light laugh and her eyes flew to Holly who was looking at her gravely. Clearly she wasn't in the mood to laugh with her and it made the atmosphere even more serious. Emma bit her lower lip. 'Sometimes he won't talk to me for days. I think once he even lasted a whole week,' she confessed in a small voice. 'Can you imagine living with someone and begging them every day for a week to talk to you? It's so frustrating and he does it because he knows how much it bothers me.'

Holly's eyes were wide and full of understanding as she listened to her every word.

Emma cleared her throat. 'When he finally does talk to me again, when I have him back to his usual self, he's incredible,' she looked at Holly and then away again into the distance. 'He could make me so happy if he just stayed that way. But he has his other side: he's possessiveness and jealous. He thinks he owns me and can tell me what to do. He hates my job unless it involves him, and puts me down all the time. Just earlier, he was furious at me because I wouldn't let him go through my phone to check my messages. I know he's going to accuse me of all sorts until I finally show him, and that's not right, is it? Or I am just expecting too much? I do love him, I really do, and perhaps I'm just really scared to get married? He's done so much for me since I've met him; I can't forget that. I didn't look like this when he first met me, but he still liked me,' she said, glancing down at her tiny figure. 'I felt so low about myself at times, and I never really believed I would meet someone to make me happy, so when I first met Charlie I used to be constantly smiling. I couldn't believe my luck. Everyone thinks we have it so perfect,' she laughed dryly, 'they think because I'm always smiling on my newsfeed I must be so happy, but it's not always true. Having the perfect social media account doesn't mean a thing in real life. I used to look at all these gorgeous women on social media when I was a size eighteen, and I used to think, if that were me, if I was as petite as them and my make-up was as perfect or abs were as toned, then I would be so happy. But I'm still not, Holly. It has absolutely nothing to do with what I look like, I understand that now. It's about what's in here,' she tapped her chest, 'and that's something I still need to work on. But Charlie has always seemed to believe in me.'

Holly was flabbergasted. 'I do understand what you're saying and I do appreciate that you're your own worst critic; you just need to learn how to be comfortable and happy in your own skin. You're beautiful, not just outside but on the inside too. Just because you were bigger back then and didn't have as many followers on Instagram doesn't mean you have to put up with the unacceptable way Charlie has been treating you. Are you supposed to be appreciative that he still wanted to be with you even though you weighed more?' 'Yes. No. I don't know,' Emma muttered. 'Nobody is perfect, right? Everyone has their flaws, I do get that. Most of the time he's such an amazing guy who makes me happy and makes me laugh.'

'Is most of the time really good enough for you, Em?' Holly questioned. 'It sounds to me like Charlie has some real issues. He's controlling you, can't you see that? What do you want to do? Have you spoken to him seriously and told him it needs to stop?' Holly looked disconcerted.

'All the time,' Emma told her, her mouth twitching uncomfortably. 'Not recently though,' she admitted. 'Maybe I need a serious talk with him and to tell him it's not acceptable any more. When we first arrived here we had a huge argument, I can't even remember what it was about now, and I made my way to the Bellagio Hotel to watch the water fountains by myself. I felt so peaceful and calm just watching the water that I wanted to just stay there and not have to face him.'

Maybe the answer was telling Charlie how serious things were though? Though deep in her heart, Emma knew it wouldn't work. She'd done and said it all before. She'd even left him around four months ago, staying in a local bed and breakfast for a few nights. He'd sweet-talked her back, and then gone back to behaving exactly how he always did once he knew she was back on side.

As Frankie had told her that day in the kitchen, once the respect had gone, it very rarely came back.

Holly's nostrils flared. 'I really don't think you should be marrying him, Emma. I know it's not my place to say, but you don't deserve to be treated that way. It's not too late and I wouldn't be a good friend if I wasn't honest about how I feel about the situation.'

They were the words Emma had been afraid of. The ones she didn't ever want to be told. Anxiety was flooding through her veins. 'I have to,' she told her, feeling panicky again. She breathed deeply. 'I do love Charlie and like I said, he can be so lovely. He does make me happy the majority of the time. I want to get married and have a family, and I have to believe that if I tell him to, he'll change. I know he's not always nice to me, but everyone argues, don't they? I think he deserves a chance. I'm not sure I'm ready to throw the towel in just yet. I don't feel like I can.'

Holly's eyes were burning with alarm. 'I think it's a really bad idea to go through with it, Em, I'm not going to lie. But I can see that it doesn't matter what I say or do – I won't change your mind, will I? You've clearly made your mind up that you're going to marry him. I think he needs some kind of help though, I really do,' she said, shaking her head and giving Emma a beady look. 'Maybe you need to see a relationship counsellor, something along those lines. Rob and I went a few times and I know it didn't work for us, but it does for lots of other couples.'

Emma was rankled by her worried expression. She was praying that Holly was going to tell her Charlie didn't sound that bad. She'd hoped she would tell her she should follow her heart and that love would conquer all their issues. But she knew even before she'd spilled her secret that Holly wasn't going to advise her to marry Charlie. She didn't ever see the nice side of him: the one that took her out to dinner and bought her gifts he knew she'd love when she was feeling down. 'I'm going to have a long discussion with him tomorrow and tell him all the things that need to change. If he sees how serious I am, I have to trust that he'll listen,' she explained, trying to convince herself just as much as Holly. 'I can't let everyone down. Everyone has made such an effort to be here for us...' she broke off, feeling her eyes begin to water. She swallowed hard.

'It's not about everyone else, Emma. It's about *you* and *your* happiness. Please don't get married for everyone else's sake. No-one would care if you didn't go ahead with it so long as you were making the right decision. It's really not something to take lightly. I'm so glad that Rob and I didn't get married, I really am. It's hard enough breaking up when there's no divorce to go through. Having to get divorced would just make it even more stressful.'

Emma faced Holly with equanimity. 'I think I'm doing the right thing, Holly. I do love him. I'll make him change. I *want* things to change so badly. We won't get divorced, I just know it. I just wanted to speak to someone about it, so thank you for listening to me.'

She stared at Holly for a few moments, suddenly feeling guilty. 'I know I haven't been there for you since you split with Rob. I'm so sorry. You know what it's like; life just seems to fly by and I've been so busy with my job and focusing on the wedding.'

Holly shook her head dismissively. 'Don't be silly. I haven't been much better, have I? It's a two-way thing and I know how manic life gets. Please don't apologize. You honestly have nothing to apologize for.'

'Thank you,' Emma said, standing up and giving her friend a tight squeeze. 'Come on, let's head back to the bar before the others wonder where we've got to.'

Holly nodded. 'If you ever need to talk, I'm here for you,' she said as they began to walk back. 'Maybe write down all the things he's done to you as well. You know, write it in a diary, something like that.'

Emma stared at her, wondering if that was really necessary.

Clearly Holly didn't have any faith in her relationship now. She obviously believed Emma may need evidence against Charlie in the future.

'And Emma,' Holly continued in a firm voice, 'you can't even think about having children with Charlie. Not until you've sorted out your relationship. It's not healthy to bring a baby into that environment.'

It was as though Emma had been winded. She craved to have her own family as soon as possible. She wanted to be a mother more than anything; it was her next goal in life. But Holly was right – there was simply no way she could bring up a baby with a father like Charlie as he was now, and Emma walked back to the others, feeling worse than she did before.

Chapter 19

Kim

Kim had no idea where Holly and Emma had gone and she was worried. Why had they just left her alone? She obviously knew Callum, Max and a few of the others, but she really wished her friends had told her where they were going. She felt a little left out and excluded, but cursed herself for being so childish. There was most likely a perfectly valid reason that they'd gone off together, but she was concerned that something was wrong.

Max walked over, handing Kim a drink.

'Hi,' he shot her a grin. 'Where've Holly and Emma gone? We got a round in at the bar.'

'I'm not sure,' Kim replied, looking at her phone to check she didn't have any messages from them. 'I'll come over to the bar and wait for them there.'

She followed Max to where the drinks were. He had been served around the other side and Kim couldn't see Callum or anyone else nearby.

'All alone,' Max said, raising his eyebrows and staring at her.

Immediately Kim started to feel uncomfortable and thoughts of earlier that day at the pool party came flashing back to her. Was he like this to everyone? She didn't want to overreact but it this felt wrong when he'd only just slept with her best friend the night before and knew she was married.

'Where's Callum gone?' Kim asked, turning her head as she looked for him in the crowds.

'He had to quickly make a phone call to his daughter. We're eight hours ahead here,' he told her, 'he'll probably be gone a while. Loves to chat to her, he does,' he replied with a smirk.

'Oh right, that's nice.' Kim sipped her drink feeling awkward and on edge. The air between them seemed to crackle with a nerve-racking tension. She almost felt like she could reach out and touch it. 'Holly and Emma didn't say where they were going, did they?' she said lightly, continuing to search for them, hoping she would see their faces and could wave them over.

'No,' he shook his head, looking pleased with himself. 'It's just you and me,' he said, staring at her as though he was enjoying her discomfort.

Kim looked into the distance, afraid to look up at him. She was unsure what he was about to say. She felt on edge waiting for him to do or say something. Max was acting strangely, exactly how he had been earlier.

'You look beautiful tonight,' he said seriously, gazing at her intensely with his light brown eyes.

'Thank you,' Kim managed to reply in a small voice. She felt a colour rush to her cheeks and hated herself for it. She didn't want him to know how discomfited she was. She didn't want him to know the effect he was having.

He moved closer to her, a hopeful glint in his eye.

'What are you doing?' She tried to laugh it off that he was edging nearer to her, but his expression remained determined.

'Oh come on, there's no-one watching us,' he expressed confidently, grinning like she was playing a game with him. His eyes were glinting as though he knew she wanted it really.

Kim could smell the alcohol on his breath and she wondered if he'd even sobered up from earlier. Kim attempted to step back but the bar was behind her, leaving her no room. 'Max, what do you mean?' she said breathlessly.

His eyes narrowed and he looked amused, his smile frozen on his lips. 'Are you really going to say you don't like me in that way?' he asked courageously. He was so cocky and arrogant. 'I won't say anything to Holly,' he whispered suggestively.

His body was pressed against hers before she had a chance to say anything and he was edging his face even closer, leaning in for a kiss.

'Get off,' Kim exploded, pushing him away. 'What the hell is wrong with you?' She gasped for breath in outrage. Her voice was shaky and her head was pulsing with blood. 'You've slept with my friend Holly if you'd forgotten that fact, and I'm not sure if it had slipped your mind, but I'm happily *married*.'

Max remained calm and collected. 'Okay, I must have read the signals wrong then,' he laughed light-heartedly. 'I was joking anyway, you don't need to get all irate about it,' he said, giving the merest little shrug.

Kim wasn't just fuming with Max, but she was upset too. How dare he think she would ever *dream* of going there with him? Not only was Holly her best friend, but she was married with two children, something he was very well aware of. Kim hated men like Max, selfish and thoughtless, and she felt awful that she was going to have to tell Holly too.

'Go to hell, Max,' Kim told him venomously before storming outside to get some fresh air.

As she marched outside alone, Kim felt homesick. Meeting Max had made her realize how lucky she was to have married such a great man like Andy all those years ago. She missed him. She missed their children and the sound of their little laughs. What would Andy make of what had just happened? One of Andy's qualities was that he wasn't a jealous man. Jealousy had never really been an issue in their relationship. Not until now. Not until Lily. Had she been crazy to jet off to Vegas without addressing their marriage problems? Had she just made it easier for Andy to hang out with Lily? The question also still remained: why had Andy entertained those flirty texts? The fact he'd liked her photo didn't sit well with her either. Kim had been sailing through life in her own little world, ignorant to the fact that as much as she was a good mother, she certainly hadn't been the most attentive wife over the years. Her throat felt tight with anxiety as she thought about how their relationship had changed so much without her really noticing it until recently. It was hard pretending everything was perfect to everyone.

A tear fell down Kim's cheek just as Frankie emerged from around the corner. His face fell as soon as he spotted her, and Kim felt flustered that he'd caught her crying alone. She hadn't spoken to him very much since she'd arrived and didn't really know him well enough to be comforted by him.

'Are you okay?' he asked, looking concerned. 'It's Kim, isn't it?'

Kim sniffed and nodded, her eyes flicking downwards to her new black heels self-consciously. 'I'm fine, honestly.'

'You're clearly not fine,' he stated, his brow furrowed. 'Do you want to talk about it?' he asked sensitively.

Kim shook her head. 'I can't…' she broke off. 'Please just go inside, don't worry about me, I'll be fine in a moment.'

She wanted to tell him. She just wanted to let *someone* know all her problems, but she hardly knew Frankie. He reminded Kim a little of Callum; Frankie was one of those people you just trusted instantly, but had no idea why. He came across as genuine and sweet and she could tell he really cared about the wedding by the way he was always offering to help Emma.

She sat on a wall and Frankie sat beside her. He wasn't going anywhere and she felt better with him beside her.

'Where are your friends?' he asked.

'I'm not sure,' she answered helplessly. 'Maybe the toilets, I haven't seen them in a while.'

'That's not why you're crying though, is it?' Frankie asked seriously.

A loud laugh escaped Kim's lips. 'No, of course not. It was...' she paused for a few seconds, 'it was Max, okay? It was something he did.' She wouldn't tell him about with her marriage worries, but perhaps he should know this part. Kim wouldn't protect Max and his behaviour.

Frankie didn't look at all surprised. 'Ah, Max.'

Kim nodded, looking directly in front of her at an elderly couple waiting for a taxi.

'Let me guess,' Frankie continued in a soft voice, 'he tried it on with you?'

Kim's jaw dropped open. 'Yes, how did you know?'

Frankie clicked his tongue. 'I don't even know him that well. He comes out sometimes when I go out with Charlie, and I often see him when I go to the gym, but that's about it. He mentioned something earlier that led me to believe he would make a move on you. He can be silly boys at times; I've heard about some of his antics through Charlie,' he said with disapproval. 'He gets overenthusiastic, like a child in a sweet shop thinking he can try everything all at once. I heard Callum tell him not to do it. Max is the type of man who likes a challenge though. He'll get himself in real trouble one day.'

Kim exhaled. 'I'm scared to tell Holly. She's going to be so upset.'

'Don't say I said, but it's probably going to be a good thing she finds out what Max is like. I'm sure Holly will see it as a lucky escape.'

Kim found a tissue in her bag and blew her nose. 'Emma and Charlie are really lucky to have you,' she told him sincerely. 'I know you've helped Emma loads for the wedding. She speaks very highly of you. I was worried about Emma when she had the panic attack in the bridal store. It was so scary to see. Did she tell you about it? Do you think something is wrong with her?' she asked him. He seemed to care so much about Emma that she was keen to hear his take on it.

He sighed, as though it had also been playing on his mind. 'When she got back she mentioned it to me and Charlie as we were in their room on the balcony playing cards. I do think it's a little worrying, yes. I hate to think of Emma feeling anxious or worried. I did offer to take her to see a doctor here, but Charlie thought it was over the top and unnecessary.'

How was it that Frankie was more concerned than Emma's own fiancé? It seemed like such a shame, and Kim couldn't help but feel a little unnerved about Emma agreeing to spend the rest of her life with Charlie. He seemed so different to Frankie and not in a good way. Frankie was just so thoughtful and caring.

'He does care,' Frankie added quickly, as though reading her mind, 'he just doesn't think it's worth seeing a doctor over when it's likely there's nothing they can do. He thinks it's pretty normal to feel a little stressed before your wedding, and perhaps he's right?'

'You're very loyal to him, aren't you?' Kim noticed.

'My father died when I was younger and Charlie and his family were there for me,' he told her.

'Sorry to hear that,' Kim replied compassionately, 'That must have been hard. I can't imagine not having my dad around.'

He nodded. 'It was a long time ago now. Charlie's mum, Jean, is my mum's sister and they're really close. Charlie's family helped us out a lot after my father died and because my mum worked all the time, I spent most of my time at Charlie's house. Jean took care of me after school and even most weekends. Jean is like a second mum to me. Charlie was a bit of a pain when he was a teenager, rebelling against everything and often getting into trouble. Jean was at her wits' end and she used to confide in me, try to get me to talk sense into Charlie, that kind of thing. I know she wished he was more manageable and compliant like me, and

Charlie hated me for that,' he laughed drily. 'He used to apologize to Jean sarcastically for not being as perfect as I was and I guess he saw me as his annoying younger brother. I just wanted him to like me, as sad as that sounds, but I couldn't agree with how upset he made Jean at times. I could never side with him when he used to call her names. To me, she was the best mum and aunt in the world, along with mine of course. Luckily he changed as he got older, and instead of tolerating me, we become friends. He knows that without a doubt, I would do anything for him. Or his family. And Emma, well, she's just such a sweet girl and I think she deserves the perfect wedding and to be happy. I enjoy helping her and don't say I told you, but I managed to get a band that I know she wanted to play at the wedding as a surprise. She's going to be so happy,' he beamed.

'Oh Frankie, that's so sweet of you,' Kim told him, his smile contagious. 'She'll be delighted with that.'

'Sorry for getting a bit deep just then,' Frankie apologized with a chuckle. 'I didn't quite mean to, but my relationship with Charlie is a bit complicated. Kind of needed explaining.'

Kim nodded. 'Thanks for talking to me. I think I'm going to get a taxi back now. I'm not really in the mood for partying any more and I don't even know where Holly and Emma are.'

'I'll make sure you get back okay. Come on, there's a taxi coming now,' he said, standing up.

Kim appreciated the offer. Frankie seemed to be a real gentleman, but she just wanted to be alone.

'Thanks Frankie, but it's not even late and I'm okay, I promise. I would prefer you to find Holly and Emma to tell them I've gone back. My phone has ran out of battery,' she explained, holding it up. She'd forgotten to recharge it before she went out.

'You're sure?' He looked dubious at letting her leave alone.

'I'm positive,' she gave him a little hug.

'Well, I hope you're okay now?' he said, arching an eyebrow.

'Yes, thanks.'

'Don't let him take up another second of your thoughts, he's not worth it. He didn't even care that you're a married woman. Emma has told me all about your family before. I think her goal is to have what you have and be as happy as you are,' he explained, shooting her a friendly, reassuring smile, not realizing he was only making her feel worse.

She waved goodbye to him and jumped into a taxi.

She sighed deeply. Everyone thought Kim had the perfect happy family life. The ideal marriage and Kim usually felt so smug, agreeing with them. Now though, she felt uncertain, vulnerable and confused.

She wasn't sure if they were really happy at all.

Chapter 20

Holly

'Hey, where's Kim? Have you seen her?' Holly asked Max. She'd already looked for her in the nearest toilets and she couldn't work out where she'd gone. When she called her it was going straight to voicemail. It was strange; Kim had been really up for going out that night. She would never normally just leave somewhere without so much as a text message to explain her reasons. Holly was bewildered.

'She was here earlier. I'm not sure where she went though,' Max shrugged as though it was no big deal.

'I saw her outside and she got in a taxi to take her back,' Frankie explained, walking over to Holly. 'She told me she's tired and not in the mood,' his eyes narrowed at Max as he spoke.

Holly's brows lifted. 'Home? Are you sure?' She checked her mobile for the tenth time, puzzled that it still remained blank. She attempted to call her again and sighed when it went straight to voicemail.

'No point as her battery has died,' Frankie told her. 'Don't worry, she's okay.'

'I don't know what to do,' Holly said, feeling torn. Frankie was saying she was fine, but it seemed odd to Holly that Kim had just left. She needed to go back to the room to check she was okay with her own eyes. How could Holly just go out and enjoy herself if there was something wrong with Kim?

'Hey,' Max put his arms round her waist, his eyes opened wide as he spoke to her, 'I'm sure she's fine. It doesn't mean you have to go anywhere. Like Frankie said, she's tired. She'll probably just be sleeping now anyway. Stay out with us. I don't want you to go anywhere.'

Holly wanted to stay with him, but she'd always prided herself on being a good friend. She was loyal and she could sense that Kim just leaving without waiting for Holly to get back was out of character. She felt terrible now for going off with Emma for the chat without telling Kim where they were going. When Emma had walked off, Holly had just followed without realizing how long they were going to be. Surely she hadn't gone back to the hotel room just because she was annoyed about that, had she?

'I got you another drink,' Max said, handing her a large white wine.

'Thanks,' Holly smiled, her mind elsewhere. 'I'll just have this last one though and then I'll most likely head back.'

'She looked fine to me,' Max said casually, 'she'll be fine. Stop worrying. You don't need to go back just because she's being boring,' he said, almost sounding fed up with Kim for ruining his time with Holly. He was acting like a spoilt child who wasn't getting his own way, without a single thought for what could be wrong with Holly's best friend.

'Mate,' Callum interjected, seeing it from Holly's point of view, 'I think it's fair enough if Holly wants to check her friend is alright.'

'Yeah, course. Whatever she needs to do. I'm going for a smoke,' he announced moodily.

'A smoke?' Holly echoed in surprise. 'I didn't know you smoked.' It was something so small, yet something so big. It

163

reminded Holly that Max was a stranger; she didn't really know anything about him. She hated smoking with a passion and immediately she felt disconcerted. As Holly stood there in the bar in Vegas, staring at Max as he fumbled in his jacket pocket for his cigarettes, she felt unnerved. How had she not known that Max had smoked? She'd never smelt it on his breath before and she was certain he'd never smoked around her either. He was a personal trainer; weren't they supposed to be against smoking and anything bad for your health? It made her start thinking about the huge list of other things she didn't know about him. Here she was, thinking a few days ago she was developing feelings for him, and she never even knew this important piece of information. She would never allow smoking in her home that she'd worked hard for. She would never let someone smoke cigarettes around her children and their precious little lungs. Of course she couldn't tell Max that.

I know you've known me for less than a week, but do you mind not smoking any more? That's it. Stub it out like a good little boy.

He would feel like telling her where to go and she couldn't blame him. But the fact he smoked was a real turn-off.

'I don't smoke that often,' Max finally answered, sounding so offhand about it. 'Just now and again. Usually when I drink,' he informed her. 'You don't want one, do you?' He offered.

'No,' Holly replied, wrinkling her nose. 'I don't smoke.'

Max walked away leaving Holly and Callum alone.

'Do you smoke too?' Holly asked Callum in wonderment. Perhaps they both did?

'Me? No.'

Holly nodded in satisfaction.

'How's your little girl doing?' he asked.

'She's okay. Thanks for asking. I felt so much better after talking to her. It's hard being this far away, but I know she's fine. She's spending the time with Rob and Nikki, his new girlfriend, and he's sent me loads of photos,' she said, showing him a couple. 'I think after a lot of grovelling for accusing him of neglect, he's finally forgiven me.' She pulled an embarrassed face.

'He sounds like a decent bloke,' Callum told her.

'I just need to stop jumping to conclusions,' Holly declared, tucking her hair behind her ear. 'I need to give him more credit for being such a good dad. Perhaps it was because I knew he was with Nikki, and it's all still new, I don't know. I guess I was feeling guilty about Max too; I've been out here enjoying myself and having fun and now Lottie has ended up in hospital. It was wrong of me to go off at Rob like that. We promised each other we would never be like that. I feel a bit ashamed.'

'You were shocked and worried, that's all. You took it out on Rob because he was the one who called you. You shot the messenger so to speak. Everyone is allowed to make mistakes sometimes, eh? Being a parent is scary and challenging; I'm certainly not perfect. I remember once when I had Eva and she woke up early at five. I just put the television on quietly so she could watch cartoons in bed. I didn't plan to go back to sleep but drifted off and I didn't wake up until eight o'clock! How irresponsible is that?' He laughed, but had a look of guilt in his green eyes. 'I felt awful afterwards. I think Eva was loving it though. She'd never been allowed to have so much screen time before.'

Holly smiled warmly. 'Lack of sleep can be horrendous, can't it? I think I would have sold my soul for more sleep when my kids were young. They're quite good at sleeping now, but if one of them wakes up I feel so groggy and grumpy,' she admitted.

'Awful, isn't it? I used to have to get up early for work, but when Eva was a baby, it was a different level of tiredness entirely.'

Holly agreed, thinking back to when she'd been pregnant with Lottie. Towards the end of her pregnancy she'd had insomnia. She told herself it was her body's way of preparing her for when the baby arrived and she wouldn't get as much sleep any more. It had been frustrating, but not too awful. She was *ready* for it. She could cope with it just as well as the next person. But then Lottie was actually born and Holly realized that it wasn't like having pregnancy insomnia at all – not in the slightest. She couldn't just lie there and read a book. She had to drag herself out of her warm bed into the cold night, creeping round like a burglar so she didn't wake Rob and trying to console a hungry baby with a dummy until she finally fed her.

'It's funny isn't it, that despite their constant demands and the fact they wear you out to a point you never knew possible, that you wouldn't change a thing about them?' Callum chuckled. 'I'd actually love more kids someday. Eva would love another brother or sister.'

Holly smiled at him and when his gaze held hers for a little longer than expected, she felt a flutter in her stomach, looking away quickly and feeling flustered by a sudden shift in the atmosphere.

Emma walked over to them.

'Where's Kim?' she asked, looking at Callum and Holly.

'She's tired so she's gone back to the room,' Holly told her. 'I'm going to drink this and then go check on her.'

'Do you really think she's just tired? It's odd that she didn't say goodbye. I feel bad for taking you away for a chat now.'

'Don't be silly. I'm always here to chat, you know that.' Holly leaned in and kissed her cheek. 'I'll see you in the morning for the hair trial.'

'Let me know she's okay,' Emma said, as Holly kissed her on the cheek goodbye. 'I've asked Frankie to be at the trial too as I want a man's opinion. So I'll text you his room number.'

'Perfect,' Holly said. She turned to Callum then, feeling regretful that they couldn't continue chatting. She enjoyed their conversations.

'I guess I'll see you tomorrow at some point,' she pecked him on the cheek.

'See you, Holly.'

Holly was pleased to walk into Max who was on his way back in.

166

His expression changed to one of disappointment when he noticed her in front of him. 'You're not leaving now, surely?' he asked her, his voice unusually whiny.

'Afraid so,' Holly responded, gazing up at his dejected expression. He placed his hands firmly either side of her hips, staring into her eyes.

'Why? It's early yet,' he moaned.

'I need to check Kim is okay. Her phone is off, and besides, it's probably best because I'm doing Emma's hair trial tomorrow and I don't want to have much to drink,' she explained again. 'I also want to check Lottie is okay so I'm going to call home.'

'Didn't you speak to her earlier?' he asked, as though she was making a big deal about nothing. He had absolutely no clue what it was like to be a parent. He didn't have the faintest idea that the moment your baby was born, you would worry about them for life.

'Why don't you check Kim's okay and then come back to my room for a few drinks later or something?' he offered, shooting her a lop-sided, mischievous grin.

Holly felt just as turned off as she did when she found out that Max smoked. It made her feel that sleeping with her was all he wanted her for. His eagerness to get her back into bed was off-putting. She knew she was partly to blame for sleeping with him so soon. Had she just slept with Max to convince herself and everyone else she was over Rob? Holly wasn't entirely sure now she thought about it. Max was the first person she'd been with since Rob and she couldn't deny that she hadn't even thought about getting involved with anyone until she'd had Rob's girlfriend news sprung on her. She thought she was being so cool about it. She'd felt so mature and affable keeping composed and so blasé about the whole thing.

'I'm probably just going to have an early night,' Holly said firmly. She didn't want him to be persistent. It would make things even worse.

'Really?' he asked again sulkily. 'Okay, suit yourself,' he said, his eyes flicking behind her as though he was distracted and had seen something else more interesting.

He kissed her quickly on the lips. 'I'll see you tomorrow or something,' he gave a cool shrug, like he wasn't really fussed either way. He wasn't really bothered about her, she could tell it a mile off, and Holly couldn't deny that it did hurt a little, despite not being sold on him either. Was Max really as dreamy as she'd first thought when she'd met him? He was devastatingly handsome, but he was immature, selfish and careless. She couldn't imagine she would ever be able to trust him if they were a couple; he was constantly looking at every woman who so much as walked into his line of vision. Looking at him now, Kim was right; he just wasn't boyfriend material. He was someone to have fun with, but not settle down with. She wasn't sure she could ever introduce someone like Max to her children either; she could never imagine him being interested in her kids and wanting to spend time with them rather than going out and partying. He just wasn't there yet and perhaps he would never be. The thought of asking him to join her for a day out with her children just seemed ludicrous. It would like asking Lottie to spend the day with her shopping for furniture; quite frankly, she would hate it. Just like Lottie, Holly knew Max would be bored. She hadn't really thought about any of this until now, and again, Holly wondered whether it was because subconsciously she always knew that Max was just a fling and would never be anything more.

Lottie and Jacob were Holly's priority. When she dated in future, it wasn't just herself she had to think about. Her children were part of the package and they had to get on with her boyfriend too. Holly was starting to understand how different it was to date when you had children.

There was something else bothering Holly too. The more time she spent with Callum, the more she realized how much they had in common and how much she enjoyed his company. Even tonight, she hadn't really wanted to leave him. Holly could kick herself. There was nothing she could do about it now.

She'd chosen the wrong one.

Fifteen minutes later, Holly inhaled before swiping her room key card in the hotel door. She felt anxious and she wasn't sure why. She had known Kim since she was five, and she just knew, more than anything, that something was up. She could sense it. Holly could see a lampshade on in their bedroom as she walked past the bathroom.

'Kim?'

Kim was sitting on the bed in her dressing gown. Her eyes were slightly bloodshot and puffy, and Holly could see that she'd been crying.

'Are you okay?' Holly asked gingerly. 'I tried calling you several times but it went through to voicemail. What's wrong?'

'Sorry,' Kim answered, her voice croaky. 'I was on the phone to Andy. Just wanted to check on him and the children back home. I didn't feel great and decided to come back. Sorry I didn't wait for you. Where did you and Emma get to anyway?' she asked, her voice weak.

Holly sat on the edge of the bed, sighing in relief as she took her heels off. She hardly ever wore heels in the UK. Flats were her thing. Sandals, trainers, boots; she wore them all, so long as they were nice, flat and comfortable. Since becoming a mother, it was all she ever had on. Gone were the days of achy feet and burning soles, and Holly was looking forward to putting her heels to the back of her cupboard when she got home.

'Emma needed to talk to me,' she explained, leaning back on the bed. 'It's a long story and not really my place to say. I'm sure she'll tell you about it all in her own time though.'

Kim nodded understandingly. 'Fair enough.'

'So what's wrong then? How are you feeling?' Holly pressed.

Kim didn't look *ill*. She looked upset.

'I don't even know where to begin. Did you see Max before you left?'

'Yes. Did you know he smokes? I couldn't believe it when he said he was going outside for a cigarette. I hate smoking. I've always said I'd never get with somebody that smokes.'

'No, I didn't have the faintest idea,' Kim replied.

'Well he does. He wanted me to go back to his room after coming back to check on you,' Holly rolled her eyes. 'Can you believe he really thought I was going to wait up until he got back to the room after a night of partying to go round there?'

Kim sat in silence chewing her lip and studying her nails.

'He just seems a bit… I don't know, keen on one thing only.'

Kim closed her eyes for a few moments before speaking. 'He tried it on with me, Holly. I didn't want to tell you, but I can't listen to you talk about him when he behaved the way he did towards me,' she said ruefully. 'He has no respect for you and didn't care in the slightest if you had walked around the corner and caught him. He tried to kiss me.'

Holly was stunned. She felt like she'd been slapped round the face. Fair enough, she knew Max liked the ladies, but she couldn't imagine he would be that much of a shit to try something with her best friend.

'Please say something,' Kim begged. 'I know you did like him, and I'm really sorry. I had to tell you. You would have done the same for me, wouldn't you?'

Holly felt a bit sick. She was mortified and couldn't believe that Max would actually stoop so low and make her feel so worthless. It was beyond disrespectful. Did he think she was stupid or something? Did he honestly believe that Kim wouldn't have told her? 'I can't believe it,' Holly said breathlessly. 'Tell me exactly what he did.'

Kim explained what had happened reluctantly. 'I'm certain he likes you though, Holly. But I just wouldn't trust him.'

'*Likes* me?' Holly let out a short bark of laughter, breathing heavily. 'Kim, are you crazy? What kind of man tries it on with the best friend of the girl he likes? I'm a big girl now. I get it.'

'I can't believe he really thought I'd go for it; you should have seen how confident he was.'

'Thank you for telling me,' Holly responded, sitting on the bed. 'As much as I'm annoyed at how badly he's behaved, I'm not actually that bothered about him, Kim, so please don't feel bad about anything. None of this is your fault.'

Kim's expression changed to one of bewilderment. 'What? I thought you liked him? You were only saying this morning…'

'Changed my mind,' Holly interrupted, shooting her a quick smile. 'Max is gorgeous, anyone can see that. But he's not for me, Kim; you were right. I've been thinking about it tonight and realize I'm still trying to get used to the idea that Rob has now moved on with someone else. That's probably why I did what I did with Max so soon. I know it sounds bad, but the fact it was more my decision that Rob and I split up meant a part of me always assumed he would just be waiting there in the background in case I changed my mind. It's stupid and selfish of me, but I just thought Rob would always be an option for me. Does that sound awful? Of course he wasn't going to wait around.'

Kim looked thoughtful. 'No, Holly. I think even a part of me thought you would probably get back together too. Now he's met someone else it seems more final. There aren't any rules as to how you should feel when your ex meets someone new and I do see why you've probably jumped in a bit quick with Max. I'll be honest, I thought you were taking the whole Rob and Nikki thing surprisingly well.'

Holly smiled wryly. 'Turns out that maybe I'm not; I haven't even been on a date with someone else. How has he fallen in love without me knowing?'

'I don't know. No-one knows what lies ahead for you either though. You've always said you weren't bothered about meeting someone else after Rob, but maybe, if you met the right person one day, you would change your mind?'

Holly nibbled her thumbnail. 'Maybe. I'm in my thirties with two children who are my world; they will always come first before anything. I do wish I'd been wise enough not to fall for Max and his charm and it hasn't made me feel any better about Rob like perhaps I was hoping. If I ever meet anyone again, they need to be mature and trustworthy. Loyal and dependable. Someone who is kind and cares about me. Someone...'

'Like Callum?' Kim suggested.

Holly gave a brittle laugh. 'Well, I guess someone like him, yes. I can't just move onto Max's friend though, can I?' she asked, looking over and studying Kim's expression, keen to known her thoughts.

'You mean like he did? I think it would be up to Callum to make his own mind up,' Kim advised before glancing at Holly inquisitively. 'If it was something you wanted to pursue, that is?'

Holly exhaled loudly. 'I can't. I just can't do that now. I've already made the mistake of getting together with Max.' Holly put her face in her hands morosely. Kim was right; she had always told herself she didn't want to get into another relationship after Rob. She was done with men for good, and just wanted to focus on her beautiful children. She'd told herself that relationships were more hassle than they were worth. But somehow, with Rob meeting Nikki and her going to Las Vegas, she seemed to have become more open to the idea. If she was ever going to bring a man into her children's lives, he needed to be special. She just felt a bit gutted that she'd started to have feelings for Callum, but she'd already blown it, before she even had the chance to work these feelings out. Before she'd even had the chance to see if he felt the same way. Of course, Holly had no idea if he was even interested or if they would even work together, but she couldn't ignore the way she had started feeling around him, and she just felt so disappointed with herself that she'd slept with his mate.

There was no way he would even consider her as anything more than a friend now.

'Do you like Callum in that way?' Kim asked, looking intrigued.

'I think I do, yes. But it doesn't matter, does it? It probably wouldn't make me any better than Max if I did something about it.'

'I don't really think you should be worrying about Max and his feelings after tonight, so if you think there's anything between you and Callum, my advice is to go for it.'

Holly shook her head. 'It's too late. I'm such an idiot,' she said, feeling really annoyed with herself. She breathed out slowly. 'I'm going to get some sleep,' Holly told Kim, slipping into her pyjamas. 'Don't worry about the whole Max thing though, Kim. If it wasn't you, I'm certain it would be somebody else.'

'Yes, you're probably right.'

Holly went to the bathroom to brush her teeth and Kim switched off the lamp when Holly got into bed.

'How was Andy?' Holly asked in the darkness. 'How are the kids? I called my mum on the way back here, and then Rob so I could speak to Lottie. All is fine at home.'

'Yes, everything is fine. He said how much they all miss me,' she said groggily, sounding half asleep.

'Ah, that's so lovely,' Holly said sleepily with a yawn. 'Not that I'm surprised he said such a lovely thing. He adores you.'

'You *think* we have the perfect relationship, Holly,' Kim replied in a tiny, sleepy voice. 'No-one knows what goes on behind closed doors.'

It took a while for Holly to realize what she'd said. 'What do you mean?' she asked curiously.

Silence filled the room until she heard Kim's soft snores in the darkness.

Chapter 21

Emma

It was the day before Emma was due to be married and she couldn't believe it. She lay in bed imagining how she was going to feel the next day. Would she be nervous? Would she spend the entire morning feeling anxious about walking down the aisle, terrified and silent as Holly did her hair and her make-up artist worked her magic? Would she be drinking far too much Prosecco to calm her nerves, her legs as wobbly as she walked down the aisle as though they were made out of jelly? The wedding had been the main topic of conversation ever since she and Charlie had got engaged and one of the only things she had thought about in months, and now it was here. Even her fans on social media were excited and as Holly picked up her mobile, her Instagram inbox was full of messages.

Eeeek wedding day tomorrow! You're going to be the most stunning bride!
Wishing you luck for your big day! I can't wait to see your dress!

Emma's messages were making her feel even more over-whelmed and she wished everyone would just leave her alone for once. She hadn't posted anything the night before. She just hadn't been in the mood.

She was pleased she hadn't drunk too much the previous evening; she felt fresh and awake. Her mind was clear. She cuddled up to Charlie who was still sleeping, enjoying the warmth emanating from his body. She felt better now she had spoken to Holly about her worries. She had shared her fears with someone and had made up her mind that she was going to talk to Charlie, to make sure he understood that she would go ahead and marry him, providing he agreed they got professional help of some kind. She was going to look into couple counselling as soon as she got the chance. Holly was right, their relationship wasn't exactly normal and they just needed a bit of guidance. Emma knew she had to try. Emma remembered when Hannah, a family friend, had raved about it.

'We see a man called Mr Carver and he's done wonders for our relationship, honestly,' she recalled her saying over coffee one summer's day. 'Honestly, Ben even helps with the cooking, cleaning and washing now, he's like a new man.'

Perhaps Emma would get onto Hannah and find out Mr Carver's details. She could certainly do with Charlie becoming a 'new man'.

Charlie needed to understand that things couldn't go on the way they were and perhaps, if someone else pointed out what needed to change, he would actually listen? She also needed to talk to him about his involvement in her career.

She had no idea what time he'd got back the previous night; she'd been so tired she'd fallen asleep straight away. He hadn't wanted to come back with her again, but that was nothing new and Emma told herself it was just something she was going to have to get used to. Charlie liked his nights out and there was nothing wrong with that. She did wish he cared a little more if she got home safe or not, but perhaps she was just being oversensitive? Charlie stirred and turned to her with a smile.

Emma could tell he was in a good mood. She could tell from his twinkling eyes, the lines round them crinkling. She was going to be rewarded with the nice Charlie today. The one who made her delirious with happiness and love, like when they'd first got together. The Charlie she wished he would always be and the one that she *wanted* to marry.

'Morning, wife to be,' he said, kissing her lightly on the lips.

Emma was suddenly apprehensive about mentioning the counselling and emails as it would ruin the good mood. It seemed such a shame when he was clearly in such good spirits. But she knew that she had to. Time was running out. The wedding was tomorrow.

'Did you have a good night?' she asked him.

'Yeah, it was good,' he replied. 'We ended up in a club in The Mirage. The Oak, I think it was called. I actually didn't come back too late in the end; maybe just after two.'

Emma nodded. 'I was out like a light. I didn't hear a thing.'

'I noticed,' Charlie smiled in amusement. 'You need to save yourself for the big day tomorrow,' he said, pulling her in close to his chest. 'Talking of the big day, we need to drive over to get our wedding licence this morning. Can't get married without it and I think it's about six miles away.'

'Okay. We'll go after breakfast and before my hair trial.' He was so warm and Emma felt safe and comfortable. She would have given anything to just stay like that with him all day. To forget about all his faults and all the little things about their relationship she just knew she couldn't ignore. If only it were that simple.

'Who went out with you in the end?' she enquired.

'Dan, Carl and a few of my mates. Max and Callum came too,' he laughed as he remembered the evening. 'I think Max got lucky with one of the waitresses – I saw him going off with her at the end.'

Emma gasped. 'You're kidding?' She clicked her tongue loudly, feeling a bit disgusted with him. Since she'd met Max at the gym, they'd become fairly close. Max could be a nice guy, but he didn't seem to have much respect for women. As soon as he went out with one, he was on to the next. She probably should have warned Holly off him from the start, but even Emma hadn't known he was *this* bad; sleeping with anyone who was willing. Holly was going to be crushed. Holly didn't let her guard down easily, and meeting people like Max wasn't helping. He was a joke.

'Nope. Small blonde girl with long hair.'

Emma shook her head. 'Poor Holly.'

'He's not her boyfriend,' Charlie pointed out.

'Yes I know that, but still. He was only with her the night before; I think it's gross. He needs to grow up.'

He stared at her with a faint smile on his lips.

'What?' she asked him, feeling confused.

'You're just so considerate of others' feelings,' he replied fondly, 'you're so caring. I think it's sweet how you think about others all the time.' He gazed at her intently. 'I'm a lucky man to be marrying you,' he said, sliding his hand into hers under the bed sheets.

Emma smiled back at him, knowing it was now or never. 'Charlie,' she began hesitantly. 'We need to talk,' she told him seriously.

He instantly looked alarmed, sitting up in bed and leaning on his elbow. 'Of course. What's wrong?'

Emma tucked her hair behind her ears. 'Charlie, things can't go on the way they are with us,' she stated with certainty. Her stomach was dancing with nerves wondering how he was going to take it. 'I really mean it. I love you with all my heart and there's nothing I want more than to be your wife, but I think you need help. Sorry, that came out wrong,' she muttered. 'I think *we,* as a couple, need help. I want to try couples counselling when we get home. We have to change the way things are, Charlie. I'm not so certain I can handle your mood swings for the rest of my life.'

There, she'd said it. Emma had finally been strong enough to admit the truth to him. It was like she'd been struggling under water for all this time and now she'd finally come out for air. Either Charlie changed or she couldn't be with him. She held her breath waiting for his answer.

'Of course,' he said gently, as though he'd been expecting her to say that. 'I agree.' He rubbed her shoulder tentatively. 'I'll go anywhere you want me to,' he told her. 'Please don't tell me you're having second thoughts about marrying me?' he said in a shaky voice. There was an expression on his face she didn't recognize; Charlie appeared nervous.

'No,' she lied. 'But I need things to change between us, Charlie. I need you to promise me that they'll change. There's something else too…' she broke off anxiously.

'What is it?'

She took a deep breath. 'Firstly, I appreciate you've helped me with my career and how far I've come, but recently I've seen emails, Charlie. Ones I didn't know anything about. There was one the other day from a sportswear company, saying they wanted to go ahead with us modelling their clothes? What on earth is all that about? Why were you emailing and signing off as me? You've never once spoken to me about it. Then there're all these other companies you've emailed. I saw them when I looked at the sent items.'

Charlie was taken aback. 'What sportswear company?' he asked, looking puzzled, before the light dawned on him. 'Oh, I know the one,' he shrugged his shoulders looking unconcerned. 'I thought it would be good for the both of us, that's all. A nice thing to do together where we could make some money too. What's the problem?'

'Yes, but you didn't run it past me. I feel like sometimes you're using my name to get jobs you want without even mentioning it to me. Are there other things you've done like that behind my back other than the things I've recently seen?' She kept her voice soft. She didn't want to argue, but she knew she had to say it.

Charlie huffed. 'Big deal, I used your name. You were getting involved in it too, weren't you?'

'Yes, but that's because I'm the one with the large amount of followers.' She hated saying it. She didn't want to mention that he would never get to do it without her. Brands wanted exposure and they would only get that through her. She didn't want to ever hurt his feelings, but Emma couldn't help but feel he was using her. Was he so interested in her career because he wanted a piece of it too? She hoped not, but couldn't stop wondering now.

'Not *everything* is about you, Emma,' he shot back spitefully. 'Were you worried I was going to take a bit of your limelight or something?'

'What are you talking about?' Emma sighed, incredulous at his words.

'It's so *easy* for you,' he continued. 'Everyone wants you to wear their clothes and promote their brand. So what if I wanted do something myself for a change. I've helped you enough in the past, haven't I? Don't I deserve a bit of spare cash too?'

Holly's brows formed a perplexed frown. 'Charlie, you're acting jealous,' she remarked. She was feeling more confident than usual because she was marrying him tomorrow and this was her last chance to say how she felt. He was in a good mood too, so she knew he wouldn't be as aggressive and exasperated as he could sometimes be. 'I don't mind helping you to do the things you want, of course I don't. I want you to be successful too; I've never, ever wanted it to be all about me, you know I'm not like that. But you should have *asked* me first. It looks a little sly doing things like that behind my back and not keeping me in the loop over my own emails. Even the other day at the florists I felt embarrassed that you'd got the price even lower and I knew nothing about it.'

'Surely you're not going to complain about me saving us money?' He looked aggrieved.

Emma shook her head. 'I just don't think it's a good idea if you get involved in my business any more. It doesn't mean I'm not grateful or appreciate the things you've done. It doesn't mean I won't help you either. But you always did it because *you* wanted to. I never asked, Charlie. You've always insisted. I just don't feel comfortable with it any more,' she confessed bravely.

He showed his palms. 'Fine, I won't help any more,' he said, looking beaten and as though he was worried that if he objected, he would lose her. He held her hand to his heart. 'I promise, whatever you want, Em. Things will be different. Just tell me you're going to marry me tomorrow.' He laughed nervously.

Emma paused, staring at him. Was he just saying what he knew Emma wanted to hear? She wasn't certain she believed he would stay out of her business, but she decided she had to believe him.

'Yes,' she said finally, unable to help but smile. 'Why can't you be like this all the time?' she asked in a quieter voice, willing him to see how happy he made her when he was so easy-going and caring. *Just stay exactly like this and everything will be fine.*

He kissed her then and she felt her worries starting to drift away.

'Before you know it, we'll be married and starting our next chapter together. I hope you get pregnant straight away,' he said wistfully.

The words made Emma's heart turn to ice and she wasn't expecting it. She wanted a baby more than anything, but not like this. Not with her relationship being the way it was. Holly had been right. It wasn't a healthy environment to bring a new innocent life into, and until they managed to sort through their problems, Emma wasn't going to be trying for a baby, but she would keep this quiet for now. She didn't want to make him angry.

'So,' Charlie said, 'sounds like you have lots planned today, doesn't it? Where are you off to? Hair trial and then the spa with the girls, did you say?'

'Yes,' Emma replied, trying to brush away her concerns about their future and only focus on the fact that Charlie said he would change. 'Then out later on afterwards. I'm not sure where to yet; Danni and Fran have arranged it.'

His tone changed to one of authority. 'Well, don't be getting too drunk, will you?' He reprimanded her as though she was a little girl who had been told to not eat all her sweets at once. 'I want you fresh and ready for tomorrow.'

'Oh lighten up,' she attempted to bring back his calm, sweet, soft side. 'We aren't even planning to drink.'

His jaw clenched and a vein pulsed in his temple. 'You'd better not.'

Just like that, the nice Charlie was gone.

Chapter 22

Kim

Kim tossed and turned in the huge bed and punched the pillows, huffing in frustration. She couldn't sleep. It had been the most terrible night, lying there, thinking about her marriage and questioning her behaviour over the years. She must have only slept for about three hours before waking up in sweat-drenched sheets, as she gasped for breath. She must have been dreaming. Or in the middle of a nightmare.

She couldn't stop thinking of the odd little comments Andy had made over the years and how she had just brushed them under the carpet. When Mylo was born, Kim had felt such an instant rush of love that she never wanted to put him down. Looking back, she had hogged him . If someone else was holding him, she couldn't help but try to steal him back, saying he needed a feed or something. Perhaps she had been a bit OTT and obsessive, but she couldn't help it. Kim had breastfed and she'd been really pleased that she'd found it so easy and natural. On the odd occasion that she'd expressed her milk and Andy fed him, Kim couldn't help but correct the way he was doing it.

'Maybe just hold his head up a little bit more?' she'd suggest. 'He likes to have a little break sometimes, to bring up any wind he has. Here, do you want me to do it?'

Andy would always end up handing him back over so Kim could show him how to do it correctly and she remembered he mentioned a few times that he felt a 'spare part,' but Kim hadn't really taken him seriously. If she was honest, she always worried that because Andy hadn't felt ready to become a father, he wouldn't *want* to do these things anyway, so she'd always told herself she would be the one to take charge. She didn't want Andy to feel as though his life had changed that much. She only ever wanted him to be happy, but perhaps she'd shut him out too much? Maybe she hadn't included him to the point that he did just feel like a spare part?

'Let's have a night off,' she recalled him saying when Mylo had been about five months old. 'My mum has agreed to stay over and have Mylo the night. Come on Kim, it will be lovely. I'm sure you wouldn't want to say no to a peaceful night's sleep. I was thinking of staying in this new hotel in London. Looks amazing it does, look at the cocktail bar!' he'd said animatedly, flapping his hand at the image on his iPad.

Kim had smiled politely, but she knew there was no way she was leaving Mylo. She would have to let him down gently. Andy just didn't seem to understand why she didn't want to leave. She was breastfeeding and Mylo would only settle with her at night. No offence to Helen, Andy's mother, either, but she wouldn't look after Mylo like Kim would. Helen did this weird baby voice whenever she was around Mylo, and instead of making him smile, Mylo usually just looked at her as though she was the most peculiar person he'd ever seen. Another time, just after Kim had fed him, Helen asked to hold him and kept doing this strange rocking motion. Kim just *knew* he was going to be sick. She'd warned Helen once, but she hadn't listened, and the next thing they knew Helen had baby puke all over her white blouse. The thought of going off without Mylo just didn't appeal to her. She knew Holly would have jumped at the chance if her mother-in-law had offered, but Kim didn't feel like she needed a break. She simply didn't want one.

Time after time, Andy would try to get her to go out, and there must have only been a couple of times since the children were born when Kim had actually agreed. She guessed she needed to loosen up a little where her children were concerned.

'I love you so much, Mylo,' Kim had said when he'd fallen over in the garden and she was comforting him, placing a plaster on his leg. 'Out of all the boys in the world, I love you the most,' she kissed him, before looking up at Andy. 'Apart from Daddy as well, of course.'

'Ha,' Andy gave a short bark of laughter. 'Don't worry, I know where I stand.'

Kim assumed he was joking so she'd just rolled her eyes at the comment, but now she was unsure. Had Andy felt jealous of their children getting all her love and affection? Was he really that guy?

The sound of Holly stirring in bed disturbed Kim from her thoughts.

Holly sat up in bed, rubbing her eyes. 'God, I need a coffee,' she said. 'Shall we go and get that really nice breakfast we had the other day in that café downstairs? I could kill for those pancakes again.'

Thirty minutes later they were tucking into breakfast.

'I can't wait to just relax in the spa today,' Holly told her, blowing her coffee. 'It's going to be so nice. I can't remember the last time I had a massage.'

'Me neither,' Kim replied, thinking back. Pampering herself was a thing of the past. 'What are you going to do when you see Max again?' she wondered aloud.

'Nothing,' she shrugged. 'If he tries to even so much as talk to me, I'm going to tell him where to go.'

Kim nodded, thankful her friend didn't blame her. 'Max is an idiot, Holly. A good-looking one, but an idiot all the same. You deserve the best man there is and he's a dick.'

Holly had a faint smile on her lips. 'I know I deserve better. I'm honestly fine though; we're just not suited. Max is a party boy and I'm a mother of two. Onwards and upwards. It was a fun, one-night fling and I'm going to leave it at that.'

Kim paused. 'Exactly. You know, being here has made me realize how I'm always so sensible and serious nowadays. I'm always focusing on being the perfect mother. I'm always so concerned about looking after my family that I guess I've forgotten about myself along the way.' She wanted to say as well as Andy too, but remained silent.

'It's sometimes hard not to,' Holly sympathized.

'I know,' Kim said. 'I think I suddenly just realized that I'm only thirty-two and getting old before my time. Seeing all the others arrive looking really excited made me want to join in. Once I got in the mood, that was it. I feel like I finally found the key and unlocked my fun side again.'

'You're such a good mum, you deserve to let your hair down. I miss the children so, so much,' Holly confessed, her eyes watering as she spoke. 'I'm usually always so desperate to get a break from them. It's not easy being a single mum to two small children, but being here, I've realized just how much I've grown up. How much I actually *adore* being with them, even though at times they drive me crazy. I can't wait to get back home to normality and doing all the everyday mundane tasks. Rob texted me this morning saying that Lottie is fine and the meet with Nikki went well. That's good of course, but it just makes me want to get back all the more.'

'Of course it does,' Kim said sympathetically, understanding where Holly was coming from. It couldn't be easy splitting up and then your ex meeting someone else when you shared children. Kim couldn't think of anything worse than another woman playing mother to her two. It was the final wake-up call she needed to realize that she had to talk to Andy about their relationship.

185

She had to find out what was going on with Lily rather than burying her head in the sand, before they destroyed their marriage. 'I feel bad for actually *enjoying* myself. Being here has made me appreciate a bit of time to myself. Just because I'm married with children doesn't mean I have to lock myself at home all the time and never go out. When we get back, I promise to arrange some fun things for us to do. We can arrange babysitters and invite some others along too. Girl time is important and I can see how I've somehow forgotten all about that. Since I've been here I haven't laughed as much for years. Only having to think about myself for once has seemed alien to me, but I've kind of enjoyed it. Is that bad?'

'Of course not,' Holly told her earnestly. 'Being a mum can be so hard; the job is twenty-four hours a day, seven days a week. When you do finally have some time off, why shouldn't you be able to enjoy it without feeling guilty?'

'I guess you're right,' Kim nodded, deep in thought. She was going to do her very best to enjoy herself in the last few days, but she couldn't shift the dreaded feeling in the pit of her stomach, no matter how hard she tried. Kim knew she was going to have to have a serious chat with Andy as soon as possible.

She just hoped that it wouldn't devastate her perfect little family.

Chapter 23

Holly

Holly felt as though she was choking on hair spray and chuckled when Frankie started having a coughing fit.

'Bloody hell, how much of that stuff does she really need in her hair?'

'We need it to hold it in place,' she informed him. 'Trust me, the last thing she would want on her wedding day is her hair coming out,' she said, pinning the last piece.

They were in Emma's room that she'd booked to stay in that night alone, so she wouldn't see Charlie on the morning of the wedding.

'Though to be fair you would still be there to pin it back,' Emma noted, 'but nonetheless I do want perfect hair for my wedding day,' she smiled.

'So,' Holly said, as she added the last pin and ran the mermaid waves through her fingers. 'What do you think of this?'

Holly span Emma's chair round so she was facing Frankie and handed her a small hand-held mirror so she could see the back.

Frankie stared at Emma in silence. 'I think it looks perfect,' he said, voice full of confidence. 'Really beautiful. Charlie will love it like that.'

'Oh wow, Em, it looks so nice,' Kim chimed in.

'Holly, you're so talented,' Emma said, her face aglow with delight. 'I'm so glad you're my friend,' she giggled. 'This is exactly the sort of thing I wanted. I actually think you've nailed it in one go.'

'I agree,' Frankie said with certainty. 'Your hair suits you wavy, Emma. Honestly, you're going to look incredible.'

Emma blushed a little. 'Ah Frankie, you're so sweet. That's why I brought you today, for comments like that,' she joked. 'Do you think we should try it up anyway? Just in case?'

'I honestly don't think you need to,' Frankie announced. 'You never wear your hair up, do you? I think having half up and half down is perfect.'

'I agree,' Kim said with a nod. 'It looks like bridal hair, but still like you.'

Emma looked in the mirror for a few more seconds. 'Well, that's it then,' she beamed, 'my wedding hair is all sorted. I'm starting to feel nervous now; there's nothing else to do, is there?'

'I picked up the wedding table plan this morning,' Frankie told her. 'You're going to love it.'

'Oh, thanks so much, Frankie. I'd forgotten all about that,' Emma flashed him a gracious smile. 'How do the rose-gold flowers look on there?' She turned to Kim and Holly, 'I've got this gorgeous rose-gold photo frame with this pretty faux flower design on one side. Frankie found the company that did them here.'

'Honestly, it's bang on. You will love it,' Frankie said.

'That's good,' Holly replied, looking satisfied.

'You seem like a great help,' Holly told Frankie. 'If I ever get married, I may employ you to help me,' she laughed.

'Ha. Weirdly enough, I've actually quite liked helping out. I know Emma's taste so well now, I feel like I could pick things out myself without even asking her.'

'You're right, to be fair. Frankie even picked the flowers,' Emma said, looking thankful. 'He knows how much I've appreciated every little thing he's done.'

Frankie looked away, as though he was a little flustered by all the praise. 'So girls, where are you all off to now?'

'Spa,' Kim said. 'I cannot wait to just relax and unwind for the day.'

'Me too,' Emma said.

'In that case, I'm going to love and leave you girls. Maybe we'll see you later on or something.'

'Thanks so much for coming, Frankie,' Emma said, jumping up to hug him. 'And for everything. I couldn't have done it without you.'

The spa was everything Holly had imagined. Warm, with the scent of eucalyptus and rosemary; soft, calming music playing in the background, romantically lit with tea-lights everywhere. Even the staff spoke in tranquil, soothing voices. Dressed in her luxuriously fluffy dressing gown and slippers, Holly felt quite sleepy.

'We'll have our massages first,' Emma said, speaking in a lowered voice to not disturb the peaceful atmosphere. 'Then we'll all meet in the hot tub and pool area and then head for our Prosecco lunch.'

'Sounds like heaven,' Kim replied dreamily. 'I had so little sleep last night that I wouldn't be surprised if I drift off during the massage.'

Holly had to admit, it did sound like bliss. Her last spa trip had definitely been before Lottie and Jacob were born; maybe they could organize more days out together like this when they were home? Everyone needed a bit of rest and recreation sometimes.

Kim and the other girls were called by their masseurs and taken off into various treatment rooms leaving Holly and Emma alone.

'How are you feeling after last night? Did you speak to him? Did you manage to tell Charlie how you feel?'

'Yes,' Emma whispered. 'It's all okay. We're going to be fine,' she said enthusiastically. Her smile didn't reach her eyes though, and Holly couldn't help but think she looked a little lost.

'You don't have to go through with it unless you're one hundred per cent,' Holly ventured. 'It's still not too late, Emma. I can run off with you if you wanted to; I'm sure we could convince Kim to come along too. We wouldn't need to tell anyone.' She let out a little laugh to lighten the mood, but she wasn't actually joking. If Emma wanted out, then Holly would be by her side supporting her all the way.

Emma laughed and then looked serious. 'Thanks, Holly. We're going to see someone when we get home. I'm sure that's all we need really. Just a bit of help. I'm actually feeling excited about the wedding now,' she explained. Her bright, cheerful tone sounded forced though and it was clear to Holly that Emma was trying to convince herself she was doing the right thing.

Emma had made her mind up, and Holly would support her decision whatever happened, so she nodded at her friend and smiled to signify she was behind her, even though she was really concerned. 'It's going to be a beautiful wedding.'

'I know,' Emma replied, 'I'm so glad we've decided to do it in Vegas. I could live here. I just love it.'

'For a holiday maybe,' Holly laughed lightly. 'I'm not sure I could actually live here. A constant hangover doesn't sound like fun. It's a bit too hyper for me. I need some quiet time every once in a while. What are you going to do about trying for a baby now?' Holly asked curiously.

It was the first time Emma's happy expression cracked.

'He wants to try straight away,' she explained, looking distressed by this fact. 'But I won't do that,' she stated with certainty.

'What did Charlie say? Was he upset?'

'I never actually told him we wouldn't be trying…'

'Emma,' Holly clenched her jaw, 'maybe you should have explained that part before you get married.'

'I know, Holly, okay?' She rubbed her temples as though the thought was giving her a headache. 'I will tell him that when I'm ready. I just want to sort things out between us first.'

Holly nodded, not wanting to make Emma feel worse. It was strange to be about to marry someone that you were afraid to have children with. To Holly, it was just another sign that Emma shouldn't be going ahead with it. She changed the subject. 'Did you hear about Max last night?' she raised an eyebrow. She hadn't wanted to mention it earlier with Frankie in the room.

'What, sleeping with that waitress?' Emma asked, throwing her eyes to heaven. 'Honestly, Holly, I didn't realize quite how bad he was around women otherwise I would have warned you off from the start. I'm sorry I ever introduced you to him now. I mean I know he's not your boyfriend or anything, but we're all in this small group for our wedding and I just think it's so disrespectful when he knows you're likely to find out. Men, eh?'

'Emma?' A gentle voice came from a lady dressed in a matching white uniform to the others. 'Would you like to come with me?'

'I'll see you after,' Emma said quietly to Holly, before walking away.

Holly's masseur came for her a few minutes later, and before she knew it she was lying face down, every part of her body being massaged and relaxed. It was pure bliss. She was warm, content and relaxed, with no worries or lists of things to do. She pushed Max far from her thoughts so she had nothing to think or worry about. She really wanted to rest, de-stress and think of absolutely nothing so she could drop off to sleep.

Holly was frustrated that she couldn't unwind at all though. Her brain just wouldn't switch off and there was only one thing on her mind: Callum.

Chapter 24

Emma

The massage had been heaven. Emma had really hoped that by relaxing for an hour, her anxiety about the following day would be banished, but no such luck. It was still very much there. Every time she thought about walking down the aisle, her stomach began to cramp up with nerves. She told herself it was normal because she had no choice. She *had* to believe Charlie. Yet she just wasn't certain that love was always enough.

She couldn't deny she had worries about his jealousy of her success, and she questioned whether he would really be able to not interfere with her work in the future. Charlie wanted what she had, and Emma couldn't help but wonder if her Instagram popularity was what had attracted him to her in the first place? She did believe he loved her, but their relationship was so complicated. After all, she'd been much bigger back then and Charlie was always reminding her how lucky she was he'd got together with her. He pretended he was joking, but was he?

She turned to her Instagram as a distraction, watching a replay of the footage she had filmed in the spa earlier on. To her followers, she was a bride-to-be, giddy with excitement about marrying the man of her dreams. They looked up to her. *Aspired* to be her and to find the perfect, handsome and loving man to spend the rest of their days with. She got comfort from their messages, even though she knew it was absurd. These people were *strangers*. The vast majority she'd never even seen in real life. They had no clue about what her life was really like. They didn't see her setting up each picture so it would be absolutely perfect. They didn't see the hundreds of discarded selfies. They saw what she allowed them to; what she presented to them. It was what they wanted to see. She smiled as a message appeared from Frankie.

Enjoy your day today. I've sorted out the order of the day pamphlets for tomorrow, so will take them with me and hand them out. Look forward to the big day tomorrow. If you need anything in the meantime, let me know xx

He was so thoughtful and caring and Emma marvelled, not for the first time, at how different Charlie and his cousin were. Sometimes it seemed impossible that they were related. She tapped back on her phone.

Thanks Frankie. Have a good night xx

Today she was going to enjoy herself as much as she could. She wanted to forget about her fears.

At lunch they were sitting drinking Prosecco in their dressing gowns and Emma couldn't help but appreciate how the warmth in her throat from the fizzy alcohol was helping to numb her worries. It was making her feel better, and it also gave her a sense of rebelliousness towards Charlie telling her not to drink too much. She was a grown woman and she could do what the hell she liked. This was her last attempt to show him that she was her own person; he didn't and wouldn't control her. Imagine if she ever told *him* not to drink too much; Charlie did as he pleased and would never care if she didn't want him to do something.

'So I thought we could play a few drinking games,' Danni grinned, handing everyone a piece of paper. 'Not a lot though, don't worry, Emma. We will all still be fresh for tomorrow morning. We have to guess what Emma's answers will be. Emma, here are the questions,' she informed her, handing her a sheet.

It was a game that Emma had seen at lots of hen parties before. A little bit of fun and completely harmless. The girls were giggling as they wrote their answers, looks of concentration on some of their faces as though they were sitting a school exam. As Emma read the questions though, she suddenly started to feel a little short of breath. Her head started to throb furiously.

Would you rather your future baby inherit from you or your partner the following? Write your answer next to each one.

Eyes
Height
Temperament
Smile
Brains …

The list went on down the page.

Emma held her breath as she thought about each answer. *Eyes.* Charlie's eyes would go as thin as slits when he was really angry with her. Those beautiful eyes, which attracted her in the first place, could make him look evil. *Height.* He was only five foot nine, but at times she felt as though he was bigger than that. He could make her feel tiny and vulnerable in an instant. *Temperament.* She didn't even need to think about that one. Charlie was unpredictable; living with him was like constantly walking on eggshells, tiptoeing round timidly, scared to upset him. It was like trying to be quiet when a baby was sleeping. Emma was constantly trying to be good in order to not wake up his angry side. *Smile.* Sometimes he smiled when he knew he was getting to her. When he ignored her and she begged him to speak, his lips curved up at the edges, as though he found the whole thing enjoyable. It made him look sinister. *Brains.* He was a mastermind at manipulating her to get what he wanted.

'Are you okay, Em? You look a little pale,' Holly asked, her eyes burning with apprehension.

Emma cleared her throat and took a deep breath. She downed her Prosecco. 'Girls, can we play this a bit later on?' she asked politely. 'I'm not really in the mood for games.'

'Yeah, course,' Danni shrugged.

Thirty minutes later and Emma knew she was getting drunk. She could feel the fuzziness starting to take over her head. Her legs were tingling and she had red blotches on her chest because Kim had pointed them out. She got them sometimes when she started drinking. She was forgetting the simplest things. But she didn't care. In fact, she preferred feeling like this. It meant she didn't have to face the thought of the next day. When she was drinking, she didn't feel anything.

Holly turned to her after she downed another drink.

'Em, I don't want to seem like a party pooper, but do you think you may need to slow down a little bit? It's your wedding day tomorrow. It's not like you're going to have a day to recover, is it? The last thing you're going to want is to feel ill.'

Kim nodded. 'She's right. Maybe drink water for a bit? Or a coffee even?'

'I'm fine,' Emma brushed them off. She was big enough to handle herself. She never usually suffered from bad hangovers anyway; somehow she always seemed to feel okay. Her trick was to drink water and take a paracetamol before bed. Worked like a charm every time.

She waved the waiter over, desperate to order another drink.

Chapter 25

Emma

Somewhere in the back of Emma's mind, she knew she had gone too far. Emma wasn't normally one of those people who knew this fact. She would normally just keep drinking, enjoying every moment without a care in the world until she woke up the following day . But as she walked outside in the warm Vegas air, on her way to a bar that Fran and Danni had arranged, she could tell without a doubt that she'd already gone too far. She was dizzy, swaying as she took each step. Unsteady on her feet. Telling herself she would be fine, she followed the others to a cordoned off table inside a plush bar. She wasn't even sure what hotel they were in. Was she really getting married tomorrow? She couldn't actually believe the day had arrived. Everything was going so quickly. Time was ticking away, and before she knew it she would be walking down that dreaded aisle.

'Are you feeling alright?' Kim asked Emma again. 'I'm just a bit worried that you're a little drunk; your eyes are looking a bit bloodshot. Shall I order you a coffee?' she fretted.

'Enough about the coffee, Kim.' Her voice didn't even sound

like her own, but Emma didn't care. She was fed up with caring all the time. 'I want alcohol, not coffee,' she giggled.

Holly scrutinized her. 'Okay, maybe just a bit of water before the next drink.'

'I'm fine,' Emma repeated, holding up her half-empty glass for Fran to fill it with whatever alcohol she was drinking. Champagne maybe? Her vision was a little off and the lighting was dimmed. Was it Prosecco? She couldn't tell and didn't give a damn either way.

There was a rowdy group of men on the table next to them and Emma turned up her nose as she watched them downing pints of beer. Didn't they have any consideration for anyone else? It was as though they were in their own little world. 'They're so loud,' she complained to the others.

Holly's gaze flicked over to the table. 'Maybe it's a stag do or something.'

'Whatever it is, they're so loud I can hardly hear anything else. I can't even hear what music is playing. It's annoying,' she complained. She wouldn't normally care about it, but she was in an irritable mood and they were bothering her.

When they started banging on the table making even more noise, playing a drinking game, Emma had had enough. Everyone was looking over, but no-one was brave enough to say anything.

'I'm going over there,' she announced thunderously, striding over in their direction.

Only one of the men even noticed she was standing there, hand on hips when she reached the table. The others were too busy laughing and talking loudly amongst themselves.

'You alright, sweetheart?' He had a British accent.

'Not really,' she swayed a little as she shifted on the spot. 'I'm trying to enjoy a night out over here with my good friends, and we can't hear each other because you're so loud.'

She had at least five of them paying attention now, watching her curiously as though she was some incredibly fascinating creature.

One of them shrugged. 'Sorry. Here, take some shots as an apology,' he grinned. He raised an eyebrow. 'You girls enjoying your holiday so far?'

He was being genuinely friendly, and Emma felt ashamed for talking to them so tersely.

'Yes, we are thanks,' she cleared her throat. 'We're here for a wedding. I'm getting married tomorrow,' she told them, picking up a red shot from the table and downing it. She grimaced and picked up another one, pink this time.

'You're getting married *tomorrow*?' A dark-haired man repeated.

Emma nodded, downing the pink shot. 'Yes, you heard right.'

Another man laughed loudly. 'You're not holding back on the drink for someone who is getting married tomorrow, are you? Wow.'

'I don't get hangovers,' she informed him, proudly. 'I'll be okay.'

'She's enjoying her last day of freedom,' another said in admiration. 'Good for you.'

'Why don't you girls grab your chairs and come sit with us?' the dark one chimed in again. 'You should play the drinking games with us. Boys vs girls.'

Emma was aware she should say 'no thank you'. But now she was standing there it looked like so much fun and she wanted to enjoy herself and shift her moodiness. The men were friendly and easy to chat to, despite her snippiness when she'd first gone over to them. Before Emma even knew what she was doing, she gesticulated to the others to come over and join her, pulling up chairs around the table.

'We're playing drinking games,' Emma told them, determined to beat the men. She'd always been competitive and even with drinking games, she was no different. Her mind was fudgy from alcohol though, and she didn't feel like she could focus properly. She certainly wasn't going to be at her best.

They went round the table introducing themselves before the dark-haired one, who called himself Luke, starting explaining the rules of the game. Emma did her best to concentrate on what he was saying, but the rules didn't sound as straightforward as she'd hoped. No, in fact, Emma didn't feel confident that she was going to be on the winning side.

That was the very last thing that Emma remembered before passing out for the entire night.

Chapter 26

Kim

They had been sitting with the group of men Emma had introduced them to for over an hour. Emma was looking a little dishevelled and out of it, though it was always hard to tell when she was really drunk. Perhaps she should stop drinking now though, Kim thought, her sensible, motherly side coming to the surface.

'So who's single here?' Fran asked interestedly.

A few of them nodded.

'Well, kind of,' one of the men, Greg, said with a guffaw. He had red hair but the stubble round his chin was more of a strawberry blond shade. His friends joined in.

'Don't go getting involved with this one,' another laughed loudly, 'he's trouble.'

'How so?' Danni questioned, flicking her hair flirtatiously.

'He's seeing a married woman,' the red-haired man couldn't wait to announce. 'Some cougar who has three kids.'

Greg looked down at the floor, but seemed far from embarrassed. If anything, Kim would say he looked a little proud of himself and it irritated the hell out of her.

'No way!' Fran replied, loving the gossip. 'What, does she just lie to her husband all the time? Pretend she's seeing her friends instead of you?'

'Something like that,' Greg sniggered. 'She just deletes our messages and I think she has my number saved under one of her mate's names.'

'Ah, her poor kids,' Danni said.

'Look, I don't want to break her family up, but that's down to her, isn't it? I don't know her husband. Can't blame her for wanting a piece of me, can you?' He chuckled along with some of the others.

Kim looked away, not even wanting to hear the rest of the conversation. She knew if she joined in, she would end up getting into an argument with him. How could he be boasting about having an *affair*? It was absolutely disgusting. People just had no idea of all the hurt they would be causing. It wasn't even just the woman's poor husband who would most likely be crushed, but there were children involved and most likely in-laws and friends. You were demolishing lives when you decided to be unfaithful.

Kim exhaled sharply, sipping more of her drink. She couldn't help but think of Andy again. Was he having an affair with Lily? Had the thought even crossed his mind? Her heart ached remembering those messages.

'You okay?' Holly asked her tentatively. 'You seem a little quiet?'

Kim was about to brush her comment under the carpet, like she'd be doing the whole trip, but she suddenly wondered what it would feel like to share the burden of what was going on. Holly was her best friend so why hadn't she told her? She finally wanted to come clean that she wasn't as secure in her 'perfect' marriage as everyone thought. Perhaps she felt embarrassed that she was having these troubles and worries and that Andy was paying another woman interest? Taking a long, deep breath, Kim made up her mind. 'Can we talk somewhere alone for a bit? I need to tell you something.'

Chapter 27

Holly

Kim looked distressed and Holly wondered what the matter was as she followed her through the hotel. It was strange that Emma had done a similar thing the previous night and she felt like everyone suddenly needed to tell her their troubles. They told Fran and Danni to look after Emma, who hadn't even noticed them leaving.

'How far are we actually going?' Holly asked, feeling a little tipsy and not wanting to veer too far from the rest of the group. She dreaded to think how Emma must have felt, knowing she had drunk about three times as much as her.

'I don't know,' Kim told her solemnly. 'I just have something to tell you and we need to be alone.'

They passed a coffee shop that was fairly empty and Holly pointed to it. 'What about in here? I could do with a coffee to sober up a bit. I feel like today is getting a bit out of control. Aren't we supposed to be chilling out and relaxing before the big day instead of getting drunk? I don't know how Emma does it and I'm not really sure this is a good idea. It wasn't part of the plan, was it? It was just supposed to be a few Proseccos at lunch.'

Kim bought two Americanos and they sat there for a bit before she started talking.

'There isn't more to do with Max, is there?' Holly sighed.

'No, not Max. Don't worry,' Kim attempted a smile, but her eyes looked fearful.

'Okay. What is it then?'

Kim explained how she found the messages from Lily on Andy's phone and how she had a bad feeling in her gut about them. They were inappropriate and she was gutted that Andy was being so flirtatious with a woman he worked with. Then there was the Instagram likes and comment. She was concerned he was having an affair, and rightly so judging by the type of messages. Holly couldn't deny she was stunned. She never had Andy down as the type to look elsewhere. She'd always seen Kim and Andy's marriage as rock-solid. The last couple she would envisage splitting up. Andy was friendly and likeable, and Holly simply couldn't imagine him as being capable of betrayal. Not to Kim.

'Why have you kept this all to yourself?' Holly wondered in puzzlement. Holly was her best friend; they usually told each other everything.

'Ashamed, I guess. You've always thought that Andy and I were so strong as a couple.' Kim shrugged her shoulder with a pained expression.

'Why did you not ask Andy straight away about them? For all you know it could be absolutely nothing. I mean I know the messages are overfriendly, but you're probably assuming the worst.'

'I know it's odd that I didn't ask him about the texts, but I was too afraid of what he might say. I don't want to lose him, and if he has been unfaithful, I can't stay with him, Holly. I would never trust him again. I'm terrified.'

'I do get what you're saying, but if it were me, I wouldn't have been able to hold it back. I would have confronted him right there and then,' Holly told her. 'I just can't imagine him ever doing anything behind your back. He absolutely adores you and everyone knows how happy you two are.'

Kim's voice was laced with melancholy. 'That's the thing,' she fiddled with her wedding ring, twisting it round her finger. 'I'm not so sure Andy is happy, Holly. When I accidently fell pregnant with Mylo, I felt so guilty that I'd scuppered all the travelling plans we'd so been looking forward to. Andy wasn't ready. He wanted a bigger place and to save money before we had children. So I always wanted to make his life easy when the children were born. I didn't want him to feel that having kids earlier than planned had been a mistake, but by being the one in control of the children, I feel like I've kind of forgotten about Andy,' she confessed plaintively, before telling Holly of Andy's remarks about being left out. 'Mylo being premature and in hospital for a month was the scariest time in my life. When I saw his tiny little body, I vowed I would protect him forever. But I think I may have gone overboard. I've never even given Andy a chance to get involved with our children like he should have, and I've always made the children *my* priority. I never want to go out at home when he asks, our love life is pretty much non-existent, which has been down to me never being in the mood and I realize that I've changed so much I hardly even recognize myself.'

Holly couldn't deny that Kim had really transformed as a person. She had also noticed that Kim struggled to let go where the children were concerned. She liked to be in control of them, and Holly had always put it down to Mylo being premature and the anguish she went through. Could you be too overprotective of your children? She knew Kim never let Andy deal with the children by himself, but not to the extent that Kim was now describing. She didn't realize that having children had actually created a barrier between them. She imagined it must have been quite tough for Andy, being made to feel inferior and useless.

It was a good thing that Kim recognized her issues because

she and Andy could work through them together, and it certainly wasn't acceptable to be messaging a colleague so flirtatiously. What on earth was Andy thinking? If he felt they were having some kind of trouble, the first thing he should have done was spoken to Kim about it, not looked elsewhere for attention. They needed to communicate and resolve their issues. They had to make their relationship work. Kim and Andy were made for each other; they'd just come across a little bump in the road.

'I need to speak to Andy,' Kim said faintly. 'I need to see what's going on. I wanted to escape it all by coming here, but it's the only thing I've been able to think about. I'm petrified that I've pushed him away and it's all my fault. I'm also worried I'm not going to be able to forget about these messages either. I'm so angry with him.'

Holly squeezed Kim's hand. 'I'm sure you'll be able to sort it, Kim. There's never an excuse for being unfaithful either, despite what it's been like between you. Andy should have spoken to you about it.'

'I feel like he's tried though and I've not been listening.' Kim put her face in her hands, then looked up. 'Sorry for not telling you all this sooner. I should never have kept it all to myself, I see that now. I feel so much better for telling you about it.'

'It doesn't matter. I understand.'

'Thanks so much for listening, Holly. Right, let's get back to the others,' Kim said, standing up.

Holly nodded, standing beside her. 'I'm not drinking anything else. I feel much better after that coffee. I think we should get Emma back to her hotel room too; she needs looking after.'

As the girls arrived back at the bar, there was no sign of any of them so they tried calling Emma, Fran and Danni on their mobiles.

'There's no answer,' Holly said in puzzlement, after calling Emma yet again. 'I don't have any of the other girl's numbers, do you?'

Kim shook her head. 'Maybe they've gone back already?'

'Yes maybe,' Holly said, yawning loudly. 'Let's go back ourselves. I'm so tired and we have a big day tomorrow. I'll text Emma to let her know.'

But as the girls started walking towards the taxi rank, Holly spotted Danni and Fran and a few others walking along.

'Where's Emma?' Kim called out.

They both shrugged. 'We took her back to her room to sleep it off. See you tomorrow,' Danni called out aimlessly.

'Oh God,' Holly grumbled, 'shall we check on her? I wish we hadn't let her out of our sight.'

Kim agreed and they made their way to her hotel room, continuing to call and text her. They banged on the door when they arrived, but there was silence.

'Shall we go to reception and explain what's happened so someone can open the door so we can see she's actually okay in there?' Kim suggested.

Holly thought it was a good idea, and five minutes later after speaking to someone and going back up in the lift, they had a member of hotel staff following them to Emma's room.

'Maybe she's asleep?' Holly said hopefully. 'As soon as we see she's okay, we'll go straight to bed.'

But as the door creaked open, Holly's heart sank. Emma's room was empty.

Emma was missing.

Chapter 28

Emma

Emma's eyes peeled open and then shut again. The room was dark, but there was a crack in the curtains letting in a glimmer of light. Her heart was thumping in her chest as she gazed round the room. Where on earth was she? Her mouth felt as though it was filled with cotton balls. He head was throbbing and she had a terrible feeling in the pit of her stomach. Something was wrong. Very wrong.

Emma sat up in the unfamiliar bed and looked at the figure lying in the bed next to hers. At least he wasn't in the same one and she was pleased she was still fully clothed, wearing the skirt and top from the previous day. Who was it? She couldn't tell from the back of his head, but she was sure from the height it was a man. Then something else dawned on her suddenly. Today was her wedding day! How had this happened? She exhaled when she noticed the time on the clock by the television read 05:01. At least she hadn't overslept or anything like that, but she needed to get out of there. She could tell it wasn't Charlie lying in the bed next to her because his hair was too dark.

There was a bottle of water by the side of her bed and Emma took several gulps greedily. She was gasping, and she wiped her chin as some of the water trickled down from her mouth. She couldn't remember a single thing about what happened. She felt pleased to see her bag lying on the floor; at least she hadn't lost it. She picked up her bag and slipped her phone out, unable to believe how many missed calls and messages she had from her friends. Thankfully, there was nothing from Charlie, and Emma just hoped she would be able to creep out of the room she'd ended up in and no-one would be any the wiser. Not being able to recall what you did and how you got home was actually quite frightening, Emma realized, feeling foolish. She was about to carefully get out of bed without making a noise when she noticed something in the room that immediately made her feel more at ease. A blue pair of swimming shorts and flip flops, which she knew belonged to Frankie. She breathed out slowly, thankful he'd looked after her. Her eyes focused on a few other things she knew belonged to him too: a dark purple suitcase and a black cap with NYC written in white letters. *Thank goodness.*

Emma took another few gulps of water, knowing there was far too much on her mind to be able to fall back asleep. That was it now, she was up for the day. She knew it was selfish, but she wished that Frankie would wake up so she could ask him what had happened. She felt humiliated that she'd blacked out, but it was hardly surprising given the amount of alcohol she had consumed. What was she thinking? She had so much to do today! Her head was pounding and she desperately needed a paracetamol. Perhaps she hadn't got away with *this* particular hangover. Her eyes roamed the dark room, trying to focus on somewhere where Frankie may have put some painkillers.

Feeling more confident now she knew it was Frankie's room, she pulled the curtain open a little more, checking that her watch read the same time as the clock by the television, in case that one was wrong. That was when she saw it, and her heart was in her mouth.

There was a ring on top of her engagement ring on her wedding finger. Where had that come from? She was puzzled and suddenly felt sweaty and faint, falling back on the bed and holding her hand up, wishing she were imagining it. She'd never seen the ring before and to be honest, it looked cheap. Tacky. A garish fake diamond on a silver band she was certain would make her finger turn green. It certainly wasn't the one that Charlie was going to be placing on her finger that day, so where had it come from?

Telling herself it was probably a joke one, and maybe from a game with her friends or something the night before, Emma tried to relax, taking deep breaths. There had to be a reasonable explanation for this and she was going to laugh about it one day.

Do you remember when I woke up on the day of my wedding in Frankie's room not knowing where I was and panicking over the fake ring?

They would all laugh. It was be the joke of the year. Something they would tell their children when they were old enough.

If only she could recall what had happened. But Emma had a really awful, fearful feeling. She rubbed the ring, turning it round and round with her thumb, when a flashback popped into her head.

A trip in a taxi.

Giving over her marriage licence.

A vicar, standing in front of her.

A little wedding chapel.

A cork popping.

Frankie.

She got married.

Emma felt sick, jumping out of bed and dashing to the toilet. She'd already got married, she realized, and as she rushed past Frankie, she knew then that she was actually looking at her new husband. Emma had got so paralytic she had married *Frankie,*

209

her fiancé's cousin! It was a joke. A complete nightmare. Frankie was usually the one who rescued her, and Emma guessed he must have been in a complete state to have gone through with it. When had they met up? More importantly, why hadn't anyone stopped them? Emma began to panic, the room spinning round, wondering how on earth she was going to face the day, before spewing up in the toilet.

This had to be the worst wedding day ever.

Splashing her face with ice-cold water, she told herself to calm down. The last thing she wanted was to have another panic attack all alone in the bathroom; the previous one had been petrifying. She realized at that moment that she wouldn't actually be alone. Frankie was only just outside the bathroom door. He would hear her if she called out and she knew he would be up and by her side in an instant. *Her husband.* The thought made her almost laugh if it hadn't been so tragic. How were they going to explain this to Charlie? She couldn't even begin to imagine how furious he was going to be. It sent a chill down her spine, just thinking of it. She stared at herself in the mirror, racking her brains as to what she needed to do to fix this. Perhaps she could get the marriage annulled? She had no idea if that was even possible, and slowly walked back to her bed to Google it on her phone. When she pulled out the phone, she noticed a folded piece of paper in her bag with the title, Marriage Certificate, only confirming what she'd done. The rest of the document was blurry so she couldn't see anything about being able to take it all back. She was pathetically hoping there was a line on it reading:

If you were drunk and this was all a big mistake, please come back and we'll cancel it for you.

She highly doubted it was going to be that easy though, and as she searched on her phone to see if there was a simple solution, she discovered there was no way this was going to be sorted on time for her wedding in less than eight hours. It was like something from a film. The thought of getting married drunk in Vegas was so ridiculous; none of it felt real.

She'd have to beg for forgiveness from Charlie. What if he turned his back on her, seeing it as unforgiveable, even if she hadn't known what she was doing at the time? Would *she* have forgiven him if it had been the other way round? She would have been fuming; she would have cancelled the wedding as soon as the words had left his mouth. She pondered this for a moment and a thought occurred to her. Maybe, rather than this being the worst thing in the world, it was actually going to save her? This was going to be the excuse as to why she couldn't go through with it. So, she had married Frankie. The truth was, something actually felt right about that. Emma turned her head to look at him. As she gazed at his gentle features, relaxed in sleep, and his long lashes, she realized at that moment she would actually be happy if she were with him. If she were marrying him that morning, she didn't think she'd have any doubts about it. Frankie treated her like a queen; he was sweet and genuine. He always considered her feelings and looked out for her when Charlie didn't. Why had she not known she felt this way before? Or had she always subconsciously felt something, never daring to confess it and just suppressing her feelings ever since she'd met him?

It was wrong to care about her fiancé's cousin as more than a friend. She had her suspicions that he felt the same about her too; the way Frankie looked at her, cared for her and treated her was different to how he was with any other girl, even his previous girlfriends. But Emma had been with Charlie, and she was a loyal person, or so she had always thought. Of course, she didn't want to hurt Charlie, but a part of her felt braver with Frankie now by her side. She was done caring about Charlie and what he thought. She was through with dancing to his tune. He didn't deserve another chance, and in her heart of hearts she was fully aware that he was *never* going to change. Not as long as he was with her. He was so used to being the one in control. Always in the driver's seat, able to treat her however he felt each day, because he knew she would just take it. She would always beg for his forgiveness. Well, not this time. Being with Frankie, being his *wife*, made her feel all the more powerful and strong, even if it had all happened on a drunken whim. It was obvious they had feelings for each other; didn't the truth always come out when you were intoxicated? This time it certainly had.

Frankie was so kind, he'd even slept in the bed adjacent, rather than in hers, probably so she didn't feel uncomfortable this morning. She wondered if they'd kissed. If only she could recall the first time his lips had touched hers, but the memory was lost. Gone, with all the other things that had happened the previous evening.

There was so much to do. So much to cancel. So many people to let down and Emma just wished she could close her eyes, go back to sleep and wake up on a gorgeous desert island on her honeymoon, just her and Frankie. Thinking about it, she had never felt so content in her life. This was who she should have been with all along; if only she had met Frankie first. She felt like laughing out loud about what they'd done. It wasn't funny in the slightest, but it was so carefree and for once, Emma had done exactly what she obviously wanted. It was so *Vegas*.

She heard Frankie stir in his bed and he rolled over, squinting his eyes at the light from the outside world shining in.

'What time is it?' he asked in a groggy, sleepy voice.

'Early,' Emma told him, pleased he was awake so they could talk.

He sat up in bed, and Emma couldn't help but glance at his bare, tanned, toned chest. She longed to go over to him and feel her fingers on his soft skin.

He breathed out and turned his head to look at her, picking up his mobile to check the time. 'How are you feeling? Do you remember much about last night?'

'Honestly? Not really, no. I kind of blacked out,' she told him, feeling ashamed. 'I know about this though,' she said, staring at her ring.

'Right,' he cleared his throat, looking out of his comfort zone. 'Yes, I'm not really sure what we're going to do about that. It's all a bit of a mess, isn't it?'

Emma couldn't agree more. Everything *was* a complete mess. Did Frankie regret marrying her? He wasn't exactly in good spirits this morning and Emma felt an overwhelming sense of disappointment. What had she expected? For Frankie to come over and snuggle up to his new wife as though they hadn't done anything wrong? He had married his cousin's *fiancée*. It was hardly something to be proud of and he was obviously feeling incredibly guilty. He and Charlie were so close; they always had been since they were young.

'I'm wondering whether we can go back to the chapel this morning and explain that there's been a huge mistake. Maybe I can call them?' he suggested in a sombre tone.

Emma felt her heart sink. His words were cutting. They hurt. 'Maybe,' she managed to reply in a small voice.

'Do you not want to marry Charlie, Em? Is that it?' he asked with concern.

Wasn't it obvious? She'd got drunk and married *him*. Clearly she didn't want to marry Charlie.

'I…' she broke off, unsure what to say and how to act. This was weird. She was sitting in bed next to her new husband and he was asking her whether she wanted to marry someone else.

'It's normal to have cold feet,' he reminded her. 'Last night, you weren't exactly yourself, were you? I mean, you were so drunk,' he shook his head, 'I'm not even sure you knew what your name was. I couldn't believe they allowed the ceremony to take place in the first place. We may be able to speak to someone and sort all of this out so the wedding can go ahead today. It may not be too late. I'm not certain it was even legal and that's something we have to find out asap. Charlie loves you. Perhaps there's a way that he won't need to find out that any of this ever happened.'

Why did he want her to marry Charlie so much? Was he afraid of him? She wondered. Emma felt like crying. Why had he married her if he knew how drunk she was? It was so out of character for Frankie, and she couldn't understand why he was saying these things now. Obviously now he'd woken up, the reality of what they had done had hit him and he was feeling remorseful. She'd hoped he would wake up with plans about how they could run off together and live happily ever after, somehow avoiding Charlie so she wouldn't have to face him again. Emma was so stupid to even hope that was a possibility.

She gulped. She wanted more than anything to tell Frankie the truth. She didn't want him to make any phone calls. She didn't want him to speak to anyone at the chapel and to tell them it was all a big mistake. No, Emma wanted to leave things exactly as they were, with Frankie as her husband, even though she knew it was crazy. Maybe she needed to be a bit more crazy in her life? She knew that she should feel terrible today; guilt and horror should be eating away at her, but she didn't feel any of those things at all. She just felt relief, as though she'd been given a get out of jail free card in a game of Monopoly. How could she really not show up to her own wedding though? There wasn't a crueller thing she could do to Charlie in her opinion. Jilted at the altar. It was unthinkable.

'I don't know,' she revealed in a shaky voice. 'I'm not sure I can do it, Frankie.' She gazed at him with pleading eyes to rescue her like he usually did. She wanted him to tell her it wasn't possible now. She'd married *him*, and it was too late to marry Charlie now. There really was no turning back. She wanted their ceremony to be legal; but now she was really thinking about it, knowing that Frankie didn't have had a marriage licence, it was highly unlikely. She'd done her research before choosing Vegas as her wedding destination.

Frankie looked pale, as though he was in complete shock. 'But, why? I thought you were happy with him, Emma? He's going to be gutted. Lots of people probably feel like this on the morning of their wedding. It's really normal to feel nervous and like you want to back out. You love him; you two are the perfect couple.'

Emma shook her head. 'He's not always the same person he is in front of you. There's more to our relationship than meets the eye.' Her eyes were shiny as she stared at the wall, deep in thought. 'You know, I always thought I'd be waking up today, all excited and emotional, ready to marry the man of my dreams. Hopeful of our happy future together. Instead, I find myself hungover, having already married someone else. What does that mean, Frankie? It can't be good, can it?'

Frankie hesitated, clearly uncertain how to respond. 'You've been out and drunk too much. I think that's what it says. You won't be the first person to wake up on your day of your wedding having done something stupid and you certainly won't be the last.'

'What about you then? What's your excuse?' Emma asked him, fed up with him acting as though it was all her doing. He'd played a part in this too, and she couldn't understand why he wasn't taking any responsibility.

Frankie looked mystified, as though she was talking in another language. 'What? I'm not sure what you mean? My excuse for what?'

'What's your excuse for marrying me?' Emma demanded, 'there's obviously something in it, Frankie, even if you were as drunk as me. There's always been something between us, I knew that when I woke up today. I know it's wrong, but you shouldn't deny it. Our actions last night speak volumes. I think you agree with me deep down that we are much better suited than Charlie and I…'

'Emma, stop.' Frankie shook his head several times as though he couldn't bear for her to say another word. 'You've got it all wrong…'

'Have I?' she interjected. 'Can you honestly say it was a drunken mistake and you don't have any feelings for me?' she questioned confidently.

His brows furrowed in bafflement. 'You've honestly got it wrong, Emma. I found you at around eleven o'clock last night after calling you constantly.'

Emma had a horrible feeling in her stomach, and it turned over with anxiety. Her frown mirrored his as she stared back at him in confusion. 'We got married, didn't we? The ring...' her eyes darted down to her left hand, 'I noticed the marriage certificate in my bag. I'm actually happy, Frankie, you needn't worry. You're right that this is a huge mess, but if I'm honest, I'm glad it's made me wake up and face my true feelings for you.'

Frankie shot her a look of pity. 'Yes, Emma, *you* got married,' he looked away from her, as though he was annoyed with her careless actions, 'but not to me.'

Emma felt nauseous again.

'You were with a group of men,' Frankie told her sternly. 'I think it was Luke you got married to. I don't know. I can't really remember his name.'

She felt crestfallen. She hadn't married Frankie at all.

She had married a complete stranger.

Chapter 29

Kim

Kim woke up feeling better about everything. She felt lighter somehow having told Holly her worries. Kim had decided she was going to call Andy that morning and ask him about Lily. As much as she wanted to do it face to face, she couldn't wait a moment longer.

She stretched out in bed, her thoughts turning to Emma. She smiled, despite her nerves about the phone call she needed to make, thinking she'd most likely had a really late night somewhere; her last chance of freedom. She hoped she wasn't feeling too rough this morning, and Kim was grateful that she'd stopped drinking when she had as she had a mild headache. She rubbed her temples, turning off her alarm as it started beeping.

Holly began to stir. 'Oh my God, I feel so tired still,' she said, sitting up on the pillow.

'I feel okay,' Kim replied. 'Bit of a headache, but I'm fine.'

Holly checked her phone. 'I'm going to try Emma again. I'll need to start her hair soon, and I haven't had any replies from last night. Have you?'

Kim shook her head. 'No. She's probably still asleep or something. Let's just get washed and head to her hotel room like she told us too; I'm sure she's there. Then I'm going to call Andy. I really need to speak to him.'

'Good idea.'

When Kim tried calling Andy thirty minutes later, it went straight through to voicemail. She frowned, wondering why his phone was switched off or he didn't have any signal, and she couldn't stop her stomach from bubbling with tension. She didn't know whether it was because of what she needed to ask him or because he wasn't answering. He had the children by himself today and she couldn't help but panic that something was wrong. Kim knew she needed to stop being such a worrier, but being away from them all and not knowing what was going on was proving hard.

'I'll try him again later,' she told Holly.

Emma's room was the floor below, and as they stood outside knocking, they stood there in stunned silence that there was no answer.

'Shit,' Holly muttered. 'She's obviously not in there, is she? There is no way anyone could sleep through this banging. What on earth are we going to do?'

Kim pulled a face. 'I'm really not sure. Maybe we should just go back to our room and start getting ready? At least that way you'll only need to do Emma's hair afterwards?'

Holly looked concerned. 'She was supposed to be getting breakfast in the room at eight, and it's now ten past,' she said with concern, staring at her watch. 'I'm really worried about her.'

For once, Kim was lost for words. It wasn't exactly common to go missing on the morning of your wedding, was it? Kim thought back to the morning of her own big day; they had stayed at the venue the evening before and had limited themselves to a couple of glasses of wine with dinner. Kim had wanted to have an early night and she'd stuck to her word, being tucked up in bed by ten o'clock. She wanted to feel fresh and full of energy when she woke up. There would be no black bags underneath her eyes; Kim was determined to look her very best. To Kim, it only meant one thing that Emma had disappeared and it wasn't good at all.

The only reason someone wouldn't want to be found on the morning of their wedding was because they had changed their mind. Perhaps Emma didn't plan to get married today after all?

Just as they turned the corner of the corridor, Kim heard the loud ding of the lift up ahead, a figure slumping out.

'She's here!' Holly exclaimed with relief. 'Look, it's Emma!'

Chapter 30

Emma

She had to act normal. Frankie had instructed her that on no uncertain terms was Emma to tell anyone about her wedding ceremony to Luke the night before. He was sorting it all out so she could go ahead and marry Charlie. To put her mind at rest, he was going to call her as soon as he'd spoken to the right people. He was acting as though it was just a tiny little issue that he had to take care of. An accident, like simply falling over or losing her keys. It hadn't meant anything. After Frankie had told Emma what had happened and how he'd found her, she was literally stuck for words. She was disgraced. He'd ignored the part where she'd told him her feelings for him, and Emma felt horrified for having said anything now. She just listened to Frankie's instructions. Obediently did what she was told so she didn't ruin the biggest day of her life. He kept reiterating over and over that she loved Charlie and wasn't thinking straight before of wedding nerves. Maybe that's what he really believed? Either way, without Frankie by her side, Emma felt as though she had no choice but to go ahead with the original plan. She ignored the pain in her heart, the disappointment that Frankie hadn't whisked her away, and plastered a smile on her face when she saw Kim and Holly in front of her.

'Where have you been?' Holly asked, looking delighted to see her. 'We've been so worried about you! Haven't you seen all your missed calls?'

Emma sighed. 'It's a long story, but I'm here now. I just got drunk, that's all. I bumped into my aunt and ended up going to her room for a chat,' she fibbed, knowing they would never find out otherwise; she had a single aunt, Brenda, who had come away on the trip. 'I fell asleep by accident. I hope the make-up artist can work her magic with my face when she arrives. I look and feel awful.'

Emma opened the hotel room, grimacing when she spotted the bottle of champagne on ice. No way was she touching that this morning. 'The others are coming here at some point to get their hair done, Holly. I hope that's okay?'

'Of course,' Holly shot her a warm grin, 'I said anyone that needs hair doing, send my way. Happy to help in any way I can.'

'That's so nice of you,' Emma told her earnestly.

Emma tried to act how she would have done if she were happy with the choice she was making. She tried to imagine how normal brides were on their big day. Anxious? Giddy with excitement? Quiet? Constantly chatting away to disguise the fact they were terrified? It was difficult keeping up the bright tones and fake smiles, and Emma didn't know how to feel when she heard her phone beep and see Frankie's name pop up on the screen of her phone.

Good news. The ceremony wasn't legal. The chapel also performs ceremonies just for fun. There's nothing stopping you getting married today. I'll see you down the aisle! Frankie xx

Emma gulped, staring at the words until her eyes became watery and her nose tingled. *There's nothing stopping you.* She took a deep breath, closing her eyes, thinking about how she just needed to make it through the day. Soon it would all be over. She would be Charlie's wife and she would just have to get on with it. She'd made her bed and flown everyone out to Vegas. But she couldn't ignore the fact that it had become clear to her, now more than ever, that she really didn't want to go through with it. Emma couldn't stop thinking about Frankie and how she'd felt that morning when she thought he was her husband. There was a connection between them that felt right, she was certain of it. She'd never felt so out of control over her fate. She was so worried about disappointing everyone else, but what about her? Did her own happiness matter?

'Do you want a glass of bubbly?' Holly asked.

Emma shook her head violently. 'Absolutely not. But you two go ahead and open it, help yourselves to a glass. It's such a waste otherwise. Sorry my hair is such a mess,' she apologized. She didn't actually care. 'I quickly washed it before I came here and it's gone a little frizzy because I didn't have time to dry it properly. Thank God you're here to make it look nice.'

Holly nodded, beginning to brush it.

'You sure you don't mind us opening this? It feels wrong if you're not having any. I don't exactly feel amazing myself, but I'm hoping the hair of the dog is going to work,' Kim giggled.

'Honestly, please go ahead,' Emma insisted. *Someone* may as well have fun on her wedding day.

Emma was a master at masking her feelings when she wanted to. She remembered being at school once when she was about fourteen and overhearing Sally Bateman and Hayley Martins whispering that she would have to wear a tent to the end of year party as it was the only thing that would fit her. Too embarrassed to tell her friends why she was upset, Emma just pretended she hadn't heard it, but she'd felt dejected for weeks afterwards.

Another time, Emma had gone on a girls' weekend trip to Amsterdam, even though she didn't want to go because she couldn't afford it. She'd agreed to go initially because she hadn't realized the cost. She'd been a student at the time, and knowing she would upset the others if she pulled out because it would be an odd number, meaning someone would have to pay more for their room, she felt she had no other choice and forced herself to join in the excitement, which she really hadn't been feeling at all. She was a people pleaser – she hated letting others down. She disliked fuss and causing problems. She didn't want people to ever feel sorry for her. She was the type of person to have a splitting headache all day, but not complain. She would say yes to babysitting her friends' children, even though it meant she had to change all her plans. She was a professional at tricking people into thinking she was perfectly okay, when she wasn't. Today was no exception.

Everyone seemed to be in good spirits but Emma had never felt more alone in her life. Danni and Fran arrived with more champagne and shortly afterwards her two cousins joined them too. There were giggles and perfume being sprayed. The flashing of photographs lighting the room and hairdryers blasting out noisily made Emma feel as though she couldn't even hear herself think. From the outside, it was a typical bridal party morning.

The more people who arrived in the room, the more Emma wanted to disappear. How she wished she was just a bridesmaid, or better still, just a wedding guest. She didn't want the day to be all about her and as much as she'd got used to attracting attention on her social media pages, this was a different feeling entirely. She felt overwhelmed, like the room was closing in on her. Her chest was red and blotchy again and she was shaking uncontrollably. Was it through nerves or because of the alcohol the night before? Emma wasn't sure.

'You look amazing,' Fran commented.

'Thanks,' Emma managed.

When the make-up artist was finished, Emma turned and looked in the mirror.

'Oh wow, Emma. You look incredible,' Kim said in admiration.

'Stunning,' Holly agreed, her eyes sparkling with excitement.

She had to agree. Holly and the make-up artist had done a fabulous job and somehow, even after just a few hours' sleep, she did look nice. It was just a shame she didn't feel it and couldn't join in their enthusiasm.

'Shall we get the dress on?' Holly suggested. 'We actually don't have that long left and I'm worried about how long it takes the do the buttons up at the back.'

Emma raised a meagre smile. 'Okay.'

'You seem really calm,' Danni added. 'I'm not so sure I would be on *my* wedding day,' she laughed loudly, clearly getting a little merry from the champagne.

Holly helped her into the dress.

'Gorgeous dress, Emma,' Kim said, looking in the mirror as she applied her lip gloss.

It was a large room but there seemed to be too many people in it, and as Holly started buttoning up the dress, she felt even more like the room was closing in on her.

'Emma, Frankie has asked where you put Charlie's new cufflinks? He's on the phone now,' Fran called.

'Emma, the photographer is asking whether he should go to Charlie's room now. Shall I tell him you want him here a bit longer?' Danni asked. 'Are you dressed yet?'

'Em, did you want to go ahead with the hair piece?' Kim was asking. 'Don't want to worry you, but we should get it in before we run out of time. Holly will need to put it in.'

'God, these buttons. There's so many of them,' Holly exhaled from behind her, sounding a little stressed that time was running out. 'Beautiful dress, but my gosh, they certainly didn't take into consideration how long it would take the bride to get into it!'

'Where's your perfume, Emma? The photographer has asked to take a photo of it along with your shoes?'

Emma felt the heat creep up to her cheeks and she threw her hands up to her face, which felt as though it was on fire. She needed to get out of there. 'Just stop,' she said abruptly to Holly, who stood there open-mouthed. 'Everyone just stop,' she said, loudly this time.

Everyone stood there gawping at her as Emma picked up the train of her dress, and with no explanation ran from the room.

Chapter 31

Emma

As Emma made her way to Charlie's hotel room, she felt her stomach fizz with nerves like never before. But she had to tell him, despite how terrified she was. The wedding was off. She wouldn't and couldn't go through with it. The easy thing would be to just run away, but Emma knew she had to face up to him. Even though he could be terribly unkind, Charlie deserved more than that.

Now here she was, despite agreeing to Frankie she would go ahead with the wedding, standing outside the room where Charlie was. Where she *hoped* he still was anyway; what if he'd already left for the chapel? She felt short of breath and started to sweat, even though it was freezing with the air-conditioned on full blast. Emma tried to steady herself against the wall outside the hotel room that Charlie was staying in, taking deep breaths. The very same room where she'd slept all week. She'd booked the other room on a different floor where she was supposed to have stayed last night. The room where she was supposed to be adding the final touches right now. She wondered what the others were going to make of all this. This wedding was going to be talked about for years. The bride who changed her mind on the day of her wedding. The bride who had already got married the evening prior. It was absolutely ridiculous. Laughable.

She tapped on the door, startled when she heard laughter from inside. Then it occurred to her, that of course, Charlie had company in there. The groom didn't typically get ready alone, just like the bride. The ushers, his father and Frankie would all be in there with him.

Jason, one of Charlie's ushers opened the door, taken aback when he noticed it was Emma standing there in her dress. He paled and closed the door hastily, so he was just peeping through a crack.

'What are you doing here? I don't think you're supposed to see each other before the wedding. It's bad luck,' he informed her in a hushed voice.

Emma's mouth twitched uncomfortably as she spoke. 'I need to see Charlie. I need to speak to him, alone, and I need everyone else to leave the room. It can't wait. It's urgent,' she said boldly, her insides turning to jelly.

'What? Right now?' He gawped at her as though she'd lost the plot. 'Okay, one minute,' he closed the door.

Emma's heart galloped with nerves, wondering what was being said behind the door. She could hear muffled voices but had no idea what they were saying .

Charlie's dad opened the door, attempting a smile, coming outside and closing it behind him. 'Is everything alright, Emma? Did you need something?' His bright voice and smile didn't match his worried, narrowed eyes. His forehead was crinkled up like tin foil.

'I need to see Charlie right now. I need to speak to him and we need to be alone. This isn't a joke,' she said with urgency. 'It can't wait.'

His eyes swept over her with a look of concern and his smile vanished. 'Right,' he cleared his throat, a look of worry crossing his face. 'Very well. How long do you need? Are you sure it's not something I can help with?'

'Unfortunately not,' she said regretfully. 'We're going to need a while – I can't say how long. But I do know the sooner I see him, the better.'

He nodded obediently and then a few moments later, he was coming back out of the room along with three of Charlie's ushers and Frankie.

'Emma,' Frankie hissed as he walked past, 'what are you doing?'

'The thing I should have done this morning,' she told him with certainty. She sounded a lot braver than she felt.

He nodded then, knowing anything he said in attempt to change her mind would be futile, looking away and following the others.

Charlie's eyes were wide with fear and surprise when Emma walked into the room. 'Emma, what's going on?' He looked her up and down, becoming distracted. 'You look beautiful by the way,' he told her, his eyes roaming up and down from her hair and make-up to her dress. 'Wow.' Then his expression changed and he looked perturbed once more. 'Are you okay? Why are you here now? You're scaring me. You're the one who said how important it is that we don't see each other this morning,' he reminded her. 'Shouldn't you be getting ready with the girls? I thought you wanted to keep your dress a big surprise?'

Emma felt as though she couldn't swallow, her mouth completely dry. She felt like her heart was going to burst with its excessive beating. Her shoulders were hunched gloomily as she descended into the chair in the corner of the room. She was gasping for a drink and reaching out, she poured herself some water from a glass bottle by the television. 'You may want to sit down. I need to talk to you.'

Charlie sat on the edge of the bed, opposite her. He looked so vulnerable sitting there, waiting to hear his fate. He looked fearful, and Emma knew then that he had guessed. He wasn't going to make it over the finishing line after all. He'd pushed Emma too far and lost her.

His breathing was audible and he sounded out of breath, even though he wasn't moving.

'Charlie, I don't know how to even start,' Emma tailed off, twisting her fingers, feeling discomfited. 'I'm so, so sorry. I can't marry you. It's not right between us and I know that in my heart.'

He exhaled slowly, putting his head in his hands as though he couldn't face her. As though by not facing her he was blocking out what she was saying.

'I do love you,' Emma continued, feeling abysmal, 'but you know as well as I do that our relationship isn't healthy. I feel like I'm walking on eggshells all the time. I never know what mood you're going to be in or if certain things are going to upset you. Half the time I'm not even sure you really like me. I have to pretty much beg to get you to talk to me again.' She shook her head. 'I just feel as though our relationship isn't stable. It's unpredictable and you can get nasty. I can't live like that, Charlie.'

He looked up at her then, with pleading, watery eyes. 'I'll change, Emma. I thought we spoke about all this? I'll do anything, anything...' His voice cracked with emotion and he seemed to shrink. 'How can you do this to me? We're supposed to be to getting married. I love you. I'll change and be the man you need me to be. *Please*, Emma. Don't do this to me. You can't,' he said gently, a tear rolling down his cheek.

Emma wiped her own tears away. She knew he was going to say this, but it didn't make it any easier. It felt strange hearing him plead with her, not the other way round, and she knew she had to be strong and stick to her guns. She couldn't let him change her mind. She didn't trust it would ever work between them and she reminded herself of the relief she had felt when she thought she'd married Frankie. It wouldn't be fair on herself or Charlie if she allowed him to talk her back round.

'Charlie, I will forever be sorry for not being brave enough to end it sooner between us. I feel terrible for doing this to you right now; it's the worst timing possible. But my mind is made up. I can't marry you. I just hope one day you find it in your heart to forgive me.'

Charlie sobbed then, and Emma couldn't stop herself from putting her arms around him. She knew she had broken his heart and she felt wretched. She remembered her first-ever boyfriend who had broken up with her years ago and how she'd felt desolate afterwards. She had grieved as if he had died. She had been low for months after and she wouldn't wish that feeling on her worst enemy. Yet here she was doing the same thing to someone else. This was worse too, much worse. She caught sight of them hugging in the mirror and thought how strange they would look to an outsider. Emma looked every bit as a bride should: wearing a beautiful ivory dress, not a single hair out of place, her make-up flawless. The tell-tale red blotches remained splattered across her chest though, giving away the fact that she was hot, bothered and stressed. Charlie, who was usually full of such bravado, looked broken and frail. He appeared dazed and confused as though he'd banged his head and couldn't quite work out who and where he was.

'*Please, Emma.*' He begged again, whispering in her ear. His hands were shaking as he placed them into her own.

Emma pulled away, biting the flesh of her lower lip. 'I'm so sorry, Charlie. I really am.'

He stiffened and his jaw set. 'After everything I've done for you,' he hissed. His face screwed tight as though he was in immense pain, he walked out of the door.

Chapter 32

Holly

Fran's hand flew to her mouth in horror. 'I don't believe it!' she squawked, hanging up her phone to whoever she'd been speaking to. 'The wedding is off! That was Frankie on the phone. I can't get through to her. Has everyone tried calling Emma? What on earth is all this about?'

Fran was someone Holly would describe as a 'flapper'. She was a drama queen at the best of times, always looking stunned and concerned by the smallest things. She was the last person you would choose to have around you in a crisis. The type of person that just made things even worse.

Holly tried Emma once more, but she was sure her attempts would be in vain. If Emma had cancelled the wedding, which wasn't actually a massive surprise after the conversation they'd had, she wasn't going to want to speak to anyone. 'Straight to voicemail,' she said regretfully.

'Oh, this is just *ridiculous*,' Fran said in bafflement. 'She can't do this and then just run away.'

'I can't believe she's cancelled it, can you?' Kim said quietly so only Holly could hear her.

'I think there's a lot more to it,' Holly said carefully. 'It's better that she cancelled the wedding than went through with it and regretted it, don't you think?'

'I thought she was acting quiet this morning,' Emma's cousin said.

'Yes, she hardly said a word, did she?' Danni agreed, looking as though she was actually enjoying the commotion. 'I just thought she was nervous.'

'I don't think I've ever known this to actually happen before. I dread to think how much money has been wasted here,' Fran tutted loudly, still looking absolutely flabbergasted. 'I was really looking forward to today as well...' she tailed off, mumbling to herself.

'Shall we go try to find her?' Kim suggested.

'Yes, there's nothing else we can be doing really, is there?' Holly replied. 'She must be feeling awful.'

They slipped out the room without the others taking much notice.

'Any idea where she might be?' Kim asked, as they walked outside.

Holly stood there thoughtfully, remembering the comment Emma had made about the water fountains. If there was ever a time for peace and tranquillity, it was now. 'Actually, I do,' she told Kim as they hopped into a yellow taxi. 'Take us to the Bellagio Hotel, please.'

Ten minutes later and Holly had noticed Emma immediately. It wasn't as though you could miss her. She stood out like a sore thumb with her disconsolate expression and the fact she was still wearing her wedding dress. She was attracting stares from everyone.

'Oh my God, she's still in the dress,' Kim whispered in horror.

'Come on, let's go over there,' Emma said, making her way through the chairs and tables.

Emma's eyes flicked up at them as they sat down, but her

232

expression stayed the same, as though she'd been expecting them to come all along.

'So,' Holly began slowly, 'you changed your mind.' It was a statement rather than a question.

'How are you feeling, Em?' Kim asked.

Emma sniffed. 'You both probably think I'm a terrible person,' she said in a small voice. 'I mean, who actually dumps their fiancé just before they're supposed to get married?'

They sat in silence for a few moments.

'I actually think it's a very brave thing to do,' Holly told her honestly.

'Charlie probably hates me, but I couldn't do it. I couldn't go through with something I knew was wrong. I have to trust my gut,' Emma told them, staring into space, deep in thought. 'My phone hasn't stopped buzzing and ringing, and I'm just ignoring it. I'm ignoring everyone, running away. I've even had to delete my Instagram temporarily because of the messages from people I don't even know, wishing me a happy wedding day,' she let out a light, caustic laugh, 'which as you can see is going just to plan. Everyone thinks I have an enviable, perfect life when in reality, I was about to marry a man I knew wasn't right for me. Now I've broken up with him and am sitting in a hotel looking like a complete nutjob in my wedding dress, which still isn't even done up at the back.' She gave a real, genuine laugh then and Kim and Holly couldn't help but smile back, despite the sadness of the situation.

Emma's face darkened. 'I just wanted to be happy and settled, you know? I want so much to have my own children like you girls, start a family. The sad thing is, I actually did think Charlie was my future at one point. I'm not sure when I started to question whether I could be with him forever, but I should never have let it get this far. I love him, but sometimes love just isn't enough. When I first met him I was so self-conscious about my weight, so down about myself, and I felt so elated that he liked me anyway

233

and wanted to be with me. But then when I lost all the weight, he was constantly putting me down; reminding me that it was him who had helped me get to where I was. He was continually pointing out how much I needed him, to the point that in the end, I believed it. I felt like I couldn't be without him, but I know now that he's just controlling and manipulating me. Even being thinner, I'm not the most confident person in the world, and that's just something that I need to work on. I need to learn to love myself for who I am inside, and I'm fine with that.'

'What are you going to do?' Kim asked. 'We'll help in any way we can.'

Emma looked at them both gratefully. 'Thank you so much. I really appreciate you coming to find me. I don't know what to do now really. But I do know the first thing I need to do is get this dress off,' she half smiled. 'I'm aware of how peculiar I look.'

'Nah,' Holly smiled warmly, and squeezed her hand. 'We're in Vegas. Seeing women in wedding dresses at all hours of the day is the norm.'

They stood up, making their way to the exit.

'That reminds me,' Emma said sheepishly. 'There's something I have to tell you about what happened last night.'

Kim's phone started ringing and she answered it, looking pleased to see it was Andy calling.

'Hi, everything okay?' She stood still as she listened to Andy speak. 'I'm at the Bellagio Hotel. Something has happened. Why?' Kim turned her back on them and walked off to talk alone.

'I forgot all about that,' Emma said as they waited for Kim.

'Forgot all about what?'

'Andy. It was supposed to be a surprise. He was coming to the wedding. He's here in Vegas.'

Chapter 33

Kim

'Seriously?' Kim asked, her mouth opening in disbelief. 'Where are you? This isn't a joke, is it?'

'No, I promise you. I'm at the wedding chapel, but they're telling me it's not going ahead or something. What's going on?' he asked, bemused. 'I'm not at the wrong place, am I?"

'The wedding is off,' Kim told him gravely, a million questions going through her mind.

'Seriously?'

'Emma changed her mind. Holly and I are with her now.'

'Goodness. I guess I'll head to my hotel then if you can come and meet me.'

'Course. Where is it?'

'I actually booked a really nice room for us at The Wynn where the wedding was supposed to be happening. I arranged it all with Emma – are you surprised?'

Kim's heartbeat was echoing in her ears. 'Yes, I can't believe it,' she managed. 'Who has…'

'Your parents have the children,' he interjected, obviously

knowing this was going to be a concern for her. 'Don't worry. They couldn't wait to spend the night over at their house.'

Kim felt a mixture of happiness and worry. She couldn't actually believe that Andy was here in Vegas! She couldn't wait to see him, but she also knew it was time to have the important talk. Kim felt sick with apprehension and distress. Surely her husband still loved her if he'd come all the way out to Vegas as a surprise?

'Meet me at the hotel reception,' she told him, 'I'm leaving now.'

'See you soon.'

Kim span round to the others, unable to contain her smile as she looked at Emma's grin.

'I can't believe Andy is here and you kept it a secret! I'm so shocked!'

'He told me to keep it quiet,' she explained. 'I nearly slipped up a few times, to be honest. I bet he feels like it's a bit of a wasted trip now the wedding isn't going ahead.'

'Vegas is never a wasted trip,' Holly replied with a smile.

'I'll speak to you after, girls,' Kim said, making her way down to where the taxis were.

'Good luck,' Holly said with feeling, giving Kim's hand a quick squeeze.

Fifteen minutes later, Kim was walking through the main entrance of the Wynn Hotel.

Andy's face broke into a huge smile as he saw Kim approach in the long, floaty dusty pink dress she'd bought especially for the wedding. Her hair had been curled by Holly and then put up into a loose braid, a few tendrils coming down.

'Hello,' he greeted her, taking her into his arms and kissing her lips. 'You look absolutely beautiful.'

Kim could tell he really meant it and she realized that these days Andy rarely saw her with her make-up done and hair styled. There was hardly any point when she wasn't going anywhere nice, was there? Her appearance was something else she didn't make much effort with any more and she vowed to change this. Not every day of course, but she'd missed seeing Andy look at her in this way. She missed feeling really good about herself.

'I can't believe you're really here,' Kim said, holding onto him and feeling safe in his large arms. 'I'm so happy to see you, Andy,' she gazed at him earnestly. 'Let's go to the room; I need to talk to you.'

They walked into the suite that Andy had booked, discussing Emma's decision to call the wedding off. It was huge with a gorgeous view of the strip, a private terrace and even a hot tub in the bathroom. 'Wow, Andy. This must have cost a fortune,' Kim said, taken aback.

'I wanted to treat you,' he exclaimed, his eyes bright. 'We rarely get time to ourselves any more. I thought it would be nice.'

'It's lovely. Thank you,' she said, sitting on the bed and pulling the fabric of her dress down.

Andy sat on the bed, leaning his head on the headboard. 'What did you need to talk about?'

Kim faltered, feeling uneasy. 'I don't really know how to begin.' She paused, forcing herself to say the words. 'I'm just going to come out and say it though. I should have mentioned it the moment I stumbled upon the messages.'

His nostrils flared. 'What messages?'

Kim cleared her throat. 'Andy, is there something going on between you and Lily? You were in the garden the day I got the wedding invite to come here, and your phone beeped. I saw the messages on your phone from her.'

Andy's brow crinkled and his eyes widened as he stared at her for several beats. 'No, of course not. We're friends. There is absolutely nothing going on between us and there never will be. I can't believe you would think that.' He looked devastated.

She scrutinized him, becoming aware of her heartbeat: an urgent hammering. 'Really? Even though the messages were flirty and completely inappropriate when you're married? She called you "hot stuff" for Christ's sake. What was I supposed to think?

237

You've been liking her Instagram selfies and she's been liking your photos too and making comments. Please, don't lie to me if there is something going on. I need to know…'

'I swear to you Kim, there's nothing there. Not like that.' His voice was even and clear, his pupils huge. 'I know you won't believe me, but Lily was complaining how she never gets any likes on Instagram so I said I'd like her photos. I can't stop her liking mine. "Hot stuff" is a joke too; nobody seriously uses that term. I can assure you that's her just messing about.'

The relief that he was telling her he wasn't having an affair was instantaneous, but Kim was still dubious about what he was saying. Would Andy lie to her?

'So why have you been entertaining those messages? It's obvious she has a thing for you. I'm not stupid, Andy. Please don't treat me as if I've made all this up in my head.'

'Okay,' Andy said calmly. 'Maybe Lily does have a thing for me. She's mentioned a few things previously which leads me to believe that perhaps she likes me as more than a friend, but Kim, she knows I would never, ever dream of going there with her. I love *you* and she knows that.'

'Then why not just tell her to stop messaging you like that? Why are you even replying?' she demanded, feeling a shot of betrayal all over again. 'I would never do that to you!'

Andy stared into space and heaved a sigh, a thick vein appearing on his forehead. 'I guess I was flattered, I don't know,' he said helplessly, shaking his head and looking mortified. 'I'm sorry to say that, but I guess it's the truth. But you're right, I should have told her to stop. I wouldn't have liked it if a man had been sending you messages like that and you'd replied and entertained it. I would be angry. It was wrong of me. I'm so sorry, but I swear on Mylo and Willow's lives, that nothing has ever happened or ever will. I would never cheat on you, but I should have stopped those messages. It's disrespectful and I crossed the line.'

Kim believed him. She knew Andy couldn't lie. Thankfully, he was a terrible liar. She once caught him lying about what he'd been up to when he was arranging her surprise birthday party. He couldn't make eye contact and his cheeks turned a shade of pink; Kim had known straight away he was up to something.

'Did Lily ever make a move on you?' She had to know.

'No, nothing like that. She just flirts, that's all.'

'And you flirt back?'

'I brush her comments away and make a joke of things all the time…' he stammered, looking out of his depth, 'you know, try to lighten the mood, but I wouldn't exactly call my behaviour flirty. I just should have nipped it all in the bud from the very start and I'm sorry,' he said ruefully.

Kim was still so upset with him. She knew it would take a lot more than 'sorry' to ever get those messages out of her head. 'Are you happy with me? With us?' she ventured.

The thought of Andy entertaining Lily hurt like hell. Just the thought of another woman acting all coquettish towards her husband made her livid. But it was also a wake-up call.

Andy scratched his beard. 'Yes,' he said with certainty, 'though I would love to spend a bit more alone time together. I wish you would come out more with our friends like you used to. I kind of miss the old you. But I do understand that the children come first and things have changed…' he broke off. 'I love the kids to bits, but if I'm really honest, sometimes I think you need to relax a little with them. Let them play without following one step behind them, ready to catch them if they fall. You need to let them breathe a bit.'

'Andy, as much as I'm not happy about those messages, *I'm* also sorry,' Kim replied, swallowing hard. 'I've had a long time to think since I first found them and I've not really been the best wife over the past few years, have I? I don't agree with how you've behaved about the whole Lily thing and I'm not going to pretend I'm not angry about it, but I can't be too shocked at you for enjoying a bit of attention from her, not when I haven't been giving you any.'

Andy stared at her, looking pained. 'I still shouldn't have ever made you feel worried about us, about me. I want you to be able to trust me. Do you?'

'Yes, strangely enough, I think I do.' Kim stared into his grey eyes. 'I always felt so guilty when Mylo was born, what with the cot...'

'That was *not* your fault,' Andy reminded her.

Kim nodded. 'Do you remember how tiny he was when he was born? When I first saw how delicate he was with those tiny little tubes coming out of him, something changed inside of me. But focusing so much on him and Willow has meant that I haven't given any of my time to you, or even let you in.'

Andy looked into space thoughtfully. 'When I got that call that you were in labour, I was in such a state of shock. I was so frightened, but I knew I had to be strong for you and the baby. I didn't know whether I was coming or going. I remember one of the first things you said to me when he was whisked away to intensive care.'

'What?' Kim had been completely out of it. She was sure that Andy had never told her this before.

'You said you were sorry.' Andy blinked several times. 'Even though I told you none of it was your fault, I knew you didn't quite believe me. I knew you were struggling with it all and I did try to tell you it was just one of those things. But I should have offered you more support. I should have made you take a break from time to time rather than just letting you deal with everything because you always said you had it under control. I should have been there more and tried...'

'You *have* been there, Andy,' Kim assured him. 'I just think I've shut you out.'

'I do want to be a good father, Kim. Our family means everything to me. I'm just scared of always doing things wrong, or not how you like them to be,' he explained. 'You're a fantastic mum, the very best, so I don't want to complain about that, but I've just always felt a bit excluded and inadequate no matter how hard I've tried. I can't exactly say you make me feel wanted or particularly loved. I know how childish and pathetic that sounds,' he admitted.

Kim had been right about his feelings, as she had always known, deep down. Things had to change – now.

'I'm going to work on chilling out a bit where the children are concerned, I promise. I want it to be different and I never want you to feel like you're not needed. You are, Andy; more than you'll ever know. The children adore you. After seeing those messages and worrying about what was going on with Lily, it's made me realize I need to change my ways too.'

'I should have said how I felt before, I'm aware of that. I don't know why I haven't ever voiced these feelings to you before. I've gone about everything the wrong way,' he shook his head looking disappointed with himself. 'I should never have just pretended everything was fine. We should have talked about this a long time ago and got help.'

'I have to agree with you.'

'Do you forgive me?' He looked sick with anxiety. 'I promise I never intended for *anything* to happen between us. I love you and would never be unfaithful to you; I have far too much at stake.'

Kim exhaled slowly. 'I want to move on from this, yes. I can't say I don't feel upset with you, because I do, but I think we have something too special here to throw away just because of this.'

He appeared elated. 'It makes me so happy to hear you say that. I can promise you too, I'll have a word with Lily and tell her the texts, Instagram and whatever, needs to stop. You have my word. I'll even move schools if it makes you happy. I can't apologize enough about it, but it never meant anything. Not to me.'

'I don't know how I've changed so much, but being here and having some fun for once has made me come to the conclusion that I need to have a bit of time for myself as well as time for us too. It's so important. Somehow I got a little lost after the children were born. I won't shut you out any more,' she explained, meaning every word.

241

'Come here.' Andy patted the bed next to him.

Kim lay beside him, running her fingers through his thick, dark hair. She kissed him, unable to remember the last time they'd spent some moments like this. It felt good. Kim fell asleep the moment her head hit the pillow most nights and it always felt like before she knew it, Mylo was tapping her to wake her up or Willow was screaming from her cot. Their kissing became more heated and Kim pulled the duvet of the bed down, signalling for Andy to join her. As his hands roamed under the covers, Kim felt her body tingle, as though it was the first time they'd explored each other's bodies. Why didn't they do this more often? she asked herself as she gasped for breath. She felt the passion coming off them in waves as Andy pulled the zip of her dress down.

Just by talking through their problems, Kim already felt closer to Andy. She felt he now understood how Mylo's birth had affected her, making her feel the need to take control where their children were concerned, but in fact, she needed Andy just as much as he needed her. There was still a long way to go and it would take time to get back to how they once were, she knew that. There would be more conversations and serious discussions, but as Andy bit her lip gently, Kim decided that for now they could put it to one side.

Chapter 34

Kim

It was the day after the wedding was supposed to have taken place and instead of waking up hungover and tired next to Holly, Kim was waking up wrapped in Andy's arms feeling deliriously happy and finally at ease.

'Good morning,' Andy smiled widely, kissing her nose.

They had spent the entire day watching films, lying in bed and ordering room service. It had been *amazing*. Kim had been reminded of a time when it had been just the two of them, no interruptions, no responsibilities. She felt as though they had reconnected. Why hadn't she ever taken Andy up on his offer before?

'I've texted your mum and she said the children are fine,' Andy said, glancing at his mobile, which he took off the charger.

'Oh really? Maybe I'll call…' Kim stopped herself. 'Okay, great.' She didn't need to call. Her mother was perfectly capable of handling them for a few nights. Andy had explained the previous day that he'd changed her flight so she could stay an extra couple of days with him. Kim couldn't wait to see the children, but she told herself she and Andy needed this time together. A few nights was absolutely nothing, and Andy told Kim that her mother was thrilled to be getting them for so long.

'Shall I order breakfast in bed?' Andy raised an eyebrow.

'You know what, I think I've seen enough of this bed. Fancy going out somewhere instead?' Kim checked her phone and saw she had a few messages from Holly. 'Holly and Emma are going to a pool if you fancy it?'

'I'll have breakfast with you, go to the gym for a bit and then meet you afterwards. Sound like a plan? Unless you want to join me in the gym?'

Kim pulled a face. 'I'll meet you after,' she kissed him.

Two hours later and Kim was lying on a sun lounger next to Holly and Emma.

Emma had been too afraid to go out much the day before, embarrassed to bump into any of Charlie's or her own family. She'd switched her phone off and she and Holly had done the same thing that Kim had done with Andy: hibernated in the hotel room and eaten junk food.

'Yesterday was exactly what she needed; she'd been pretty tearful for most of the day,' Holly told Kim when Emma went to the bar.

Emma told them all about the wedding ceremony with the stranger, Luke, one of the guys they had met on the night of her hen do. Kim had been astonished; thank goodness the ceremony hadn't been legal, otherwise it would be causing Emma even more hassle and stress than she was already going through.

Emma walked back over, handing them a bottle of water each.

'So you and Andy are okay then?' Holly asked.

'I didn't even realize anything was wrong,' Emma pointed out.

'I think we are, yes,' Kim replied, explaining for Emma's sake what had been going on between them since Mylo's birth .

'I'm so glad you were able to talk it through,' Emma said.

'And now you have a few more days to just enjoy being alone together again.'

Kim nodded. 'I'm loving the idea of relaxing with Andy for a bit longer. He's so sweet coming out here and arranging it all without me knowing.'

'You'll have a lovely time, but personally I'm glad we planned to go home today. I'm dreading the thought of seeing anyone,' Emma told them as they laid out in the sunshine, rubbing suncream into their warm skin. 'I'm also so pleased that Charlie and I hadn't booked a honeymoon. That would be even more wasted money. We always said we wouldn't need one straight after Vegas and we planned to go away somewhere nice in the winter. I do hope he's doing okay,' she said, sounding glum. 'He won't reply to my messages and I really can't blame him; he probably despises me.'

'Give him time,' Holly said wisely. 'It's still so fresh and raw. He's hurting.'

'Have you had a nice time, despite me calling off the wedding?' Emma asked, squinting in the sunshine.

Holly paused. 'You know what, I've had a lovely time, but I honestly cannot wait to get home to see Lottie and Jacob. I was saying to Kim the other day, sometimes I feel like I've lost a little part of my old self being a single mum; it can be such hard work. Exhausting. But being without them, even for just a short while, makes me realize how truly lucky I am to have them. They're everything to me. They're my life,' she said, looking a little emotional. 'I feel guilty for being so eager to get away. As soon as Rob told me his news I knew I had to come here. I'm not going to beat myself up about the fact it may take a while to get used to our new set-up with Nikki in the picture now. It's a massive change in all our lives. I feel like now I've accepted it, it'll easier for me to move on and focus on myself. Maybe I'm not entirely against eventually meeting the right person when the time is right. Until then though, I'm just going to focus on spending time with my children and my friends.'

'That sounds like a plan,' Kim said. 'You shouldn't feel guilty about wanting to get away either. I agree, it's not always easy and we all need a break sometimes. This is something that I've learnt too. I know I'm thankful I came. Coming to Vegas has helped me address some important issues and now we can move on.'

Emma nodded. 'If you ever need to talk about it, we're here for you.'

'Thanks.' Kim flashed her a grateful smile.

'No matter what happens, we all have each other.'

It was the truth, and it gave Kim a surge of comfort and hope. She was incredibly lucky to have some great friends in her life and she wished she'd told them about her plight sooner. Nothing ever seemed so bad when you had people who would always be there for you.

'Oh shit,' Emma hissed, ducking down. 'Max and Callum are over there. Have they seen us?'

Kim's eyes flew over to where they were walking. Callum nodded at her in acknowledgement, and she knew there was no going back then. It was too late to hide. They were on their way over. Kim glanced at Holly who sat up, holding her head high.

'I feel so uncomfortable,' Emma whispered, squinting in the sunshine.

'Alright girls,' Max flashed them a radiant smile, full of bravado despite his recent actions.

'Hi,' Emma said gently, sitting herself up and looking a little nervous.

'How are you feeling, Em?' Callum asked softly.

'Terrible,' Emma replied gloomily. 'Guilty. Like the worst person in the world. Sad. I don't know…'

'You did what you needed to do,' Max told her reassuringly. 'If it wasn't right, it wasn't right. Charlie will find someone else one day.'

'Don't beat yourself up about it,' Callum told her kindly.

'It's not as though you made loads of people travel halfway

246

round the world or anything,' Max put in. 'That was a joke by the way.'

No-one laughed.

'When are you girls leaving?' Callum asked.

'A bit later this afternoon,' Holly replied.

'Our flight is this evening,' Callum said.

'Anyway girls, we're going to love and leave you. I'll text you Holly, yeah? We'll meet up when we're back,' Max dared to say confidently, 'go to that restaurant I was talking about or something.'

Holly laughed sardonically. 'No thanks.'

Max flinched as she said the words, clearly not the answer he was expecting. 'No?'

'The answer is no.' Her voice was cutting. Brutal. 'I think we'll leave our little romance in Vegas,' she told him in a patronizing voice. 'Probably for the best. I don't plan on being one of your *many* women, as tempting as it is. But thanks all the same.'

Max's face fell, his gaze sweeping to Kim as she looked at her nails uncomfortably. It was obvious she'd told Holly what he'd done. So what? She wanted to shout at him. *So what, Max?* As if she was going to let her best friend get involved with the likes of him. He had no respect for women. He was a complete dick.

'Fine,' he shrugged, trying to appear completely unfazed or bothered. He wasn't fooling any of them though. 'If that's the way you want to be,' he shrugged and forced a laugh. 'Your loss, not mine.'

The atmosphere was suddenly awkward and no-one knew what to say or where to look.

'Come on then, Callum, I don't think we're wanted here,' he tried to seem as though he thought the whole situation was amusing. 'See you later, girls.'

'Safe journey back,' Emma mumbled.

Callum cringed as he followed Max. 'Bye girls. Lovely meeting you all.'

They watched Max saunter over to a group of girls, Callum following behind, not paying much attention and speaking to someone on his phone before walking off alone so he could hear better.

'He's just so full of it,' Kim pointed out in distaste.

'Honestly, I'm watching him now and wondering how I was so blinded,' Holly said in disbelief, shaking her head.

'I guess he does look sleazy,' Emma turned up her nose. 'I didn't realize he was this bad, I swear to you.'

They were staring as he put his arm around a curvy blonde who seemed to edge away, only for him to get closer. She clearly wasn't interested but Max didn't seem to notice.

'It's actually embarrassing to watch,' Kim clenched her teeth. 'It's like he's doing it to show off to you, Holly. Men and their bruised egos.'

'I was thinking that,' Emma agreed. 'He wants you to see it.'

'Oh dear,' Holly giggled, when two beefy-looking men bowled over to the girls, their expressions livid. 'Looks like their boyfriends aren't too pleased with his womanizing ways.'

'Oh shit,' Kim gaffawed, 'that one just pushed him.'

The girls sat there open-mouthed as Max pushed the huge muscly man back, before being punched in the eye and falling backwards into the pool.

After seeing Max float to the top, holding his eye, which looked like it was already turning a shade of purple, and looking embarrassed, the girls burst out laughing, lying down on the sunbed and holding their stomachs.

Kim chuckled as she watched Max pulling himself from the pool looking sorry for himself. It didn't seem as though his luck was about to improve when the security man escorted him out of the party.

'I think I may have wet myself a little bit,' Holly snorted.

Emma wiped her eyes. 'That really served him right.'

It looked like Max's ego wasn't the only thing bruised that day and Kim continued to laugh a real belly laugh along with Holly and Emma. There was nothing quite like laughing with your best friends and she couldn't wait for the future; she would always make it a priority to make more time for them. They were true friends who would share joys and sorrows. There would be the inevitable twists and turns of life but their journey would be made sweeter by sharing it together.

'That's cheered me right up,' Emma giggled, holding up her glass. 'Cheers girls. To Vegas.'

'To Vegas.'

They clinked glasses for the last time that trip.

Chapter 35

Emma

Emma sat waiting in the bar anxiously, her legs crossed on the tall bar. She automatically went to click onto her Instagram account, before remembering that she'd deleted it. It was astounding how many times a day she still went to check it. She was struggling without it and she admitted that she actually relied on it to keep her company when she had spare time. Just a quick post or browse to see what others were posting. All part of her daily routine. Or was it all part of a daily obsession? Perhaps she needed it just a little too much? It had only been suspended for the past day, and already, Emma felt as though she was missing something.

'Thanks for meeting me,' she said, her heart crawling into her throat. Why did she feel so scared? 'I got you a lemonade; I assumed you wouldn't be drinking because of the flight home and remembered that was the soft drink you normally had.'

'We've actually changed our flight,' Frankie said, clearing his throat. He ran his fingers through his dark hair, sitting down next to her. 'It was Charlie's idea. He wanted to have a few days with the lads. Drown his sorrows I guess. He couldn't face going back just yet.' He was cool and straight-faced.

Emma nodded slowly. If there were ever a place to get over someone, it was Vegas. Charlie would be partying until the early hours every night, she could just imagine. Frankie, who wasn't as much as a party-goer, would just tag along and follow him; anything Charlie wanted. He was such a loyal, caring cousin, but she did at times feel as though their relationship was a bit one-sided. She recalled once how Charlie wouldn't pick Frankie up when his car broke down because it was late and he was too tired. Instead he'd sent him the phone numbers of companies that could help. Emma had been asleep at the time or she would have gone herself, and Charlie hadn't told her about it until the next morning when she woke up. Then there was the time when Frankie was moving house and needed a set of extra hands to help move all the furniture.

'Why doesn't he just get a removal company?' Charlie had huffed. 'I've been invited to the football today.'

Charlie had gone to help, but only for a few hours after the game, and that was because Emma had told him he should do it. Frankie would have done it in a heartbeat if it had been the other way round.

Then there was Charlie's mother, Jean. Charlie was always commenting that Frankie was her 'golden boy' and the 'son she wished she had.' Emma could see that Charlie was jealous of their close relationship. He wasn't overly close to either of his parents, whereas Frankie had a lovely relationship with them. Emma had always told him to make more of an effort if he felt that way, but nothing had ever changed. She'd often felt bad for Frankie; after all, it wasn't his fault that he got on so well with Charlie's mother.

She couldn't blame Charlie for staying in Vegas, but what Charlie did was none of her business any more. Not knowing what he was up to gave her a weird, uneasy feeling, but more than anything Emma just felt relieved she didn't have to worry about him any more. 'How is he?' she asked.

'Honestly?' Frankie raised his eyebrows. 'He's not doing well. I'm worried about him. He loved you, Em. It will take some time to get over the fact that you left him on the day of your wedding,' he looked up, his bright hazel eyes taking in her traumatized expression, 'but hey, I'm sure he will be fine. He's a strong man; one of the strongest I know, in fact. It's better you didn't marry him if your heart wasn't in it. How have you been holding up?' He looked as though he genuinely cared. 'I noticed you deleted your Instagram account.'

So he'd checked on her, Emma realized, the thought lifting her spirits a little. He'd noticed she was gone. 'I'm taking a break from it for a while. I'm not sure for how long yet. It's my only source of income, so I know I'll have to go back on it soon. The break feels good though. It's refreshing. I'm not feeling my best at the moment,' she revealed quietly. 'I just wish I'd ended things sooner rather than try to convince myself that everything was going to be okay. I loved Charlie, but our relationship was far more complicated than anybody realized.' She shook her head, picturing Charlie's crestfallen face when she'd broken it off. 'Listen, Frankie, I wanted to thank you for helping me on my wedding morning. Thank you for rescuing me the night before too, just like you've done so many other nights. You've always been there when I needed someone.'

'It's nothing, don't worry about it.' Frankie shot her a natural smile.

'I guess I won't be seeing much of you now Charlie and I have split up, will I? Who will look after me now?' Her eyes were bright and watery. It had only just dawned on her that she wouldn't just be losing Charlie, but Frankie too. The thought saddened her more than she liked to admit. In fact, she couldn't bear it. Couldn't they still remain friends at the very least?

'You seem to have some good friends,' Frankie said, but he sounded gloomy about the situation too.

Emma hesitated before speaking. She had nothing to lose so

she was going to just come out and say it. 'Frankie, that thing I said to you about feeling happy when I thought it was you I had married, it's the truth. I can't stop thinking about how I feel. It was like I was supposed to have been with you all along.'

Frankie looked into the distance, his mouth twitching awkwardly.

There was silence as he digested her words.

Emma continued. 'There's something between us, Frankie. I just know there is. You feel it too, don't you?' Her voice was strained and her palms were sweaty. .

Frankie groaned. 'You can't do this, Emma. You can't say these things to me. Charlie is my *cousin*. He's been there for me ever since my father died when I was twelve. Checking up on me, lending me money when I was younger and inviting me out with him. We had nothing when my father died and my mother was always working. It wasn't her fault but she was never there for me when I needed it, so Charlie's mother was like a mother figure to me. I owe them. I owe *him*.'

Emma nodded. She knew the score already. She knew how much Charlie's family meant to him. 'You feel it too though, don't you? If you don't, if I'm imagining it, then just tell me. Please. I need to know.'

'Yes, okay,' he answered, staring at her, 'I do like you. As more than a friend. I always have done. But it doesn't matter, none of it does, because I can *never* do anything about it. I could never act upon my feelings. Don't you see that?' he said sadly, squeezing her hand. 'It doesn't matter that you and Charlie are no longer together; there's an unwritten rule between us, and I can't, I won't break it. Not when Charlie has been so good to me.'

Usually when someone told you they liked you back, you felt happy, euphoric even. But not this time. Emma felt even more desolate than she had before. Their feelings for each other didn't matter. They had to be shut out. *Ignored.* At that present moment, it felt impossible. The thing was, Emma didn't even believe that

253

Charlie *had* been that good to Frankie. She knew all the snide remarks he made about him behind his back. Not that she would ever say it and hurt his feelings.

'Can we still be friends at least?' Emma asked hopefully.

'It's going to be difficult, Em. You know I don't want to lose you just as much as you don't want to lose me, but…'

'Charlie,' Emma interjected sourly, 'I get it.' She looked around the room, envious of everyone around her who seemed so relaxed and carefree. She glanced at her watch, suddenly wanting to get away. Wanting to run and cry in her own private space. 'I best get going. I need to leave soon because of my flight,' she told him. It wasn't a lie; she actually didn't have much time to spare.

Frankie nodded and stood up. He was tall and strong and she felt safe as he wrapped her in his arms. 'You take care now.' His voice was controlled, low and deep.

Emma clasped his back tightly, before pulling back. She kissed him softly on the lips and he didn't hesitate. It just felt right. 'Goodbye, Frankie.'

'Bye, Emma.'

As she walked away from him, she felt heartbroken. After how she'd treated Charlie, she deserved this pain, she told herself. As she glanced back at Frankie, her own torment was mirrored in his expression, and she understood at that moment that she loved Frankie.

But sometimes love just wasn't enough.

Chapter 36

Holly

'How has she been?' Holly asked her mother as she held Lottie tightly in her arms. She felt her eyes well up. She knew it was impossible, but Lottie looked more grown up somehow. Her hair was longer. Her feet looked like they'd grown. Had she really been that tall when Holly had left? She never wanted to let her go. Her hair smelt freshly washed like apples. Probably one of the overpriced shampoos she'd purchased with brightly coloured packaging, aimed at kids. Her children were always clean and smelt lovely when her mother took care of them.

'She's been fine, haven't you, darling?'

Lottie nodded, looking proud of herself. 'The nurse at the hospital told me I have to be very careful, Mummy.'

'You *do* have to be careful, sweetheart,' Holly smiled at her, holding her tightly once more. 'No more jumping on the bed.'

'That's like the monkey song, Mummy,' Lottie beamed at her.

'That's right,' Holly laughed warmly.

Jacob was still having his nap, but Holly had already been in to him to give him a huge kiss. Nap-time was normally her happy hour. Her hour of freedom to tidy up, catch up on her favourite Netflix series or do some laundry, but today, Holly couldn't wait for it to be over. She was longing to hold her son and kiss him all over. To have both her children by her side.

'Thank you so much for having them, Mum. I can't believe this all happened when I was away. I'm never going away without them again,' she said emotionally.

'A little break away from time to time won't hurt you, dear,' Edna said, pursing her lips thoughtfully. 'It was just terrible timing that Lottie decided to have an accident. I was terrified, honestly. Rob was so good though; he came and collected Jacob straight away. He's been on the phone constantly. His girlfriend, Nikki, seems nice too. I'd say he's picked a decent girl there; seems to have her head screwed on.'

'I still feel so bad that I thought it was his fault,' Holly said quietly so Lottie didn't overhear. 'He must think I'm such a bitch the way I spoke to him. I'll have to call him again to apologize. He's acting fine about it, but I feel terrible.'

'You were just worried, that's all. Shock can make you say things you don't mean. Anyway, I'm just glad you had a good time away, that's all. I can't believe the wedding never actually happened though. That's unheard of.'

'It was a good thing, trust me,' Holly told her, her face darkening as she thought of the man Emma almost got herself tied to. She pulled Lottie in again and kissed her cheek. 'I'm just happy to be home with my babies where I belong.'

'Meet anyone nice while you were away?' Edna raised an eyebrow.

She just couldn't help herself, Holly thought fondly. Ever the optimist that Holly would fall in love. Callum flashed through her mind, but she knew her mother would ask question after question if she so much as mentioned him, and Holly wasn't exactly sure how she would even answer. It was complicated. 'No,' Holly told her, focusing on Lottie's cast and running her fingers along the white plaster, 'no-one of importance, Mum.'

If anything, meeting Max had just reaffirmed that Holly didn't need a man in her life. It certainly wasn't something she would search for for the time being. If she met someone at some point who was right for her, then great, she wasn't opposed to the idea any longer, but if she didn't, Holly was content with her lot. She was incredibly lucky to have her family.

Edna stayed for lunch and Holly had a lovely afternoon with her children. Jacob had woken up happy, delighted that Holly had returned. He kept running back into the kitchen to check she was still there, running into her arms and chuckling with laughter. She felt as though her heart would burst with love for her children. Of course she realized she was in a happy bubble, which would eventually burst, life returning to normality. She knew that the whining would start at some point. Holly was aware that Lottie would be moaning that Jacob had picked up a piece of her puzzle or the dummy of her doll, but for now the children seemed to be just as thrilled with her return as Holly felt.

At that moment, everything was perfect.

Chapter 37

Six Months Later

Holly

Holly still couldn't believe that Lottie was now at primary school. As she waved goodbye and watched her run happily through the school gate, she felt a wave of sadness: where had her little baby gone? Jacob was sound asleep in his pushchair. It was so strange now, being just the two of them, but Lottie was loving her big school and she was thriving, so Holly was thankful for that. As Holly walked a little further along the road, she was shocked to see Callum in front of her with his daughter. She felt light-headed suddenly, nervous yet tingly with excitement. Eva was wearing the same uniform as Lottie; she'd had no idea their children attended the same school. She'd never seen him there before, but felt delighted it might mean she would be seeing him around more.

'Long time no see,' Callum grinned widely as they came face to face.

He looked taller than Holly remembered, clearly over six foot and as handsome as ever with a sharp jaw, angular cheekbones and muscular strong arms on show in his gym clothes. Somehow his smooth, flawless skin was still tanned, making his striking green eyes stand out as much as ever.

'Wait there a sec, I'll just drop Eva at the gates.'

Holly watched him kiss and cuddle his little girl before she walked off and her heart melted a little. A few moments later, Callum walked briskly back to Holly's side.

'I didn't realize Eva was at Lottie's school; she's really enjoying it there.'

'It's a really good school,' Callum told her. 'It's scary when you have to first let them go, but Eva loves it.'

'How have you been?' Holly asked, pleased to see him. 'I haven't seen you since Vegas.'

'Good. Not much new to report really. What about you? Ah, he's gorgeous,' he said, peering at Jacob lying in the pushchair. 'How old is he now?'

'Nearly two now,' Holly smiled proudly. 'He's actually quite an easy baby now. Turned a corner. I'm sure this will all change when he hits the terrible twos though,' she giggled affectionately.

'Probably,' Callum smiled at her. 'How have you been?'

'Really good thanks,' Holly replied, noticing again how striking his green eyes were. She still felt just as attracted to him as she had in Vegas. Callum had a kindness about him that Max had lacked and she would forever curse herself for not going for Callum instead. Why had Holly been blinded by Max's cockiness and arrogance? She simply didn't understand how she could've messed up so badly and gone for the wrong friend.

'How's your friend Kim?' Callum asked. 'I've haven't seen Emma in a while either – how is she doing?'

'They're both doing well; I'm going for brunch with them now, funnily enough,' Holly told him, assuming he hadn't seen Emma because she didn't go to the same gym as Charlie any more, which

Callum owned. Far too awkward in case she bumped into him.

'I've opened another gym in London,' Callum told her. 'I work there now instead of the other one where Charlie and Max are. I haven't seen them in a while either. We've kind of lost touch. Charlie has moved to Australia now.'

'Oh really, Australia?' Holly said in surprise. 'I'm walking up here,' she pointed down the road. 'Are you going this way?'

'Yeah, same,' he said.

They walked along chatting as though they'd known each other for years. Callum was so easy to get along with and it felt good to be in his company. He always seemed upbeat and positive. Someone who brought out the best in people and the type of person you wanted to be around. She couldn't help but feel disappointed when she reached her car.

'This was the closest I could get to school today,' she laughed.

'I know,' Callum nodded, 'it's always so busy round these roads in the morning.'

'Here, let me help with that,' Callum suggested kindly, putting the pushchair down for her as Holly carefully carried a sleeping Jacob into his car seat. Holly opened the boot and Callum put it inside for her.

'Thanks, you didn't have to do that,' Holly said gratefully.

'Don't be silly,' Callum said, glancing at his watch. 'I'd better be on my way. Can't be late today as a new trainer is starting and I need to show her round. My offices are in London, which is why I have to dash as I need to make the train.'

'But the train station is the other way?' Holly said, perplexed. She thought he'd said he was going in the same direction? He'd obviously just said that because he wanted to walk with her. She felt a burst of unexpected excitement. 'Yeah, it is,' he replied distractedly, looking down the road. 'Listen, Holly, do you fancy meeting up sometime? Going for a coffee or a drink or something?'

He looked unsure of himself, and Holly realized she found

this attractive about him. Unlike Max, Callum didn't know how handsome he was. He didn't even know that Holly liked him.

'I'd really like that,' Holly said shyly. She felt really good about going out with Callum, as though she was in safe hands.

Maybe they would just remain friends, but who knew? Maybe it would be more than that; Holly was eager to see what the future held. She had a very good feeling about it.

Callum smiled broadly. 'Great. I guess I'd better take your number then?'

Thirty minutes later, Holly was sitting in a café with Kim as they waited for Emma.

'Oh my goodness, really?' Kim gaped at her in amazement. 'You and Callum actually make a great couple; I think it's great you've agreed to a date,' she said encouragingly.

Holly smiled warmly at her friend. 'You're getting a bit carried away here, don't you think? It's just a coffee or a drink. It may not even lead anywhere.'

Kim eyed her suspiciously. 'I have a feeling it's going to be more than that. Call me psychic or something, I don't know. But I think this could be start of something for you.'

Holly could only smile; she had that feeling also and she had no idea why.

'We'll see. How are you and Andy doing?' she asked Kim.

Since Vegas, Kim and Andy's relationship had taken a positive direction and they'd recently had an offer accepted on a new house. Opening up to each other had actually made their relationship stronger than ever, and they had just come back from a weekend in Amsterdam without the children. Holly was so thrilled for her friend. Kim loved Andy with all her heart; it would have been such a huge waste and shame if their marriage had ended.

Kim's face burst into a smile. 'We've actually agreed that as soon as we move into the new house, we're going to try for another baby. I can't wait,' she grinned, her face beatific.

Holly beamed back at her friend. 'Oh Kim, that's wonderful news. I'm so pleased for the pair of you.'

'I know. It's so lovely spending family days out together; the kids just love being with Andy. Sometimes I feel like I'm the odd one out now!' she laughed, sipping her coffee and looking cheerful and optimistic.

Holly gaze swept over to the entrance and she smiled broadly at Emma, who was walking through the door.

Holly and Emma stood up to kiss her hello.

'God, it's cold out there,' Emma groaned, removing her jacket.

She looked so well, as always. Her skin was glowing and healthy (she'd probably been given some free facials and skin products), her hair was shiny and even down to her perfect nails, she was immaculate. There was something else about her though, Holly realized: Emma looked happy.

After Vegas, Emma had decided to be more honest on her account and she'd even stopped counting calories and going to the gym as much. She still took care of herself of course, but no longer felt the pressure to be perceived as perfect, so she posted unedited selfies with no make-up on and her feed was full of 'real' images that people could relate to. As soon as she'd reactivated her account, Emma had posted a heart-felt video telling her followers that her relationship hadn't worked out and the wedding hadn't gone ahead; the amount of support she had received was astounding and her Instagram had gone from strength to strength. People loved her sincerity. Recently, she had even been asked to create a jewellery range with a large online company. Her career was better than it had ever been.

'How's work going?' Kim asked her, eyes sparkling. 'I saw one of the necklaces you posted the other day from your range. It looks stunning, Em. You must be so proud of yourself.'

'I'm really busy, but loving every minute,' Emma smiled. 'It sounds strange, but I'm enjoying it a whole lot more now I'm not with Charlie. I feel like I'm finally in control of my own life. Deep down he hated me doing it; he used to roll his eyes every time I asked him to take a shot of me, but I think it was because he was jealous. He made me feel bad about it, as though I was a complete narcissist, obsessed with looking at images of myself.' She paused and then said brightly, 'I make sure I don't post anything at the weekends now. It's my time off from social media, unless I need post something for a company. Having a break from time to time does me the world of good. It allows me to focus on real life. I'm taking time for myself and doing the things I love too; I've started a photography course, which I've always wanted to do. I'm starting to focus on loving myself and building my self-esteem and sense of worth, which isn't always as easy as it sounds.'

'That's great,' Holly chimed supportively. 'I think it's wise to take some time away too. Everyone else does from their jobs – you should be able to as well. I remember you telling me how you always wanted to do photography too; good for you to take time out to do something you enjoy.'

'I think people love the fact you're really true and honest on your social media now too. I was reading the positive comments the other day after you posted that funny photo of you with the double chins,' Kim chuckled.

'That one was hilarious,' Holly agreed.

'Oh I know the one. I went to take a photo and my camera was on selfie mode. I clicked it by accident and the photo came out so horrendous that I couldn't help but share it,' Emma laughed. 'I guess people prefer to see that I'm an ordinary person. I don't always look flawless; nobody does. I get spots and cellulite just like the rest of the women in the world.'

'You're a great role model to young girls,' Kim commented. 'I've always worried about the effect all these unattainable body images all over social media will do for girls like Lottie and Willow when they get older. If only more people did what you do.'

The waitress came over and took their orders.

'So,' Kim said, turning to Emma, 'dating anyone?'

'No,' Emma said easily, 'it's been really nice just focusing on myself and healing from my relationship. I finally feel like the old me again, you know? It's been so refreshing only having to worry about myself for a change.'

Holly hesitated. 'Have you heard from…?'

'Frankie?' Emma cut in, as though she was ready for the question. 'The odd polite text message, but no. Not really,' she tucked her hair behind her ears, the light fading from her eyes.

Emma had told them all about the conversations she'd had with him on the flight home. She loved Frankie, and Holly knew her love for him wouldn't just disappear overnight.

'Probably for the best, eh?' Holly said, trying to sound positive.

Emma flashed them a remorseful smile. 'Yes, I'm sure it is. I heard that Charlie has moved to Australia so at least there's no chance of us two ever bumping into each other again. It would be so hard seeing him.'

'That's good,' Kim agreed. 'Seems like he's doing his best to move on.'

They spent the morning deep in conversation and Holly couldn't wait to tell Emma about bumping into Callum. Since Vegas, the girls had made more of an effort to meet up. Emma didn't even mind tagging along when they went to soft play with Jacob and Willow. They'd had a few nights out too, and it had made Holly understand just how important her friendships were to her. Being close to her friends, Holly felt as though she could do anything. They all did.

Emma's phone beeped and her mouth popped open as she read a message.

'What's up? Who is it?' Kim asked inquisitively, unable to ignore the look of surprise on Emma's face.

'It's Frankie,' Emma said in a brittle voice, looking astounded. 'He wants to meet.'

Chapter 38

Emma

Emma couldn't think straight as she waved goodbye to Kim and Holly. Her mind had been elsewhere as soon as she'd received the message from Frankie, and she hadn't been able to concentrate on anything the girls had said. He wanted to meet her. She hadn't seen him for six months, and the truth was, she'd missed him terribly. The messages she received from him just weren't enough. Looking at photos on social media just made her mind go into overdrive. Where had he been? Who had he been with? Was he seeing anyone? She tried not to look at the ones where he had been with Charlie; it was too sad looking at him after everything that had happened. Luckily, as Charlie had moved to Australia, there hadn't been any of those for months now. The guilt often ate away at her if she thought about him too much, but other than losing Frankie, Emma's life was actually going pretty well. She felt as if she'd been lost for a while and now she was finally back, ready for a new chapter in her life.

She couldn't stop wondering why Frankie wanted to meet her. He was going to her apartment now, so she didn't even have time to quickly add a bit of make-up or anything, but she knew deep down it didn't really matter. Frankie didn't care about things like that.

She felt shaky, her heart fluttering like the wings of a butterfly as she made her way to the entrance of her building. Frankie was already standing there, all six foot one of him, outside her front door wearing a navy scarf and parka coat. His dark hair had grown a little longer and he had stubble when he was usually clean-shaven. It suited him.

His whole face lit up, his hazel eyes sparkling as he noticed her and immediately Emma felt her nerves disintegrate. This was *Frankie*. She didn't have anything to worry about. They embraced as though they hadn't seen each other for six years, let alone six months. He looked better than ever.

'Hello stranger,' Emma smiled widely. 'This was a nice surprise. Come on in,' she said, opening her front door. She'd moved out of the house she'd shared with Charlie and hadn't seen him that day either. Now she was living in her new apartment, enjoying the peace and freedom of being all by herself.

Frankie looked round as he walked in. 'Wow, nice place,' he admired as he looked round. 'Oh God, look how young you are there,' he said, pointing to a photo from years back, which was on her bookcase.

'Look how much larger I am, more like!' Emma let out a small laugh, feeling as though she had to point it out. She was so used to Charlie mentioning it when she'd shown him old photographs; she felt she had to say it.

Frankie stared at the photograph and shrugged. 'I always thought it suited you when you were that size.'

Emma's brows knitted together. 'Really? I was like double the size I am now.'

'Yeah,' Frankie replied in a serious tone. 'You were just a bit curvier then, that's all; you look good either way to me.'

Emma stared at him in disbelief. He honestly didn't realize

how happy his comment made her feel. Charlie had always made it pretty clear that in his eyes, if she gained all her weight back, he would find her unattractive. He had made her believe it too in the end.

'Thanks,' Emma replied shyly.

She made him a cup of tea, remembering just how he liked it.. 'So what made you want to meet up?' she couldn't help but ask him straight away. She needed to know why he was there. She wanted to keep it short and sweet, afraid if she spent too long with him all her feelings would come flooding back, only for to walk away again, leaving her bereft and broken-hearted. She had to know what was going on. It had been a little easier to move on with her life without seeing him for the past six months.

'I just wanted to see you, that's all,' he shrugged, but she knew there was more to it. She could see it in his eyes.

Emma sipped her tea, sitting on the armchair opposite him in the lounge. 'Really? I didn't think it was a good idea, that's all. Don't get me wrong, Frankie, I'm glad you're here. It's great seeing you. I've…' she tailed away, dubious as to whether she should say she'd missed him. She'd told him how she'd felt in Vegas, after all. It hadn't mattered because of Charlie. She wasn't willing to put all her cards on the table again. It was too painful.

'Things change,' he said faintly.

'Like what?' Emma was unsatisfied.

Frankie hunched his shoulders. 'I just want you back in my life, that's all.'

'You said we couldn't see each other because of Charlie though.' Emma was puzzled. 'To be honest, Frankie, I'm not sure it's a good idea me seeing you. I'm actually doing really well and being around you would only make things confusing for me. My feelings,' she knew she had to say it, 'well, they haven't changed since Vegas, but I'm doing okay. I think not seeing you is helping and to be quite frank, I don't think I can be friends with you, I'm sorry,' she shook her head adamantly, 'it's just too difficult.'

He sat there staring at her, as though he wanted to say something but couldn't.

'Perhaps it's best you just drink up and leave,' Emma forced herself to say. 'I can't deny it's been so nice seeing you, and I really don't mean to come across as rude, but I just fear you're going to mess my head up,' she laughed light-heartedly, trying to ease the tension in the room.

'Okay,' he said, putting his coat on and standing up. 'I'm sorry, Emma,' he said. 'The last thing I want is to confuse you.'

Emma swallowed the lump in her throat and walked him to the door.

He turned, gazing at her intently.

'What, Frankie?' Emma frowned, 'what is it you want to say? Just say it,' she pleaded with him.

When he remained silent, Emma turned around to close the door, her eyes burning, threatening tears, when she felt him take her by the arm. He pulled her close and Emma melted into him as he kissed her hard on the mouth. They held each other, kissing hungrily. She couldn't count the amount of times she'd imagined this moment and Emma never wanted it to end.

She gasped for breath. 'What's changed?' she managed, needing to know he wasn't going to change his mind. 'How come you're doing this after all this time?'

'Everything,' Frankie told her seriously. 'I just can't live without you, Emma. There's no-one else for me. I can't stop thinking about you; you're on my mind every single day. I can't even concentrate at work because I want to see you so badly. I heard through the grapevine about the way Charlie had been treating you. You know, all those awful comments he used to make about your job and how he tried to control you.'

'Who did you hear that from?' Emma wondered aloud. To be

fair, she had told people the truth when they asked her why she didn't get married.

'I saw Fran and Danni a few weeks back and they told me things from your side. I only ever heard Charlie's version.'

Emma nodded. Fran and Danni knew the full story; she'd explained it all on a night out when they'd got home from Vegas and they'd been horrified. She gazed at him, wanting to hear what else he had to say.

'I felt so guilty that I hadn't noticed how unhappy he'd been making you, even when you married that random guy the night before the wedding; it had just been a call for help. I was just too blind to see it, telling myself it was just cold feet. A last-minute change of heart. I asked Charlie about his behaviour towards you after I heard about it, and he'd shrugged as though the things he did weren't a big deal. How you were just overreacting and didn't want him to share your limelight. He said some awful things and I stuck up for you, unable to believe I'd never noticed any of this before. He accused me of having feelings for you and when I didn't deny it, he turned on me. That's when he announced he was moving to Australia, telling me to do what the hell I liked because he no longer cared. He had a big falling out with Jean when he left too, and when I stuck up for her as well, he was just rude to me, calling me every name under the sun and telling me never to speak to him again. I've never seen him act so abruptly before; he looked as though he hated me. Perhaps he always has? Jean didn't deserve any of it. He's always had such a problem with our relationship, but he doesn't help himself at all. We tried speaking to him before he left, but he wasn't interested,' he explained, looking a little disconsolate about the situation. 'He's just so stubborn.'

'You don't have to tell me that,' Emma said, holding his hands. 'I'm sorry things didn't end well between you, but don't blame yourself. You've been nothing but a great friend to Charlie and he's never appreciated you.'

269

Frankie kissed her again and Emma was unable to wipe the grin off her face. 'Coming in again?' she asked him, unable to contain her happiness that Frankie was back. She belonged with him, she was certain of it. Nothing had ever felt so right in her entire life.

'You bet I am,' Frankie replied, kissing her neck.

Emma giggled merrily, closing her front door.

Acknowledgements

Firstly I would like to thank my fabulous editor, Charlotte Mursell, and the rest of the amazing team at HQ Digital. Thank you so much for all the enthusiasm and setting me on the right path. I'm so thankful for all of the hard work that goes on behind the scenes, and I'm so grateful you've made me feel so welcome from the start.

My agent at Hardman and Swainson, Hannah Ferguson, and also to the lovely Jo Swainson who was covering at the time of my two-book deal. Thank you for everything you have done.

A big cheer to my family; my husband Terry who is always helpful when I have a deadline, my twins Harry and Darcey (the reason I'm always needing time to meet the deadline), my parents whose support and excitement means everything (as well as the babysitting when I need to write) and also to my friends Danielle, Carolyn and Claire, for listening to me ramble on about my latest storyline.

Last but certainly not least, all my readers. Every message I receive from you puts a smile on my face. Thank you from the bottom of my heart – I hope you've enjoyed this book too.

If you loved *The Morning After the Wedding Before*
then turn the page for an exclusive extract from
'*Tis the Season to Be Single* …

LAURA ZIEPE

'Tis
the Season
to Be
Single

A delightfully uplifting
holiday read!

Chapter 1

'Perhaps he's going to propose?' Grace said cheerfully, her eyes sparkling with excitement as she bent down to arrange a drawer of lipsticks.

Rachel frowned anxiously, biting her lower lip as she stared at the twinkly fairy lights and sparkly giant baubles above. The Christmas decorations had just gone up and they usually put her in a good mood instantly, but not today. Her boyfriend of three years, Mark, had called on her lunch break to check she was coming straight home as he needed to talk to her.

'No, I really don't think that's it,' she replied fretfully. 'He sounded really serious on the phone and Mark is never normally like that. It was as though someone had died. Which they haven't, thank goodness, because it was the first thing I asked when I heard his sombre voice.'

'Well, getting married is a *huge* deal,' Grace pointed out, tucking her shoulder-length dark hair behind her ear. 'He's probably just nervous.' She smiled widely. 'You should have seen Simon when he proposed to me. He was shaking so much I thought he was going to drop the ring.'

Rachel gave a light laugh. 'I'm not so sure…' She tailed off, unable to imagine Mark proposing on such an ordinary day.

Firstly, it was a Wednesday and they didn't have plans that evening to do anything special, and secondly, Christmas was just around the corner. Surely if Mark was going to propose he'd choose to do so on Christmas Day? She could just imagine it at the Christmas table, surrounded by Mark's lovely family as they gushed over the beautiful diamond ring. He wouldn't do it on a random Wednesday at the beginning of November, would he? Rachel felt like she'd been waiting forever for him to propose, but try as she might, she just couldn't imagine that being the reason he needed to talk to her.

'Don't look so worried,' Grace told her, in a comforting, caring voice. 'I'm sure if it was that urgent, he would have just told you over the phone.'

Rachel forced a smile and nodded her head. 'Yes, I'm sure you're right. It's probably nothing. I bet it's to do with his work or something along those lines. He's been so stressed over work lately; perhaps he's quit his job? It wouldn't be the worst thing.'

'Has Bianca mentioned anything?' Grace questioned curiously. 'Perhaps she knows what all this is about?'

Bianca was Rachel's best friend from primary school. When Bianca had been made redundant the year before, Rachel had managed to persuade Mark to get her a job at the bank he worked for in London. Bianca had been over the moon and so grateful. Rachel's forehead wrinkled.

'No, she hasn't, and I spoke to her last night. They only work in the same building though. They're in completely different departments so I can't imagine she'd know anything anyway. It's not like they're friends or anything.' Rachel heaved a loud sigh. 'There's no point in me guessing all day. I'll just have to wait and see.'

'Exactly,' Grace said, pulling out a lipstick and taking the cap off. 'Put on a bit of red lippie to get into the festive spirit and everything will be fine,' she smiled, passing the lipstick over.

It was quiet today in Tidemans, the department store they worked in. With Christmas fast approaching, Rachel knew it was the calm before the storm and she should appreciate the peace and quiet. Right now though, she also knew that she'd welcome the distraction of some customers, as all she could think about was what Mark wanted to say to her. As much as she'd pressed him on the phone, he'd been adamant he wanted to discuss it face to face. It couldn't be anything that bad, could it? A feeling of unease crept up on her. Everything had been fine in their relationship; a little same-old and predictable maybe, but Rachel loved the feeling of being completely comfortable and they were happy, weren't they? Who cared if she no longer had the butterflies like at the beginning? That feeling didn't last forever in any relationship, and Mark was the man Rachel wanted to marry. He was *the one*. For the past year she'd been hoping he was going to propose and she couldn't deny she'd felt a little disappointed after every night out in a restaurant or trip away together when she'd still come back empty handed. What if Grace was right? What if he really was going to propose today? Rachel applied the red lipstick with a brush and puckered her lips together. At least she could make sure she looked nice if he was going to pop the question.

Rachel loved working with Grace on the make-up counter for Pop Cosmetics and they'd become great friends over the years. They knew practically everything about each other, and Rachel was so glad she'd decided to take the job five years ago, despite having reservations about working in retail. There were usually three of them, but their colleague, Amber, was away in Thailand, due to arrive back in a few days' time.

'Good luck,' Grace said, leaning in for a kiss a few hours later when they were leaving. 'Let me know straightaway if you get engaged,' she said, her lips curving at the edges. 'What a lovely early Christmas present that would be.'

Rachel waved goodbye, feeling sick with nerves.

Their flat was empty when she got home, so Rachel put the kettle on, making a cup of tea for something to do. She was looking forward to decorating their flat for Christmas; they usually drank mulled wine and listened to Christmas songs to get them in the mood. She remembered amusedly how the year before they'd ended up pretty drunk and covered in glitter.

She was pouring the milk into the tea when she heard the front door open and Mark walk in.

'Hi!' Rachel attempted a smile and a breezy tone, swivelling round to face Mark as he walked into the kitchen. Her heart plummeted, as she instantly knew that whatever it was he was going to tell her, it wasn't good news. There was definitely going to be no proposal tonight, of that she was certain.

'Hi. Rach, do you mind sitting down?' Mark asked gravely, walking over to the kitchen table with a slight stoop to his shoulders. His face was white as a sheet.

Rachel swallowed hard, knowing she should have trusted her gut instinct that something was wrong when he had called her that afternoon. Maybe he'd been sacked from his job and they were going to struggle to pay the bills? She could handle that though and would offer to work extra hours at Tidemans and start doing freelance make-up like she'd promised herself she would years ago. Or perhaps someone was sick? Rachel was annoyed that she'd allowed Grace to get her hopes up that maybe, just maybe, he was going to propose and everything was going to be amazing in her life. She needed to stop telling herself that if she just had an engagement ring, everything would perfect.

'I've made you a cup of tea,' she said, placing the mug in front of him and sitting opposite. 'Can you tell me what's up now, please? You're starting to scare me,' she confessed, feeling awkward in front of him for the first time since they'd met.

Mark's breathing was shallow and audible as he fidgeted in his seat and stared at his hands uncomfortably. Two red blotches suddenly appeared on his pale neck. He closed his eyes momentarily.

'Look, there's no easy way for me to say this, Rachel, but I'm moving out. I can't be with you anymore,' he stated, matter-of-factly.

Rachel felt as though she'd been winded, her mouth popping open in shock. She was completely speechless, the room spinning round as she stared at him in disbelief.

'I'm so sorry to do this to you, I really am, but I can't live a lie any longer and pretend that everything is okay, when it isn't. You're such an amazing person, Rach, you really are. Someone is going to be so lucky to have you one day,' he said in pitying tones, 'but I don't love you the way I should anymore. You deserve better than me.'

A sense of deep foreboding washed over Rachel like a powerful waterfall. He couldn't be serious? But as she gazed at Mark, praying he was just trying to wind her up, her eyes swept over his guilty, tormented expression, hunched shoulders and unsteady hands, and she knew that her life was about to change forever. This was definitely no joke, and Rachel felt physically sick, her mouth too dry to speak. She blinked several times and squinted her eyes at him. 'But why? What's changed?' she managed to ask, her voice cracking with emotion. 'I thought things were fine. I thought we were happy, Mark. I even, stupidly, thought we would get engaged soon,' Rachel whispered breathlessly. 'I imagined we'd be getting married next year and that maybe we could have a nice Christmas wedding like we'd discussed or…'

'Rach, please don't,' he interjected, looking as though it was painful for him to talk, his eyes trailing to the window like he couldn't bear to look at her. 'It's nothing you've done. You've been great, you *are* great in fact. It's me.' He winced. 'Oh God, I don't want to be the guy that gives you the cliché "it's not you it's me".'

'Then don't be,' Rachel retorted, her voice now razor sharp and unrecognisable. Her heart was beating so fast it felt like it might explode at any second.

'I don't want to hurt you,' he whimpered. 'I don't deserve you, like I said. You deserve so much better than me.'

Even breaking up with her, Mark was being nice about it. He was so well spoken and polite that for some reason it made it more of a slap in the face because she couldn't hate him. How on earth was this happening? How had it come to this? Rachel hadn't gone after a bad boy, trying to tame him unsuccessfully. Rachel had chosen Mark. Mark with the kind, gentle features and smiley face who was friendly to everybody. The type of man to help an old lady crossing the road or to buy the homeless man on the street a cup of coffee. She'd settled for the good guy; the one who wasn't supposed to break your heart after three years together. The one who was supposed to be proposing!

'What's changed?' Rachel asked in a demanding voice. She needed an explanation. Rachel wasn't giving up without a fight. They had so many plans for the future. Rachel had been looking forward to hosting Christmas for Mark's entire family, like she'd done every year since they'd met. She'd been looking forward to playing board games with his sister, Lottie, who was just as competitive as Rachel, handing her presents out, which she'd put a lot of thought into, and pulling Christmas crackers at the table, with Mark's father making them read the terrible jokes inside one by one. She had even been looking forward to Mark's mother getting drunk, mumbling all her words and not making any sense by 9 p.m. Was she really going to be losing everyone in one fell swoop? It was devastating. Brutal.

Mark looked at her then, as though she was a poor little dog he was about to put down. 'I have. Things have just changed. I love you, Rach, you know I do. But I think it's more like a friend.'

It would have hurt less if he'd stabbed her and suddenly Rachel felt angry.

'Right, well that's just great then,' she said, pushing her chair back to stand up, which made a loud scraping sound. 'I'll just get my things and go. There's nothing I can do if you're telling me that you only love me as a friend,' she said, hating the fact that her face was scrunching up and her eyes were filling with tears.

'Please, don't, Rach. I already feel terrible enough,' Mark replied, putting his head in his hands.

'What do you want me to say, Mark? I love you, and not just as a friend. I thought we were going to be together forever, and now suddenly out of the blue you come home and tell me you no longer love me!' Tears cascaded down her cheeks. 'I feel like such an idiot.'

'You're not an idiot. I'm the idiot. I don't know what I'm doing anymore,' he sighed, rubbing his eyes with the palms of his hands.

'You're breaking up with me,' Rachel stated, brushing her tears away roughly. 'I'll leave and make things easier for you,' she told him, making her way into their bedroom to pack a bag.

'No, I'll leave,' Mark said, jumping up to follow her, 'I should be the one to go.'

'No, you won't,' Rachel snapped at him. 'You won't be the one who gets to break up with me and then walk away. I don't want to be here alone, in our flat. There are too many memories. It's all yours.'

'You don't have to go right now,' he mumbled guiltily, his eyes downcast. The dark shadows under his eyes and his blotchy skin gave the impression that the situation was making him ill. Well, good. Rachel hoped he was suffering just as much as she was.

'What shall I do then, Mark? Sleep next to you in bed knowing that you don't love me? Sleep on the sofa knowing that you're next door where I usually sleep? I can't believe you're doing this, Mark. Just before Christmas too.'

'There was never a right time. After Christmas it's your birthday, then Valentine's Day, then our anniversary. When would the right time be, Rach? I could sleep on the sofa,' she heard him say, before she slammed the door to cry alone.

Rachel sobbed, trying to hold it together until she left. She was utterly heartbroken, but she didn't want Mark to see how distraught she truly was. She felt humiliated and foolish. Mark seemed a complete stranger and not the man she'd laid beside for the past three years. Where had all this come from and how had Rachel not seen it coming? If he no longer loved her, there was really no going back now, was there? There was simply nothing she could do about it.

'Where are you going to go?' Mark asked her, his voice laced with sympathy and sadness as she opened the bedroom door with a suitcase.

'I don't know,' Rachel responded honestly. 'Home I guess. Not that it should concern you now.'

'Yes, I suppose home to your parents is best. Rachel, I'm so sorry,' he said pathetically, looking as though he didn't know what to do with himself.

Rachel sniffed loudly, still unable to believe they were breaking up. 'So am I, Mark. So am I.'

She closed the front door behind her, not looking back at him, and made her way to her car before her face crumpled and she cried her heart out.

Fifteen minutes later and Rachel was still crying. She was dreading going home to her parents and explaining what had happened. Her parents would be so disappointed; she could just see her mother's sorrowful expression wondering how Mark had done this to her daughter. Her mother and father adored Mark. They were always telling her what a lovely young man he was and that she couldn't have picked better.

I definitely could have picked better, Mum, the bastard has left me, she thought wryly as she stopped at the traffic lights.

Rachel's mother had been harping on about grandchildren ever since she could remember and now she felt like she'd somehow let her down. She wondered if it would be better going to Bianca's? Bianca lived alone in her flat and had a spare room she could stay in. They'd been best friends since childhood and Rachel felt completely at ease being a snivelling wreck in Bianca's presence. Rachel was always there for Bianca when she was feeling down; she couldn't count the number of times she'd been on the phone until 1 a.m. listening to Bianca ramble on about some guy who hadn't called her back. Deciding this was the best idea, Rachel put her foot down hard on the accelerator and made her way there.

'Rachel?' Bianca looked as though she'd seen a ghost as she opened the front door. Her eyes were open wide with concern and shock as she gazed at Rachel standing there.

'Oh Bee, it's all gone horribly wrong. Can I stay here?' Rachel sniffed, wiping her nose with a crumpled tissue she'd found in the bottom of her handbag.

'Of course.' Bianca opened the door and took Rachel in her arms. 'What's happened? Is it Mark?' she asked gently.

Rachel nodded, her eyes filling with tears again. 'We've broken up,' she croaked. 'He doesn't love me anymore.' Rachel's face wrinkled as she said the words.

'Oh Rachel, I'm so sorry. I'm just so, so sorry. Come through to the lounge. Let me get you a drink,' Bianca suggested kindly.

Rachel let Bianca lead her into the lounge and sat on the sofa. 'It's come out of nowhere. I don't know what I'm going to do,' Rachel said, feeling helpless. The rug had been pulled from under her feet. She couldn't believe she was here, instead of at home making dinner and wondering what to watch on television for the evening. Everything had happened so quickly.

Bianca looked awkward. She felt really bad for Rachel and it was a surprise seeing her in such a vulnerable state. Rachel was the strong one in their friendship. Rachel didn't get upset about the little things like Bianca did. She was the one who was normally comforting and reassuring Bianca for whatever reason. Rachel had been the lucky one. She was the one with the job she loved and the boyfriend she adored. She was the first one to kiss a boy, lose her virginity and get into a serious relationship. It was Bianca who went out on the countless bad dates and struggled to find a nice man to settle down with.

'Can I get you a drink? I can open a bottle of wine if you like?' Bianca offered.

'No, I'm fine,' Rachel exhaled. 'Well, I'm not fine, I'm completely heartbroken, but the thought of eating or drinking makes me feel sick.'

Bianca gave a little nod and sat down slowly opposite Rachel. 'What did he say?' Bianca asked in a small voice, her large brown eyes full of sympathy.

'That he loves me like a friend,' Rachel confessed, rolling her eyes. 'Just what every woman wants to hear,' she said sarcastically. 'There's nothing I can do about that, is there? I can't make it better. I can't say I'll stop nagging him as much, or that I won't be as possessive or whatever other things men hate. Because I don't do any of those things and it's not because I've done anything wrong, it's because he doesn't love me anymore. It's the worst possible thing he could say.' She closed her eyes trying to prevent the tears again. 'I'm just hoping he says he's made a mistake. I'm praying that because I've actually left him, he'll change his mind.' She laughed uncontrollably. 'I'm pitiable, aren't I? I just don't know what's going on anymore. I just want him to want me back.'

Bianca shifted on the armchair and stared at Rachel with a frown. 'Perhaps it's for the best?' she replied optimistically. 'You'll meet someone else, Rach, you know you will. You always do. Maybe Mark just wasn't for you?'

'I don't want to meet someone else,' Rachel moaned, shaking her head and blowing her nose. 'Mark was nice. He was reliable, loyal and dependable. My parents love him. My friends love him. He was *the one*,' she stated firmly, her chin wobbling. 'I thought I was going to be spending the rest of my life with him. I can't explain it…' She broke off. Bianca had never had a long-term boyfriend, so she couldn't possibly know how she felt. Bianca's relationships usually lasted no longer than a month. She had no idea what Rachel was going through, couldn't ever know the pain she was feeling – not that Rachel was about to voice this for fear of hurting her feelings.

'I just keep thinking I should have known,' Rachel continued. 'But I didn't. I honestly thought everything was fine between us. I knew things weren't perfect, but that's life, right? No one's relationship is perfect. The longer you're together the more comfortable and relaxed you get. That's just how it goes. What does he actually want?' Rachel said, raising her shoulders.

Bianca sat quietly looking down at the floor. 'You'll meet someone else,' she practically whispered.

'I'm sure I will eventually,' Rachel nodded, rubbing her nose and desperately trying to find some positivity. She knew this was going to be difficult, but she *would* get through it. She had great friends and family around her for support. She wasn't the first person to go through a break up and she certainly wouldn't be the last. She was aware things could be much worse. Somehow, it would be okay again one day, she did know that deep down. She just needed to get over the shock and hurt. 'I really thought I had the right man,' she explained, shaking her head in puzzlement. Then the thought suddenly hit her, as though a light switch had been turned on inside her head. 'Oh my God. Say he's already seeing someone else? I didn't even ask him. How could I not have asked him? He could be leaving me for another woman. Have you seen him with anyone at work? Do you ever speak to him?'

Bianca's eyes darted around the room, like she was afraid to answer and Rachel instantly felt tension in the room.

'No, I don't see him at work. Well, sometimes I see him. Like occasionally, but it's not often… I… he… we work on different floors,' Bianca replied, appearing a little flustered and uncomfortable.

Rachel frowned, wondering if Bianca was hiding something from her, when her eyes landed on a black jacket hanging up outside in the hallway. A feeling of sheer dread hit her like a tidal wave. She felt sick to the core as she stood up and walked over to it, her hands shaking as she reached out for the jacket.

'Rach? What's wrong? What are you doing?' Bianca asked, watching in horror as she picked up the jacket and opened it.

Rachel prayed that she was wrong. She hoped with every single fibre of her being that it couldn't possibly be true. She opened the

285

jacket and when she saw the pink nail varnish stain inside by the pocket, it took her breath away as though she'd been punched. She knew then exactly why Mark had broken up with her. She pivoted and stared at Bianca in disbelief.

'This is Mark's jacket,' she stated calmly, adrenaline pumping through her.

'No it's not,' Bianca replied quickly, her face turning a shade of pink. She let out a nervous laugh. 'Why on earth would Mark's jacket be here?'

'It's Mark's jacket,' Rachel stated with certainty, ignoring her, her index finger touching the stain. 'I had just painted my nails once when he asked me to grab his phone from the pocket because he was in the bath. You see this mark here?' Rachel pointed to the pink smudge. 'This was because my nails were wet still. I felt really bad about it afterwards, though you can't see the stain from the outside. Mark was always particular about his clothes. He takes good care of them.' She shot Bianca an intense gaze. 'Why is Mark's jacket here?'

Bianca's eyes were as round as saucers. 'Rachel, please let me explain…'

'I got you that job at Mark's firm,' Rachel interrupted. 'It was me, you know. I begged him to get you in there. I told him how down you were and how bad I felt for you getting made redundant. He didn't want to get involved at first; he kept telling me it was a bad idea in case you weren't any good and he'd been the one to recommend you so it wouldn't look good on him, but I kept on about it, singing your praises and persuading him to do it. I've been a good friend to you, haven't I?'

Bianca gave a weak nod, looking away.

'Yes, I have. So I think it's about time you were honest with me, don't you?' Rachel could feel herself growing angrier with every second. All those late nights Mark had been working flashed through Rachel's mind. All the times that Bianca hadn't answered the phone and then made excuses as to why she couldn't meet up, Rachel had just assumed she'd been really busy, and she supposed she had been –

with *her* boyfriend!

'I don't know what you mean…'

'Bee, just cut the crap, okay?' Rachel interjected hotly, rolling her eyes and feeling as if her head was about to explode in rage. 'How long have you been seeing Mark for? How long have you been seeing *my* boyfriend?' She couldn't believe she was even saying the words. She glared at Bianca, feeling the tension emanating from her.

Bianca fiddled with her hair, at least having the decency to look ashamed. She looked at the floor; she'd clearly rather be anywhere else in the world at that very second.

'Rachel, I'm so sorry,' she said finally, tears filling her eyes. 'I never meant for any of this to happen. We both didn't.'

'*We*? So you and Mark are a *we* now?' A loud laugh escaped her lips. 'Tell me, for how long? How long have you both been lying to me?' she snapped, feeling more hurt and betrayed than she ever knew was possible.

'Oh God, I know you're upset, but the last thing we ever wanted was to hurt you. We've both felt so bad, Rachel. Please believe me. It's been going on for about two months, that's all. I told him I wanted to stop. I couldn't carry on until things were sorted between you two,' she sniffed loudly.

Rachel gazed at Bianca noticing her mascara was smudged, her eyes focusing on the black smear underneath her chocolate brown eyes. She looked around the room at the colourful scatter cushions on the sofa with the sequins which scratched your skin, the full magazine rack with magazines piled messily around it and Bianca's pink fluffy slippers lying in the middle of the room. Mark wouldn't care much for her untidiness. He'd hate it in fact. It would grate on him eventually, but perhaps he didn't even know that side to Bianca just yet. Or maybe it didn't bother him right now because everything was so new, sexy and exciting. She could just imagine the thrill of their sordid meetings, worrying that Rachel may or may not catch them and find out. How could the two of them have got together behind her back? At what point had Bianca become appealing to Mark? He'd never seemed remotely bothered about her before. They'd always gotten along of course, but just on a normal boyfriend/best friend level. There had been absolutely nothing remarkable about their relationship. In fact, she distinctly remembered Mark calling Bianca 'quite the chatterbox,' implying it was a bad thing. So when had the chatterbox become irresistible to him? Nothing between the two of them had ever told Rachel to watch out because, if she wasn't careful, one day they'd hook up and ditch her. They hadn't even flirted in front of her before. Rachel felt as though it was all a bad dream; she was frail and shaky and thought she might pass out from the shock at any second. How could they both do that to her?

Bianca began to weep and Rachel had to stop herself from comforting her out of habit. This was certainly not the time to make her so-called best friend feel better.

'So you've really been seeing Mark then?' she asked, a nasty bitter taste flooding her mouth.

Bianca nodded, her nose beginning to run. 'I think I'm in love with him,' she cried. 'I'm so sorry. It's all just such a mess. We just got chatting at work one day in the lunch canteen. We were talking about you, but there was just this spark between us. I can't explain it. I know you're going to hate me,' she sobbed, 'and I deserve it. I really do deserve it.'

Love? It was as though the word was lodged in Rachel's throat and she couldn't swallow. So it wasn't just a fling then? It wasn't a mistake. Bianca was planning to steal Mark because she couldn't live without him. Supposedly *loved* him. Her Mark. What had happened? Had they started a conversation about her and then realized that actually, they would make a better couple? *How about we both lose Rachel and get together instead?* The world had gone crazy.

'I don't know what to say to you,' Rachel said, filled with a wave of disbelief, her eyes suddenly dry. She was too stunned and hurt to cry at that moment. The shock had dried up her ability to show any emotion. 'I just need to get out of here. I need to be away from *you.*'

'Please just believe that we're sorry, okay?' Bianca pleaded. 'You can't just leave like this.'

Again, the word 'we're', to show that they'd become a secret couple, while Rachel had just been happily living her ordinary little life in ignorance. 'Wrong. I can do whatever the hell I like,' Rachel retorted, her head throbbing like it did when she had a migraine coming on. 'I don't owe you anything, Bianca. You want my boyfriend? You're welcome to him. Don't ever contact me again.'

Rachel marched to the front door, slamming it behind her. She took a deep breath wondering what on earth she was going to do.

What a very merry Christmas this was going to be.

Dear Reader,

Thank you so much for taking the time to read this book – we hope you enjoyed it! If you did, we'd be so appreciative if you left a review.

Here at HQ Digital we are dedicated to publishing fiction that will keep you turning the pages into the early hours. We publish a variety of genres, from heartwarming romance, to thrilling crime and sweeping historical fiction.

To find out more about our books, enter competitions and discover exclusive content, please join our community of readers by following us at:

🐦 *@HQDigitalUK*

f *facebook.com/HQDigitalUK*

Are you a budding writer? We're also looking
for authors to join the HQ Digital family!
Please submit your manuscript to:

HQDigital@harpercollins.co.uk.

Hope to hear from you soon!

**If you enjoyed *The Morning After the Wedding Before*
then why not try another delightfully uplifting romance
from HQ Digital?**

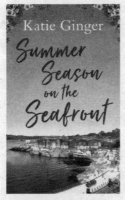